Praise

Very funny... Induced
laugh in ju
Kevin Samp

'Finally, a rock 'n' roll novel that people can
properly relate to'
Ciaran Jeremiah,
The Feeling

'Hilarious – it's *The Inbetweeners* meets *Spinal Tap*!'
Alex Marsh, author of
Sex & Bowls & Rock and Roll

MOCKSTARS

FOUR BOYS – ONE BAND – NO CHANCE

Christopher Russell

This edition published in 2020 by Farrago,
an imprint of Duckworth Books Group Ltd
1 Golden Court, Richmond, TW9 1EU, United Kingdom

www.farragobooks.com

First published by Red Button Publishing in 2014.

ISBN: 978-1-78842-220-8

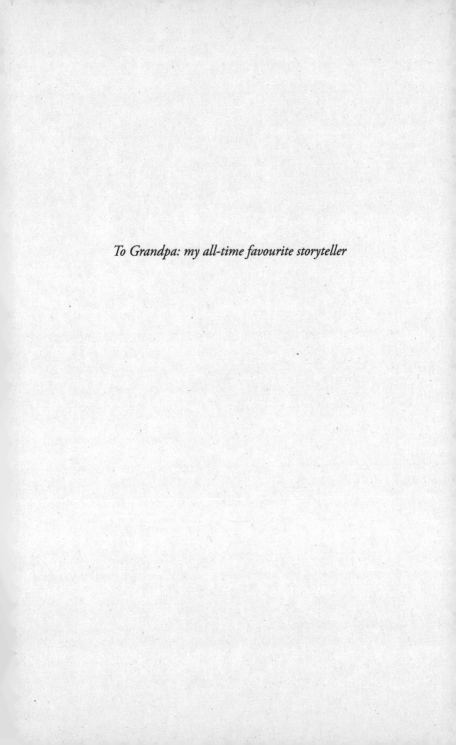

To Grandpa: my all-time favourite storyteller

Some of this actually happened.

1

I've never been in a fight before. 'Come on then.'

There are many, many reasons for this. 'Don't you talk, mate, or what?'

Being built like one of those pipe-cleaner people you make in nursery school is definitely one of them.

'Oi. Mate.'

My floppy hair is another, because judging by the complete absence of cold fear in this man's eyes, floppy hair is not particularly menacing.

'We need to have a private chat, you and me.'

He presses against my ribcage and corkscrews a meaty fist around the front of my shirt. I can see hundreds of tiny, angry pores opening across his nose and cheeks.

Say something. Diffuse the tension. 'Hello there.'

Hello there? *Hello there?* Who says that in a combat situation?

'Bet you think that was a pretty funny stunt, yeah?'

'No, not at all… um… Sir.'

He lifts me two inches off the ground, pushing air through his nostrils like a bull. My feet dangle in space.

'There are two thousand people in here tonight. You got no regard for Elfin Safety?'

I *could* reply that the safety of elves is the least of my concerns right now, but I don't think he'd find it that funny.

'Sorry… I won't do it again.'

'Damn right you won't.'

I could try punching him. Shall I punch him? I won't punch him.

'I've been watching you,' he says, venting a gust of stale breath into my face. It smells of pork scratchings. On the other side of the curtain heaves the sweaty might of the London Astoria, ripple and pulse, a beast in the dark.

'You weekend rockstars, you're all the same. Think you own the place.'

'No, I—'

'But you don't. You get me?'

One hand still clamped fast around my shirt, he slowly curls the other into a tight red boulder. His gaze darts downwards to admire the fist, then rolls back up to face me.

OK. This is now going to happen. My lungs empty of air.

Every muscle tightens.

His elbow spring-loads backwards, and I close my eyes.

ONE MONTH EARLIER

The Statue of Liberty stands tall and proud above a crowd of onlookers, its famous crown a jagged silhouette against the afternoon sun. Fingers point, feet jostle, cameras flicker and click.

'How does he stay so still, bruv?'

'Dunno, he's like actually the stillest person I has ever seen.'

'Nah way, he's moving! Like a lickle tiny bit.'

'What's he s'posed to be?'

'Think he might be that Statue of Liberties.'

Coins clatter on the cobbles.

'Hey bruv, how do you stay so still? You broken?'

The Statue of Liberty stirs disdainfully, like an old cat disturbed in sleep, a tired scowl trapped beneath caked-on green paint. All around, Covent Garden is buzzing with tourists and fizzing with noise, a circus of shoppers and street performers. Weaving through the crowd, George and I are striding the red carpet towards the Rock Garden, instruments in hand.

'Slow down, lads. Bands only.'

The bouncer blocking our path is thug-faced and chunky, his big, bald, neckless head encased in a mobile-phone headset.

He looks like an egg in a call centre.

'It's fine: we're one of the bands. Satellite.'

He sniffs, looks me up and down and shakes his head. 'You don't look like a band.'

'We've got instruments, though,' I protest, pointing at my keyboard case.

'I can't just let any old chancer with a saxophone in here, can I?'

'It's a keyboard,' I reply, wounded. The Egg crosses his arms.

'Whatever it is, it's blocking the thoroughfare.' I'll block your thoroughfare if you're not careful.

'Nobody panic!' comes a disembodied voice from the stairwell, and seconds later a figure emerges from the dark. A perky-eared man-boy with surprised hair, he's dressed in a wonkily knotted black tie and a shiny burgundy suit that glints in the sun. He looks like you could dunk him in the bath and he'd come out dry.

'You must be ChrisnGeorge,' he says in a triple-distilled Irish accent. 'Shawn. Apparently I'm in charge here.'

Shawn grips George in a double-armed handshake which makes both their fringes quiver. Watching me from the corner of his eye, the Egg clears his throat and quietly adjusts his headset.

'So, listen, welcome to the Rock Garden. You'll love this place – it's a total craphole.' His mouth widens into the shape of a laugh, but no sound comes out. 'Just kidding. Follow me.'

Leaving the sunny bustle of Covent Garden, we follow Shawn through the doorway and begin a spiralling descent into the bowels of the building. Within seconds, the noise of London has dissolved in the underground black.

Shawn is bouncing down the staircase in front of us. 'Have you come far?' he calls back.

'Berkshire, near Reading,' I reply, struggling beneath the weight of my piano.

'Aaaah, the Royal County of BERK-shire. Windsor Castle, Legoland. You got the works out there.'

We reach the bottom of the stairs and I set my keyboard down, struggling for breath. Shawn claps his hands together and winks at us.

'So what's the party scene like in Reading, boys?'

George thinks for a moment.

'Doesn't have one. It's got a massive PC World, though.'

'Well, that's grand,' replies Shawn, doing his silent laugh-shape again. 'Now, follow me…'

Draping his arms around our shoulders, Shawn guides us proudly into the main room. A kaleidoscope of coloured light floods my eyes, momentarily blinding me, before gradually diffusing to reveal an empty venue with a small stage, wiggly leather sofas and a blue, back-lit bar. The tables are set with ashtrays and winking tea-lights, and a large silver glitterball rotates above the dancefloor. Onstage, a dark-eyed stage technician is soundchecking the drum kit, dumbly pounding the kick drum. *Dmmb. Dmmb. Dmm-dmmb.* Behind him hangs a banner that reads: 'LONDON INDEPENDENT MUSIC AWARDS – *highlighting the very best in emerging live music*'.

'So there's the stage, obviously, over by the toilets that's the sound desk, and this door leads backstage to the dressing room.'

George's eyes meet mine. A dressing room? Hello Wembley.

'We're running a *weeeee* bit late on the old soundcheck, but don't worry. You're in safe hands with our man Dan.'

Shawn gestures towards a rusting metal cage at the back of the room, dimly lit and deathly silent. The faint outline of a hunched back, motionless black shoulders.

'Dan's an absolute biscuit, best in the business. Used to be monitor engineer for Dexy's Midnight Runners. Now' – Shawn whips a pen and paper from his back pocket and I tug my gaze away from the beast in the soundcage – 'while I've got you here, how am I introducing you tonight? Y'know, maybe a few words to sum up your sound and whatnot?'

Shawn is looking at George. George is pointing at me. 'Christoph's really good at this.'

Shawn turns on his heel.

'We-ell, um. OK.' I touch a finger to my lips. 'So you know acoustic pop like, err, like Crowded House obviously, and then there's a bit of Turin Brakes type stuff in there as well and I suppose Belle and Sebastian, although I went to see them once and it was just all these limp-armed students mincing about drinking Diet Coke and it kind of made me want to kill myself.'

Shawn blinks.

'So anyway, so… um… so really it's a *new* kind of melodic pop, with influences spanning rock, alternative and singer-songwriter, that manifests as this commercial-sounding, vocal-based acoustica that isn't folk – definitely not folk – although I suppose, sometimes, it is a bit folky.'

Shawn's eyes flicker down to his empty notepad.

'Ooo-kay. Good. We can work with that. You seen the VIP area?'

He points to a smallish enclave in the corner of the venue, separated from the main room by a black and gold rope.

'Bit daft, really, but the labels love it.'

I peer inside the low-lit room. Across the tabletops, rows and rows of empty champagne flutes are lined up like tiny glass soldiers.

'Speaking of labels,' Shawn continues, 'I've one more thing to tell you before I go…'

He throws a quick backwards glance at the venue.

'Bit of industry banter for you… secret, like.' He drops his voice to a whisper. 'It's all to do with this one fella, *ve-ery* important guy. He's coming to the show tonight, great pal of mine, works for City Records – one of the *majors*. Head of A and R, complete genius and whatnot. Known him for years. Anyway, he's under a *laaaht* of pressure at work right now for his next signing to, y'know… come good. Y'know?'

We both nod.

'So he comes to me, does Paul, and he says: "Shawn, I can't be arsed with this scouting crap anymore. You're a man with your finger on the pulse, where should I be looking?"' Shawn laughs to himself. 'Daft. Anyway, he seems to think I know what I'm talking about, and he wants one of my bands. One of my "nominated acts". And that, my boys, could be you.'

He winks at us again. 'No pressure.'

My eyes lead me back to the black of the soundcage. Inside, nothing stirs.

'You know these sorta people, right? They work fast and they don't take prisoners, which means tonight could be the start of something big… but only for the right band, and there's some pretty stiff competition this year.' He looks at us both for a moment, his gaze suddenly intense. 'So you two just do whatever it is you need to do tonight, OK? Whatever it takes.'

We both nod in unison. Shawn pops a trilby on his head and steps away from the stage.

'I'll be off then, the boys from Satellite.' He waves a casual hand at the Beast in the Soundcage. 'I'll leave you with Dan. You're in safe hands with Dan, he used to be monitor engineer for Dexy's Midnight Runners.'

As Shawn saunters off through a nearby doorway, George hoists his guitar onto his shoulder and grins his valley-wide grin.

'Shall we?'

Mounting the small stage, we ease into our well-practised process of unzip, plug in, turn on and tap-tap, all beneath the gaze of the Beast in the Soundcage. Within five minutes we're ready to go, and I play a few test chords on my piano. The sound coming back through the monitors is thin and harsh, a ghostly old piano straining through broken radio.

I lean into the mic. 'Um… Dan?'

My words are met with a hard silence, and I strain in the inky blackness for signs of life inside the cage. After a few seconds, the creature stirs, a single lantern casting a mournful orange glow across its jagged, stubble-wrecked features. Dust mites cluster in the gloom.

'Um… excuse me… Dan?'

With Frankensteinian effort, the creature drags its twisted frame forwards so that its eyes hover a mere heartbeat away from the wire mesh of the cage. Freezing breath escapes its nose in rhythmic, billowing clouds, and flecks of starlight from the slowly spinning glitterball reveal a haunted look hanging half off its face like dead skin; the terrible visage of a beast that, in some long-forgotten past life, danced but fleetingly in the warm fire of its one true love, only to be so soon plunged into an accursed existence of darkness, bondage and despair.

'*What?*' comes the voice from the dark. Nails along sandpaper.

'Sorry… nothing,' I reply, shrinking back behind my keyboard.

'So here we are,' says George, standing centre stage with his legs wide apart. 'Le Garden Du Rock. I think tonight might just be our night, Christoph.'

He strums a triumphant, ringing chord on his guitar, and I gaze out into the shadows, Shawn's words echoing loud and clear in my mind. *Just do whatever you need to do.*

I look over at George again, and he smiles.

It's a smile I've seen before, and it makes me uneasy.

2

Buzzing like a wind-up toy through the stubbly mess of wannabe rockstars, a chatterbox onslaught of frizzy red hair is doing the rounds. Strapped across her chest is a string of My New Favourite Band badges, gleaming under dancefloor spotlights. Her name is Ellen, although many know her simply as… the Noise.

'She wants to climb inside your pants again.'

George has appeared by my shoulder. He is sucking Coca-Cola through a straw. I clear my throat.

'Not necessarily.'

8:22 p.m. All around us, the Rock Garden is filling up. Skinny boys in bands, pretty girls in gangs, record-label suits glued to BlackBerry phones. Something trendy pumping on the sound system.

'Trust me,' continues George, slinging an arm around my neck, 'she's heard that you're back on the market, and the girl's about to burst.'

'Yeah, well. That was a long time ago.'

I brave a glance at my piano, waiting in the darkness at the back of the stage.

'I'm telling you, you can't look away. The Noise is sucking you in. She's like a sexy hoover.'

Over by the merchandise stand, the Noise is yapping breathlessly at Shawn, who is edging imperceptibly backwards. George slurps at his drink and pokes at the ice with a straw.

'Where did you go with her again?'

'You know where we went.'

'That's true, but I like hearing the story.'

He smiles dashingly at me. My feet do a tiny shuffle. 'We went to Melton Mowbray.'

'That's what I thought. You filthy little rascal.'

8:26 p.m. Sixty-four minutes to go. The air in the venue is hot and stifling, and strangers shout across the dark, clinking glasses. Above our heads, Covent Garden rumbles and thrums.

'Christoph.'

George is leaning rakishly against the bar, blue eyes gleaming. A barmaid busies herself behind him. I peer over his shoulder.

'Are you hiding something behind there?'

'The day we met, Christoph, I made a vow to always make our lives together spectacularly, ridiculously brilliant.'

Suspicion narrows my eyes.

'And as you well know, I'm a man of my word.'

He moves aside to reveal a pair of triangular cocktail glasses with little paper umbrellas sticking out of them. Both are filled to the brim with a cloudy white liquid and have a veiny, oval-shaped lump sitting at the bottom.

'What are those?'

'They're our drinks.'

'They look expensive.'

He grins.

'Don't you worry about that, old chum – I just got paid for my last website. Crowmarsh Gifford Horticultural Society, and it was, I don't mind admitting, an absolute cracker. Coding so slick it was practically erotic. And anyway,' he continues, squeezing my cheeks together, 'you're worth it, kiddo.'

'I wanted a Beck's,' I reply, between squashed cheeks.

'You always drink Beck's. Beck's is magnolia. This is a *lychee martini*.'

I rub my jaw and frown at the drink.

'It looks like a testicle in skimmed milk.'

'I know,' agrees George, watching a guitarist tune up onstage. 'Great, isn't it?'

Then it happens. The urban mess of pumping music and barking voices and bottle-tops popping and cash tills ringing begins to swirl and cluster around the moving sonic vortex of the Noise as she advances upon us, all frizz and eyes and fingers, and as she crashes into our lives she sucks the entire evening up into her face and a rushing, pounding silence seizes the air like a vice and time and space and matter all collapse into nothing and just as quickly are launched back out of her mouth in a terrifying tirade of ginger hair and teeth.

'Hi guys how's it gooooing this is soooo wicked everyone's REALLY nice Shawn's so *funny* is he Irish I think he's Irish he's so *funny* have you been here before I haven't it's weird the Rock Garden is SO weird I mean it's just really *dark* in here don't you think?'

Somewhere in London, a single tap drips.

'Did you guys bring merch I could sell it for you I don't mind I brought my Satellite T-shirt with me anyway so I could do it if you want what are you drinking it looks weird?!'

'Martini,' replies George, his eyes glazing over with a giddy sort of fear.

'Oh my god my cousin makes the BEST martinis but he worked behind the bar at Richard Branson's fiftieth birthday party so he's like totally a professional they had a fairground there and everything you're doing "Girl on the Radio" tonight aren't you?'

The bones in my face are beginning to grind together like I'm being slowly trampled by goats.

'Ye-es... we are...'

'I saw the setlist on the stage I like the set it's good you're playing all my favourites except "Fool In Love" you're not doing that one I don't really know why hey do you guys know Sophi Without An E?'

I shake my head robotically.

'Oh my god you have to meet her George she is so ACTUALLY in love with you come on she's over here I'll introduce you,' she squeals, grabbing George by the wrist. George reaches out for my shirtsleeve as she pulls him away and, for a moment, I lose my footing and stumble backwards into a body behind me.

'Oi, watch it!'

'Cripes, sorry.'

Disentangling myself from the stranger, I watch as George is dragged away across the dancefloor, mouthing 'KILL ME NOW' and tugging at an invisible noose. I turn round to inspect the damage and find a girl with dark wavy hair, bent double and brushing spilt drink from her legs. She's wearing a high-collared red leather jacket and very tight jeans.

'Can't bloody believe this,' she says, looking up at me for the first time. All breath leaves my lungs.

She's absolutely gorgeous. But she is also soggy.

'Sorry, sorry. Sorry. Let me buy you another drink.'

Her dark-chocolate eyes are fiery, almost fierce, and make me feel strangely helpless. I examine the puddle on the floor.

'What were you drinking there? Was it... erm...'

Think. What would a cool cat like her drink in a place like this?

'Cinzano?'

She stares back at me.

'It's not the eighties, mate.'

'Right. Yes. Of course. So would you... like a Cinzano?'

Stop going on about Cinzano. You don't even know what it is.

'I'm all right for Cinzano, thanks,' she says, her eyes passing over the row of illuminated bottles on the back wall. Her accent is a curious mix of Cockney and posh which I can't quite place.

'What's that?' she asks, nodding at my drink. Oh no.

I am holding a lychee martini. I AM HOLDING A LYCHEE MARTINI.

'It's not mine.'

She stares back at me, chewing gum. 'You nicked it?'

'No! No. No. I'm obviously...'

Obviously what?

'...holding it for a friend.'

She chews at me some more. I glance across the room towards George, who is being talked at by both the Noise and Sophi Without An E at the same time.

'What the hell is it, anyway?'

I tell you what this is. It's a very camp cocktail, that's what it is. 'This would be a lychee martini.'

Stupid drink's sapping my manly allure. I need a macho prop, like a cigar, or an enormous moustache. Or an axe.

'Never seen one of them before,' she says, flicking a rich lock of hair over her shoulder. I take a sip, grimacing as the salty gloop creeps down my throat.

'Oh, haven't you? I believe James Bond drinks one in, er…'

She cocks her head at me. If only I'd even once in my life seen a single Bond film.

'*James Bond and the Giant… Russian…*'

Giant Russian what? Giant Russian Doll? Giant Russian Peasant Uprising?!

'*James Bond and the Giant Russian.*' Pillock.

'Look, I'll just have a whiskey, yeah? Double, no ice.'

Double whiskey? This woman is amazing.

'Comin' atcha,' I reply, immediately wincing. She rifles impatiently through her handbag as I order her drink.

Elbows on the counter, I take a slow, deep breath and clear my mind. Come on, squire. It's like George always says: being in a rock 'n' roll band is very sexy, even when you're only the keyboard player and your idea of the perfect Saturday night actually amounts to a bubble bath, a Richard Curtis boxset and a seafood linguine.

'So, yeah,' I continue, swinging both arms, 'I'm just hangin' out here, hangin' tough, waiting to do the gig.'

She squints at me. 'What?'

This is your chance. Just play it casual, man. *Play it casual.* 'Oh, I play piano, the, uh… piano. Yeah, just in, like, one of the bands or whatever.'

'*Piano?*' she replies, with a snort, touching up her lipstick in a pocket mirror. 'You a jazz band, then?'

'No… rock band. Well, I mean, it's sort of acoustic, but it's influenced by a big rock sound? Like, um, you know Simon and Garfunkel?'

No response.

'Well, anyway, not that. I mean, we're more into the Beatles or Bon Jovi really, and George used to listen to a lot of Dire Straits when he was growing up, so we've ended up with this kind of soft-rock influenced, emotional pop sound with an almost indefinable international flavour that, *I* think anyway, is reminiscent of the songs of the Finn Brothers or, say, the early work of Adam F. Duritz.'

She is now curling her eyelashes. 'So… yep.'

The barman selects a whiskey bottle from the shelf and a long, awkward silence descends. The girl yawns. Onstage, Shawn is introducing the opening act, a jazz-funk band, all white suits and saxophones. I lean casually against the bar.

'You know… playing the piano… it's…'

Not that. You promised never to say that again after the incident with the sexy cellist in the Kashmir Klub.

'Playing the piano is a lot like making love to a beautiful woman.'

My head rolls off the back of my neck and down onto the floor with a bony thud, leaving the exposed spine wriggling about on the stump like a little worm. The jazz-funk band start up onstage.

'What did you say?' she shouts back over the music. Thank God for that. Literally, *thank God*. Thank you, God.

'I was just saying that… the DJ looks a bit like my friend Ben.'

'Oh.'

'But it's not Ben.'

'Right.'

This is horrible. What happens now? Should I say more words?

'Five sixty,' says the barman, setting down the whiskey. While I fumble for my wallet, the girl plucks the glass from the bar.

'Catch you later, yeah,' she says, downing the drink in one go and disappearing into the crowd.

***

8:48 p.m. George and I are standing at the back of the venue, hot and squashed among the gathering masses, waiting for Shawn to introduce the next band. Onstage, a short, stocky guy with a buzz cut is tuning his guitar while something jagged by Franz Ferdinand hacks through the sound system. I brave a careful glance into the soundcage, making momentary eye contact with the Beast. He shifts in his seat and I look away.

'So when are we on again?' asks George, sucking thoughtfully on a lychee.

'I've told you this about a hundred million times.'

'Yeah, course. Course. So… when are we on?'

8:56 p.m. Thirty-four minutes.

'Half an hour.'

'Right, yeah. So what time's that?'

'Nine thirty.'

'Cool. *Coolio*. Kick-off nine thirty.' He swallows the fruit. 'So what time is it now?'

'Five to nine.'

'Five to… right.' He pauses. 'And we're on at ten thirty?'

'Nine thirty.'

'Nine thirty.' He points at his temple. 'Roger that.'

Shawn steps up to the microphone, adjusts his trilby and addresses the crowd.

'Okaaay, listen up people. We've got one of our nominated acts for you now, and these kids are something *special*. We set up the London Independent Music Awards to recognise the unsung heroes of the unsigned circuit and, year after year, the band we've picked for Best New Act have gone on to huge things. Chart hits, worldwide touring, you name it.'

He gestures at the guitarist with one outstretched thumb.

'Now, this band, they're up for that award this year, and in about ten seconds you'll find out why. Without further ado, people, straight outta Shoreditch, let's make a totally obscene amount of noise for the Black Cats!'

The stocky buzz cut guy slices out a sharp, brittle riff on his guitar. It's an angry, wasp-in-a-box sound, angular and rhythmic, the insistent chop-chop of a factory blade. There's a palpable excitement in the room, the crowd suddenly swelling in numbers and volume. Over the racket of the fans chanting someone's name, I can hear my heart beating in my ears.

Whoever this is, they're our direct competition.

To the din of enthusiastic whooping, onto the stage steps one of the most beautiful women I have ever seen. She's dressed in a high-collared red leather jacket and is carrying a half-empty bottle of Jack Daniel's.

'You... are... *kidding* me...'

The girl grabs the microphone, slides it from the clip and, gripping the stand by its head, drags it slowly across the floor and past her chest, holding it outstretched on the far side of her body. Then she starts to half-sing, half-talk into the mic, almost a rap, but strangely melodic. Buzz Cut Guy intensifies his riff, and she ducks and dives around the rhythms, tuneful rapping breaking occasionally into long, sustained notes. Her singing voice is hard and pure, with just a hint of smoker's ripsaw.

'I know her.'

'What?' replies George, entranced, nodding his head to the beat.

'I mean, I don't *know* her... I just met her. At the bar.'

'Hey, fast work, old chum!' he laughs, turning to face me.

'Although... you didn't use your piano-is-like-making-love line, did you?'

I don't reply. George throws one arm around me and points at the girl.

'She doesn't seem like your type, Christoph, I have to say.'

'No... no, she isn't,' I agree, watching her break from the mic and swig from the whiskey bottle. Then I add, quietly: 'She really isn't.'

Despite the band's basic, stripped-down arrangement, the room is beginning to move. There's a crackle in the air, a surging in the dark, and even without a drummer or a bass player, it's a frighteningly powerful sound. The duo tear through five punky, funky numbers, each no more than three minutes long, each time teasing louder and more impassioned applause from the crowd.

'These guys are amazing,' says George, shaking his head. 'I feel sorry for whoever has to follow this.'

'George.'

He's not listening. '*George.*'

He raises his eyebrows at me. 'Uh-huh?'

'It's us. *We* have to follow this.'

'Oh, right. Well if it's us, that's different.'

He beams at me and goes back to watching the band.

'So yeah, we're Heidi and the Black Cats, and if you wanna see us again before awards night we're headlining the Water Rats next Friday,' the girl is saying in her stark, unplaceable accent. 'After that we got our first international tour, Germany and that, so I dunno, hit us up if you're out there.'

Someone in the back row shouts, 'We love you!' and Heidi flicks her dark hair ostentatiously over her shoulder, something which makes me fancy her and dislike her at the same time.

An international tour? How is that *possible?*

'Thanks for listening, yeah? And if you wanna hear us with the full band – Water Rats next Friday. This is our last song, s'called "Tank".'

I turn to George. He has gone unusually quiet. 'Did she just say...?'

He nods, slowly.

'How can they be touring Europe?' I continue. 'It doesn't make sense, they're not even signed.'

Heidi and her singular Black Cat kick into their final song, and I check my watch. 9:22 p.m. Time is running down.

'ChrisnGeorge.'

A hand lands on each of our shoulders, and we turn to find Shawn standing behind us, lights from the stage dancing in his eyes. He nods towards the band.

'It's time.'

***

The small, dark space beside the stage is cramped and hot, little more than a storage area for amps. George and I are crammed in together next to Shawn, who is pointing past the stage towards the dancefloor where a scruffy-haired suit is loitering by the stage.

'That's him, lads, Paul. City Records.'

The man's tie is slung loosely around his neck, and his unironed shirt hangs out wrinkled over the top of his jeans. He looks like his mum made him dress up smartly for a family party.

'Now, I was with Paul earlier, and he's had a few sherbets, but I've tipped him off about you fellas. You do your thing, and I'll get down there and chat him up for you.' City Records empties a champagne flute and is almost immediately handed a fresh one by a passing waitress. He yawns and looks at his watch. Shawn pats me on the shoulder as he passes. 'Best of luck, boys.'

Striding out onto the stage, Shawn shakes the guitarist by the hand and looks out across the venue, smiling widely at the animated crowd. Heidi is standing behind the microphone, soaking up the applause, silent in simple victory. When the adulation eventually dies down, she turns, picks up the whiskey bottle and walks out of the spotlight. Shawn takes the microphone.

'Ladies and gents, Heidi and the Black Cats! How 'bout that?!'

'You all right, Christoph?' asks George, ruffling my hair. The band are leaving the stage, and I am watching City Records, silently, as he watches Heidi.

'Mm-hmm.'

'This is just another gig, old chum. This is what we do.'

'Yep.'

'Hey, buster. Yo. Look at me.'

George is poking me in the back. With a sigh, I turn round to face him.

'Put it this way,' he continues, staring right at me. 'What's the one thing you're best at in the entire world?'

I think for a moment. 'Probably Scrabble.'

'Now, these guys are new to the Rock Garden,' Shawn is saying, 'they're young, they're hard-working, and give 'em six months and they'll be bigger than U2...'

When Heidi reaches the bottom of the steps, City Records is there waiting for her. He touches her arm, and she flinches. Putting up a hand, he explains something while pointing at the stage, and gestures towards the VIP area. She pauses, shrugs, and walks with him across the room.

'Ladies and gentlemen, also up for Best New Act this year, please welcome the incredible... Satellite!'

The room thunders, lights tumble and swirl, and we step out onto the stage.

3

Standing in the hot, summer-sticky glare of the stage lights, I clutch the end of my piano and survey the crowd. A few familiar faces pitch camp among a forest of strangers. George fires a millisecond of ocean-blue eyes at me, and I stand up straight.

'So er... we're Satellite,' I begin, touching my fingers to the piano keys. 'This song's called "Ben Are You Coming Home".'

As George releases the opening guitar chords, I stare out into the black of the soundcage, but there's no movement inside. The applause, crackling like hot oil in a pan, spatters and snaps over the rise of the music and chatter in the room drops off word by word. A silence settles over the heads of the audience, evening mist sinking into wet grass, and I test a few notes on my piano. Slowly, stumbling, it coughs out through the monitor.

I can barely hear it.

'*I sat idle yesterday, I thought about a lot to make me smile...*'

George is singing the opening lines, and his voice is clear as glass, but my piano is still the cracked, fragmented ghost from before, struggling out through a broken radio. In the dark of the soundcage, still no movement.

I can't play the gig like this.

'*I thought about our masterplan... and I thought of all the things that we'd done...*'

A blurp of feedback, the fizzle of distortion, and my piano chokes through the aged speakers. I search the audience for reactions, but our spotlights are blinding and I can't make out faces.

'Now here I am just sitting, waiting, in the dark,' sings George, *'for you to come home...'*

Then, in the soundcage, the orange light flickers, the beast's face is a-glow, and I see fevered hands turning dials and pulling faders. Something is changing. The keyboard falters, disappears and, in one glorious sweep of sound, the speakers gasp open and crystal-clear piano floods the room, sinking down deep into guitar and voice.

I look over at George, and he nods back. We've arrived.

'We can set this old world right... and have a beer before you disappear again...'

The music gathers pace as our instruments sing, the guitar light and bright, the piano rich and smooth. Out in the room, no sign of City Records, and no sign of Heidi. Shawn is at the bar, chatting up barmaids. Closest to the stage stands the Noise, talking at Sophi Without An E and pointing towards George. She is telling the story behind the song.

'For in these later days, we're just so busy breaking out and making our own ways...'

We sink into the bridge and, along with the familiar lyrics, fragments of memory float to the surface. Black-and-white tiny-films wash by me like driftwood, months and months of gigging, night after night, in London's darkened acoustic clubs, Mondays at the Spice of Life, Sundays at the Bedford, Wednesdays at the Troubadour. Winning fans, one by one, people to learn the words, fill the spaces, wear the badges. Selling home-made EPs from a torn cardboard box.

'And sometimes all you need is to see a friendly face...'

The chorus hits and we're running, travelling, weaving through the music with ten years of momentum behind us. Nods and smiles from the crowd, feet tapping, heads bobbing.

'Ben, are you coming home? What I'd give to see you...'

Verse becomes chorus becomes solo becomes climax, and our voices entangle over the rising chords. New people join us from the bar.

'I'm out of my mind, just waiting here, as all of my friends disappear...'

29

Finally, over the vanishing music, the closing lyric fades into silence and the track reaches its end. The clitter-pa-clatter of applause greets us on the other side, sudden and noisy like rain on a tin roof.

'Thanks very much, cheers. This one's called "Emily".'

We move through the set as cats across car-tops, darting from song to song on feet as light as air. 'Emily' bursts open like a pop tangerine; 'Sleepless' smoulders and soars in the dark; 'Girl on the Radio' slows time to a standstill and everybody – everybody – listens.

And then it's time for our final number. I turn to George, and he smiles at me in the red burning lights. It's that same smile, the one from soundcheck, and it stirs a memory inside my head.

Just do whatever you need to do.

He leans into the microphone.

'Hi people! I'm George. Thanks again for listening…'

This is wrong. George never does the talking.

'So we're Satellite, we're from Goring, which is this little village on the Thames, and… erm…'

What is he doing?

'…we're really excited to be here 'cos this is our last gig before our world tour kicks off next week…'

WHAT?!

'There's details on our website if you want to check it out – gig dates and everything.'

There are scattered whoops from the crowd. I stand, rooted to the spot, helpless and mute under naked white light.

'For now, though, here's our last song… and we'll see you guys at the awards ceremony! This is "Callsign".'

Slipping a capo onto the neck of his guitar, George starts strumming the strings hard. 'Callsign'? I don't know this song. I mean, we rehearsed it once, but that was a month ago, and it's not on the setlist. Why is he doing this?

'George.'

I call to him off-mic, but he can't hear me. I'm trapped behind my piano.

'I don't know this song. *George*. Seriously.'

I have no idea what the chords are. Is he playing a… C sharp? I can't concentrate. I'm not playing anything. He's going to start singing, and I'm *still not playing*.

I close my eyes. I can't think in this heat, this dark. It's not right. The chorus is nearly here, and I'm still not playing.

I look up and catch George's eye. He smiles his curious smile.

The stage lights turn green, to orange, to yellow, to red.

*****

'What the hell was that about?'

Tunk. Tunk. Tunk. A barman hammers three glasses onto the metal counter, flips a silver shaker and in one swift motion fills them all with a red cocktail mixture. I am leaning against the back wall, breathing double time, clothes clingy with sweat.

'I don't know what you mean, Christoph,' says George, chasing a lychee around his empty glass.

'You ended on a song I barely even know. And more importantly, you just told a roomful of people we've got our own world tour.'

'Clever, huh?'

'You can't just make stuff up.'

'"Visualise your goals, and they will spring forth like slick round eggs from a turtle." I think Mother Theresa said that.'

'I'm not convinced she did.'

'Think about it, Christoph. I'm *competing*. Those other chaps, wasserface, Horny and the Fat Cats—'

'Heidi and the Black Cats.'

'… they've done their thing, it was – *all right* – and now we're doing ours, and our thing is *obviously better*. I'm competing.'

'With a made-up tour.'

'Hey, I'm just laying the groundwork. This is where you come in and, y'know… actually book it.'

He goes in to skewer the lychee with a straw, misses and accidentally fires it across the bar into a bowl of peanuts.

'It's not that simple.'

George conducts a quick search for the owner of the peanuts, then hides the straw behind his back.

'Uh-huh.'

'George, the furthest we've ever travelled for a gig is Bracknell.'

'Yeah, exactly. Easy. Now c'mon, let's go see if the barman knows how to make a Dribbly Wizard.'

***

Eleven fifteen. The evening is crawling to an end, and the final act are pounding out their angsty indie-pop to a slowly thinning crowd. Alone in the dressing room, packing away my keyboard, I am surrounded by discarded old socks, dusty instrument cases and boxes of industrial bleach. Funny… I always imagined my first backstage area would be a nirvana of fresh fruit and champagne.

The sound of drumming, thumping through the whitewashed walls, suddenly triples in volume as the door swings open.

'Oi! Piano Man!'

Startled, I fall backwards over my keyboard case and land spreadeagled on a mountain of toilet rolls. The pile is disintegrating beneath me but, with some difficulty, I manage to scramble back onto my feet. Along with Heidi, who has appeared in the doorway, I watch as a succession of rolls trundle away across the floor.

Eventually, they come to a stop. 'Hello there.'

She stares at me. 'What are you doing?'

'Nothing, nothing. Just… checking the… toilet-roll situation.' Another roll tumbles off the pile. 'Which is all good, obviously.'

She has this thing she does with her face, not quite a snarl, not quite a smirk. A snark.

'Yeah, y'know, just thought I'd hang backstage for a while.' I fake a yawn, but it doesn't work, so I turn it into a very, very weird smile. 'You guys played a great set tonight.'

'Yeah, cheers. You lot are all right too. Kinda like The Beautiful South, but less shit. You wanna support us at the Water Rats?'

She collects a handful of dark hair and spins it deftly into a bun on top of her head. I stand up, still for some reason holding a toilet roll in each hand.

'You want *us*… to support you?'

She shrugs, and lights up a cigarette.

'Um, yes! Yes. Brilliant.' I clear my throat a few times. 'I mean… I have to check if someone can cover my shift.'

'Day job? Wouldn't catch me doing that.'

'Whatever, it's no big deal. I just make beds and do the coffees and things at some crappy hotel, it's no biggie.'

She stares at me again. I remember I am still holding toilet rolls, and make a careful tower on a nearby windowsill.

'You're a hotel maid?'

'Um… no.'

She's right. All of my colleagues are named Vera.

'Anyway, you'll need to bring your whole band, obviously. It's a proper electric gig, rhythm section and that. You cool?'

'Ah. Well, technically—'

'We're in,' comes George's voice from behind me. 'I'll text our drummer right now.'

George is standing in the doorway, faux texting. I bulge my eyes at him, but he isn't looking.

'Who are you?' demands Heidi, puffing smoke into the stale air.

'I'm the singer.'

'You look like Jon Bon Jovi in the nineties.'

George grins. I'm not convinced she meant that as a compliment.

'I'll Myspace you the details,' concludes Heidi, hitching a handbag onto her shoulder. 'Gonna be a sell-out, so tell your fans to get there early.'

Dragging long and hard on her cigarette, she gives us one last look, a flash of that trademark snark, and walks out the door.

'She seems nice,' says George, hopping across the scattered toilet rolls.

'She's not. I don't trust her.'

'But you do fancy her.'

'I never actually said that.'

'And hey, the Water Rats! That's a great gig.' I run both hands through my hair.

'Except there's no way we can do it, because we don't have a proper band.'

'Patience, Christoph. All in good time. I mean, did Mao Tse-tung have that funny hat when he started?'

'What?'

'Mao Tse-tung. When he started, did he have his own hat?'

'I'm not sure that's relevant.'

'I believe Mao would disagree.'

I slump down on a nearby chair.

'We're in a very strong position,' continues George, hands on hips. 'You know, Jesus once fed five million people with just an old shoe and a packet of fishfingers.'

'No he didn't.'

'Ladies and gents,' comes Shawn's voice through the open door, 'that's the live music done for tonight, but make sure you stick around for DJ Spicy, who'll be taking us into the wee small hours with a cocktail of hard house and Japanese techno-pop hits. And don't forget, LIMA Ceremony, three weeks from now, twenty-ninth of April at the London Astoria. We'll see you there...'

I hoist my keyboard case up from the floor. 'We should go.'

'Sure, sure. Any minute now. But first, you and I have a date with these Mexican Fireballs.'

George presents me with two fresh cocktails, traffic-light coloured and foamy at the top. I peer behind his back.

'Where'd they come from?'

'I don't know. Mexico.'

'Seriously, George, I'm on the early shift tomorrow.'

'Come on, buddy, the night is young and so are we. What's the worst that could happen?'

He passes me my drink, and I examine its hat of fuzzy red foam.

'I could wake up in a skip in Canary Wharf being licked at by tramps.'

'Exactly,' he concludes, lifting his glass. 'Chin-chin, old fruit.'

4

'Sweetheart, mind lifting your juice?'

Mum slides a glass coaster under my drink and I drop it back down. In front of me, my laptop screen is filled with familiar names, songs and album covers. Crowded House, Billy Joel, Counting Crows. *August and Everything After*, *Crossroads*, *A Rush of Blood to the Head*. It's taken some time, but an afternoon's contemplation and experimentation has propelled this playlist to near perfection.

Part three of *Chris & George's Ultimate List Of The Greatest Rock & Roll Tracks Ever In Existence* is complete. It's a list that's composed in part-chronological, part-thematic order. For example, both 'November Rain' by Guns N' Roses and 'Cat's in the Cradle' by Ugly Kid Joe easily won their place in the line-up and, if you're adhering to chronology, strictly speaking they should appear consecutively. But obviously you wouldn't put those two songs next to each other on an album, so we used 'My Guitar Lies Bleeding in My Arms', from Bon Jovi's *These Days*, as a buffer, even though it was released at least three years later. Musically, this bridges the gap between the two songs while at the same time expanding on the theme of companionship and the need to make your own way in the world.

It's devilishly clever.

'Hello, son.'

Dad is in the doorway, holding a big yellow torch.

'Hey.'

'How was last night, any exciting developments?' he asks, fiddling with the battery compartment lid and nudging his spectacles up his nose.

'There was someone there from a major label.'

'Great! Great. And he liked the band?'

I fidget in my chair. Outside, in the calm of the countryside, a dog barks and a flock of birds scatter. 'Well, um… he didn't actually see us play.'

'Ah. Still, it's not *what* you know, you know. This torch is kaput.'

Sticking out his bottom lip, Dad taps the battery case with a screwdriver and shakes his head. Mum appears behind him and pops a hand on his shoulder.

'Post for you, darling.'

She passes me an envelope, a heavy cream one with the address typed in a luxurious font. It looks unfamiliar: clearly not a bank statement, or a mobile phone bill, or an update from Student Loans, and that doesn't leave much else. On the back is a watermark that reads *Harley Bourne Group*.

A name I haven't heard in over eighteen months.

***

Upstairs, I'm sitting on the bed in a towel, freshly showered, staring at the unfolded letter. I have now read it six times.

> *Harley Bourne Group*
> *Golden Square*
> *London W1F 9EP*
>
> *Dear Christopher*
>
> *Following our correspondence in September 2002, we are writing to inform you that—*

'Chris!'

Mum's voice, from downstairs. A flurry of conversation in the hallway.

'Chris: George!'

The front door slams shut and George's eager footsteps rumble upwards through the house. Stuffing the letter back into its envelope, my fingers fumble at the sound of his approach and the paper slips from my hands and floats slowly to the carpet and George reaches the top step and his hand hits the door handle and I stretch out and zip the letter under the bed with one socked foot.

He bursts in.

The cat, startled, leaps off the bed and flies from the room.

'Christoph!'

I smile at him, not breathing. He frowns. 'Everything all right?'

'Mm-hmm. Yep.'

'Sure? You look a bit... weird.'

With the heel of my foot, I nudge the letter further under the bed.

'No, nothing.'

A grin spreads across his face.

'Have you bumped someone off? Buddy...? You have, haven't you? You've bumped someone off.'

I do a short, hollow laugh.

'So how's the world of hotel housekeeping?'

Six hours, thirty-five identical bedrooms, a thousand mini shampoos, shortbread biscuits, toilet rolls, hospital corners, overpriced peanuts, home.

'Every time I walk inside that place, a little piece of me dies forever.'

'Jolly good. So I've been thinking...'

He nudges me along, and perches on the end of the bed.

'...about this European tour, you know, from last night, about finding ourselves a band.'

'Right... OK.'

'Christoph, this is our chance to get out of Goring and see the world.'

'What do you mean, our "chance"? There *is* no chance, you just made it up.'

'Everyone's leaving,' he continues, slumping back against the headboard. 'All of our friends are moving to London to seek their fortunes. This is the great exodus, and if we don't do something about it we'll be left behind, sitting around in our dressing gowns with our mums watching endless *Bergerac*.'

Radio 2 clicks on downstairs. Terry Wogan is talking about cheese.

'OK, but… OK.'

'I've made a plan, I've done my research, and I know where to find our band. The Tour Bus is outside, full tank of petrol, and we're leaving right now.'

I blink back at him.

'Can I put some pants on first?'

'This is rock 'n' roll – you don't need pants.'

'I think I do need pants.'

He shrugs, slides a random book from the shelf and starts flicking through pages. I open a drawer and rifle through clean clothes. Under the bed, one corner of the letter is just visible, poking out of the dark.

'Where are we going, then?'

'The centre of the universe, old chum. You're gonna love it.'

***

LOCK-UP-YOUR-DAUGHTERS ROCK FESTIVAL
Live bands from 6pm–2am every night this week!!
Headline sets from Noodle Muffin & The Pig Squints,
Bordering On Retarded and Penis De Milo
… PLUS MUCH, MUCH MORE!!
12 Bar Club, Soho

The poster is bright pink and gaffer-taped to the side of a transit van. Underneath Bordering On Retarded, somebody has written 'your mums in this band'.

'Watch it, mate.'

A thick voice from behind shoulders me off the pavement and into the gutter. Fetid rainwater seeps in through a hole in my shoe and, as I step from the puddle, my sock slowly moistens.

'This is it, then?'

'That's right, my friend. Denmark Street: the centre of London's musical universe.' George squints into a nearby store, stroking his chin. 'At least, that's what it says on Wikipedia.'

All around, in every direction, are musicians. Tall ones, short ones, fat ones, angry ones, old ones, bored ones, beardy ones, greasy ones, the lank-haired, the dark-eyed, the scruffy-jeaned, the pale of face. Music shops are crammed like slum shacks onto both sides of the street and a constant stream of musicians file in and out, guitars strapped to backs like snail shells, drumsticks poking out of back pockets. Vintage rock music farts through doorways from knackered speakers, shop signs yell at us from every direction (WE BUY USED GUITARS!, LOWEST PRICES ANYWHERE!!) and the pungent, tin-foil tang of cheap Chinese takeaway chokes the air.

George is pushing his way through the travelling caterpillar of people, and I follow behind, squirming past pork-armed bikers in Motörhead T-shirts. When the herd eventually spits me out, I find myself standing in front of a cramped, one-room guitar shop. Inside, bent-backed teenage boys twiddle riffs.

Two shop employees are taking a break by the doorway.

'No, Dave, listen,' one is saying to the other, waving his cigarette in the air. 'There's no point in even considering the PB1000 for that job. Yeah, there's room for a pre-amp *booster*, but you get the same thing with the UPC-424, and that's just way more giggable…'

Flecks of cold rain park on my cheeks as I search the street for George. He is nowhere to be seen. The One Who Wasn't Dave flicks his spent cigarette butt and it rebounds off my wet shoe, spilling ash.

'This way, Christoph.'

George pops his head out of a narrow alleyway running alongside Andy's Guitars, and almost immediately disappears again. I follow him through the gap and down the crooked path, and light fades into shadow.

The alleyway is dank and smells of kebabs. A brown network of urine stains snakes down the crumbling brickwork and into the gutter, and above, covering most of the wall, is a sprawling, multi-layered crust of adverts, posters and business cards, peeling and torn. A notice at the top reads: 'MUSICIANS WANTED'.

'This is definitely it,' George is murmuring to himself, tracing a finger down the forest of papers. 'The rest of our band are on here somewhere, I can feel it.'

A black-and-white poster shouts at me from the wall. It is letter-headed with a crudely drawn skull and crossbones and, beneath that, a bulging cartoon phallus.

> **Drummer wanted for neo-medieval crunkcore sludge-metal act BUMSNOGGER. Major labels interested!!! and *genuine* offer on the table from Top Banana Management. Must be into: cybergrind, deathgrind, Anthrax, Carcass, Spineshank, Suicidal Tendencies, piercings, fetish culture and sharing groupies.**

'I'm not sure about this,' I reflect dubiously, glancing across at George. He is engrossed in a poster of his own.

'Huh?'

'What's a Spineshank? Is that a *thing*... or a band?'

'Say what?'

'Nothing.'

I move on to the next one.

> **Guitarist wanted for Australian hip-hop / black ambient / Celtic-reggae crossover 6-piece THE F*CKING C*NTS. No time-wasters please.**

'Ha! This is amazing.'

George is pointing at a piece of card on the wall, eyes wide.

'What?'

'This guy can play the bassoon *and* the Renaissance lute.'

The flabby grumble of a motorcycle engine slops past in the street behind us. I return to my investigation.

BASSIST SEEKS BAND

This sounds more promising.

> **Been playin for 30 yrs, just kicked the junk, lookin for new direction & some durty supa-sick beats. Influences mainly in late 90s German skankmetal e.g. Hanzel und Gretyl, Jürgen Skull, Das AquaFaggots.**

This is absolutely useless. I'll bet not one of these people has ever sat down and had a really good listen to *The Best of the Housemartins*.

'Now we're talking…'

George is tapping a flyer on the wall in front of him.

'This is our man. I've found him.'

Plucking the piece of paper from the wall, George bounds over to me and waves it in my face.

'He's a drummer, he's toured with Bryan Ferry and Tom Jones and he's looking for "a quality pop/rock band with prospects". You should call him.'

'Why me?'

He shrugs.

'Because you're better at… you know.'

'What?'

'Speaking and that.'

He smiles and lobs a stick of gum into his mouth. Reluctantly, I key in the contact number and the phone begins to ring.

'Should I…? I mean, wha—… Oh, bugger.'

'This is Calvin's phone, here comes the beep, you know what to do.'

Beeeeep.

'Um… so. Hi. So. Hello. I just found your number in… erm… well, down this sort of back passage in Soho.'

This isn't a *Carry On* film, you twerp.

'What do I say?' I hiss at George. He is casually inspecting some mud beneath his fingernails.

'Just tell him about our vibe and get him to call us back.'

'Vibe? What do you mean "vibe"? We don't have any vibe.'

He grins at me, chewing.

'So anyway, we're looking for a drummer for our band, and… er… our *vibe* is, um, acoustic trad ballad, heavily influenced by, erm, by Chris de Burgh and…'

George is shaking his head and miming the slitting of his throat.

'…although obviously not Chris de Burgh, because he's rubbish. More like the English Crowded House meets…'

George is dancing a jig and pointing at his shoes. When I raise an eyebrow at him, he abandons the jig in favour of pretending to ride a very small horse.

'…meets a modern-day, um… Herman's Hermits. So… yep. So… give me a call. OK, cheerio. OK. Bye.'

I slump back against the wall.

'Well, that was utterly awful.'

'It wasn't that bad.'

'And what was that thing you were doing, with the jig, and the horse-riding?'

He smiles at me

'Counting Crows.'

'Why didn't you mime somebody *counting crows* then?'

'Too obvious. Anyway, chin up, old fruit. He'll be calling us back any minute. D'you leave a number?'

I glare at my phone.

'Pants.'

George steps back from the wall and cranes his neck backwards to gaze up into the cosmos.

'What now?' I ask, a chill settling slowly in my bones.

'Now,' muses George, 'we stop, and we think. There's got to be… something…'

Thump.

Thump.

THUMP.

From deep within the bowels of Denmark Street has risen a heavy, steady thump, like the darkening heartbeat of the city. It pauses for a moment, then returns.

Thump.

Thump.

THUMP.

'D'you hear that...?' says George, his eyes sparking alight. 'Sounds like... drums...'

Carefully, he rests one ear on the wall and touches both palms against the brickwork. A queer silence descends, and the thumping slows, very, very nearly, to a stop.

Then, in an instant, the beating heart explodes in a splintering pandemonium of rhythm and quiver and crash that fractures the very air into a million sonic splinters and shakes the whole building until it buckles under the force and propels George backwards into the opposite wall at six hundred miles an hour, shattering concrete and filling the alleyway with grey-green smoke. Ten seconds later, when the smoke has cleared, he pops out of the building onto the cobbles below like a cookie from a cutter, leaving a George-shaped indentation in the wall. A dust cloud settles in his hair. He sits up and shakes his head.

'That's the greatest drumming I've ever heard.'

He springs to his feet and chases the sound down the alleyway. The Drummer has settled into the beat now and the air is fizzing with excitement. Thump, smash, thunder, roar. I follow George down the narrow passageway and out into a small courtyard area crowded with ventilation shafts and barbed wire, hidden away from the bustle of the city. The drums are behind us now, all guns, thunder and warfare.

A large notice is painted on the wall.

"THE FAMOUS" 12 BAR CLUB
Time Out 'BEST LIVE MUSIC VENUE' '95/'96

Underneath, a tacked-on poster.

LOCK-UP-YOUR-DAUGHTERS ROCK FESTIVAL
Every night this week!!!

George's face widens into a thousand-mile smile.

'He's in there. Where's the door?'

And he's gone again, back down the alley. Thump, smash, thunder, roar. The momentum scoops me up and is pulling me along when a painted sign on an abandoned black door catches my eye.

'George. Back here.'

Sandwiched in between a flapping sheet of tarpaulin and a knackered air-conditioning unit is a notice reading 'CLUB ENTRANCE'. George leans into the door and listens.

'Somewhere on the other side of this doorway,' he says, palm pressed against the wood, 'is Our Drummer. You game?'

After the tiniest beat, he throws the door open and is sucked up inside the building like a penny into a vacuum cleaner.

5

Ahead, the 12 Bar Club is throbbing with noise and crawling with people. Glasses clink, beer taps squirt and cash tills thrum. In a distant room, the drums thunder. I make a move to follow George and a fat hand clamps onto my wrist.

'Oi. Princess.'

Inside a grubby-windowed booth sits a bloated, leathery woman with bulging bug eyes and a scrapyard of metal piercings hanging off her face. She groans in towards me, tightening her grip on my arm and, as her mouth yawns open, the chemical sting of cheap vodka fills my nostrils.

'The squid's a nightmare.'

How very odd.

'Sorry… squid?'

'Yeah.'

Bug-Eyed Metalface is counting piles of pound coins from a tin. I brave a glance into the club but George is, once again, lost.

'I don't really know what you mean.'

'Wha'?'

'You seem to be telling me about a squid?'

'Wha'? Six queers in the Nile mate,' she burps, steadily counting pounds. I raise a tentative finger.

'Thing is, I'm not entirely sure wh—'

'Six. Quid. In. Tonight. MATE.'

She leers at me with a faceful of ironwork, and I fumble for change in my wallet.

'Paying for your brother?'

'Sorry?'

'Freddy Freeloader.'

I follow her greasy finger in George's direction.

'Oh. Yes. He's not actually my brother though, we're—'

'Juzwell, mate.' She burps again. 'We don't do Family Tickets.'

I slide twelve pounds across the counter, and she waves me away.

'G'on then.'

Mumbling half-formed thanks into my chin, I tumble into the 12 Bar Club and the crowd snatches me by the scruff of the neck. Brawny shoulders jostle me back and forth, and wooden table corners prod my thighs. My nose twitches at the sweaty tang of belly-stretched T-shirts, the distant whiff of urinals and the gritty pong of stale beer and ashtrays. Big bearded rockers in denim jackets laugh beefily at each other's jokes and drain pints in two swigs, paint peels off the walls and posters plaster every surface advertising gigs by bands called Daddy's Ballbag, Mary & The Meat Puppets and Not Now I'm Naked. Cobwebs of congealing lager foam cling to empty glasses, and above the bubbling stew of greasy nest-haired heads, a thick duvet of smoke clings to the ceiling like factory smog.

'This place is champion.'

George is back by my side, blue eyes firing.

'Shall we go poach ourselves a drummer?'

We're choking through the crowds, wedging past the bar, squeezing along the walls, all the while following the sound of the pounding drums. Beyond the curve of George's neck I can make out a tiny stage in the distance, hot with action, shuddering with movement, and as we slip through the doorway into the live room, the drum kit gasps suddenly open like a hundred thousand brass keys exploding into an aircraft hangar, and the air shatters in a cacophonous smithereen of battling metallic rhythms and ringing cymbals. Behind the kit thunders a rolling army of drummer and drumsticks, opening his mouth wide every few bars to belt powerful high notes into a microphone.

We stand, transfixed, our eyes bolted onto the blur of sticks and hair and rhythm exploding from the corner of the tiny stage. George lays a hand on my shoulder.

'Elvis has entered the building.'

I've never heard a sound like it. It's devastating. The bassist and guitar player are ropey, and the singer seems half drunk, but it doesn't matter. The drums are carrying everything. And if *this* guy was in *our* band…

When the song clatters to a noisy end and the room collapses into slapdash applause, the band begin to dismantle. The Drummer spins both sticks, slips them into his back pocket and drops down off the stage.

'We need to buy this guy a drink,' suggests George, one hand on my arm. 'Seduce him.'

'What, now?'

'Now or never, Christoph.'

Pushing through the crowd, we pinball between shoulders and backs on a beeline for the Drummer. He is heading for the bar, where the queue is six people deep, and our access is blocked by a fortress of barrel-bodied rockers in leather jackets. Squeezing through, I soon find myself stuck fast between two large, T-shirted beer bellies. Both men are looking down at me as if I were a horny dog humping at their legs.

'Hello there.'

Beer Belly One takes half a step back.

'Keep your hands to yourself, mate. We've only just met.'

Beer Belly Two sniggers at this and takes a noisy gulp from his pint. Nervously, I watch as the lager drains from his glass, my heart thudding in my chest. Maybe I'm not cut out for all this. Maybe I'm just an extra from *The Archers* who got lost looking for the bric-a-brac sale and accidentally wandered into an orgy.

'Ha, yes! I'll be… I'll be asking for your number next!' I venture, catastrophically.

Neither Beer Belly finds this amusing.

Still being watched like a tiny panicking dog, I squeeze free from the prison of paunches and crane my neck for signs of the

Drummer. He is standing several rows in front of me, tapping a rhythm on his chest. George, meanwhile, is chattering at a middle-aged woman at the far end of the bar. She sits cross-legged on a tall stool, limbs curling over one another, black mini-skirt holding on for dear life against the squeeze of her thigh. She touches him on the arm, revealing a cluster of red-painted nails.

Pushing on, I establish a foothold at the bar and sidle up next to the Drummer. He is nodding along to some secret rhythm in his head.

This is it.

Got to make a strong first impression.

Adopt a power stance.

What would Rod Stewart do?

A-ha! Got it.

I rest my elbow on the counter, and my chin on my fist. This looks good. This looks *great*. 'Hey, dude.'

To emphasise my greeting I also poke him in the arm. He turns around and is immediately drawn to my chin-on-fist stance. Hmm. I was aiming for Nonchalant Bohemian, but now that I think about it, this is actually Effeminate Wrestler.

'Great gig, dude. Wanna pint?'

Why do I keep saying 'dude'? He's not a Ninja Turtle.

'Yeah, sure,' he shrugs, still nodding along to his secret drumbeat. I furtively scan his strong, Viking-like features. His face looks like it was hewn from the rock of an ancient Baltic cliff face.

'So, do you…'

Whatever you do, don't say 'come here often'.

'…come here often?'

You dreadful idiot.

'Now and again. Played here forty, maybe fifty times.'

'Wow. What a… lot of times.' I scan the beer taps. 'Amstel OK for you…?'

'Tony,' he replies, offering a hand. 'Amstel's fine, yeah.'

We shake, the muscles in my hand shrinking at his blacksmith's grip.

'I'm Chris.'

His face shifts into a crooked smile.

'You're a gent, Chris. Big Butt Trumpet fan then?'

Wow. WOW. That was a peculiar opening gambit.

'Sorry… what?'

'You like Butt Trumpet?'

OK, so I didn't mishear that.

'Sorry, but it did sound rather like you asked me if I like butt trumpets.'

'I did.'

Just agree. Always best to agree.

'I suppose butt trumpets are… nice…?'

'You know I'm talking about the band, right?' he replies, gesturing at the stage.

'Oh, the *band*! The band. Yes. Obviously. The band is called Butt Trumpet.'

THE BAND IS CALLED BUTT TRUMPET.

'Yeah.'

I smile weirdly at him. This isn't going entirely to plan.

'Anyway, um. No, they're not really my thing.'

Well, that definitely ought to do it. Tony picks up his pint and makes a move to walk away.

'I mean, what I meant was, I'm not really into them, no. I'm actually more of a fan of… you.'

Ugh. That was a bit creepy. Need a diversion.

'Christoph!'

George appears at my side and slots a fifty-pence piece into the tip jar. One of the prettier barmaids eyes him up.

'You're never going to believe this,' he is saying, 'but I was just talking to a woman over there – she works for Island. Island *Records*. In the *accounts* department. That means she's done tax returns for, I don't know… probably everyone in the entire history of music.'

My mouth opens very, very slowly and I raise one finger.

'She wanted to know all about the band and you and me and what it's like living in the countryside and do we have girlfriends and do we have a manager and then I was telling her about the time we cooked that four-foot-long burrito, do you remember?'

'George.'

'Yes, old chum?'

'This is Tony.'

As I step aside, George's eyes open like parachutes.

'No way – it's you! First time I heard your drumming I thought my ears were going to fall off.'

Tony flicks his chin in appreciation and, as I make my way down the bar, George begins to unleash conversation on him. When I return some minutes later, laden with beers, George is still in full flow and Tony seems to have moved a step or two backwards.

'...then, when I finished the Satellite website, I thought why not start my own business? So now I do wireframes, and CSS, and HTML coding, and there's this new open-source content management system called WordPress which is basically software script with tons of plug-ins and widgets and stuff...'

Tony's hand has moved instinctively to the drumsticks in his back pocket.

'Here you go,' I interrupt, distributing pints. We clink glasses and there is a short, loaded silence.

'So Tony, you been with, er... Butt Trumpet long?'

'Nah, I'm just sitting in for a mate. Bit of a weird lot, to be honest. I'm in tons of bands right now, but, I dunno, I'm looking for something new.'

George kicks me in the shin, quite hard.

'OWW-we've got a rock band,' I blurt. Tony glances about the room.

'Who's we?'

'We two. The us. Me and George.'

An expression of baffled astonishment spreads across Tony's face. He's looking at me as if I just told him I was head of the KGB.

'You two... are a band?'

'Yep, since we were thirteen,' beams George, whacking me on the back and spilling my pint.

'We've just been nominated for Best New Act at the Independent Music Awards.'

'Oh yeah, what's that? Rings a bell. Battle of the Bands?'

'No, it's a proper awards ceremony,' I insist. Tony looks unconvinced. 'They've got a logo and everything.'

He shrugs and demolishes nearly a third of his pint.

Ask him. Just ask him. What have you got to lose?

'Speaking of the band, we're actually looking for...'

I'll tell you what you've got to lose. He could say no. He could reject you outright. He could tell you he wouldn't join your band even if there'd been a cataclysmic holocaust and you were the last musicians in Christendom and this cruel rebuke could send you into a gruesome downward spiral that drives you first to drink and then to intravenous drug abuse in some urine-stained stairwell where you remain in hopeless purgatory and a puddle of your own fluids until, thirty years from now, forever rejected from the bosom of mainstream society, you find yourself sitting at bus stops all day weighing twenty-five stone, wearing fluorescent sunglasses and plastic bags for shoes, smelling of cheeseburgers and quacking at pigeons.

That's what you've got to lose.

'...we're looking for a new drummer.'

Tony falls silent for several seconds, the faintest gleam in his eyes. He takes another slug of his beer.

'What happened to your old one?'

'Oh,' replies George, 'we've never h—'

'He lost all his arms,' I interrupt, hastily.

Hmm. That didn't sound quite as good out loud as it did in my head.

'In a... terrible gardening accident,' I add, as if that makes it any better.

'The drummer from Def Leppard lost an arm once,' reflects George.

'Yes,' I reply, 'but he still has the other arm left.'

'I s'pose.'

'What do you mean "I suppose"? *That's how he drums.* With his one arm. How could a person without any arms *at all* be a drummer?'

'I'm just saying. Anything's possible.'

'No it isn't.'

George grins at me, and I look back at Tony. He is watching us, curiously, beneath lowered brow.

'Anyway... um. Yep. We need a new drummer.'

'What kind of band you got?'

George stares thoughtfully at the ceiling. I take a breath to speak, then stop, then open my mouth again.

'Well... I think the *best* way to describe it would be Anglo-American-influenced melodic rock/pop acoustica underpinned by a powerful sense of melody, vocal harmony and shot through with a lyrical singer-songwriter integrity.'

Tony's face of hewn rock is unmoving.

'Basically,' jumps in George, 'we do uplifting acoustic ballads with a rock edge, and loads of two-part harmonies. And we're looking for a third harmony to go on top.'

'That way, we can achieve a fuller, more intense sound that's somewhere between Toad the Wet Sprocket and a slightly less self-conscious Matchbox 20.'

After considering us for a moment, Tony whips his sticks from his back pocket and drains the rest of his pint in one go.

'Let's meet for a jam. Next week.'

'Hoorah,' I agree, obviously regretting the use of the word 'hoorah' with immediate effect. 'We can Do A Jam. Let's jam.'

How do you jam?

'This is my number,' adds Tony, scrawling his digits onto a nearby beer mat in black marker. 'I know a place in Penge called Hell's Palace. I'll see you there.'

Just as he's about to leave, he stops, thinks, and points at George.

'You got an electric guitar?'

'Yep.'

'Bring it.'

And with that, he hands us the beer mat, pockets the pen and walks away.

6

The letter is open on my desk.

It lifts ever so slightly in the cool April breeze drifting in through my bedroom window, and I trap it with one finger. Outside, Dad appears from the greenhouse, brandishing spring onions, nudging his specs. Beyond the garden is the old playing field, and beyond the playing field, endless hills and meadows and rolling countryside, the occasional farmhouse, a cluster of trees.

My gaze falls back to the letter.

It happened in the autumn after we finished university. A pretty weird time for most arts graduates, a professional no-man's land, and until the letter arrived I'd forgotten about it almost entirely. It was a bit pointless applying for those jobs in the first place, to be honest. I never actually *wanted* them, and I wouldn't have said yes even if I'd had offers. The truth is, there was part of me that just didn't want to disappoint people – my parents, my grandparents, my tutors. Part of me that was strangely compelled to keep up appearances.

Harley Bourne was just another name on the list.

Harley Bourne Group
Golden Square
London W1F 9EP

Dear Christopher

Following our correspondence in September 2002, we are writing to inform you that a position has opened up which we feel would be directly suited to your skills and experience. We have kept your information on file since your interview and, now that the role of Junior Account Manager has reopened, we would like to formally extend the offer. The starting salary is £22,000 per annum, with benefits.
We look forward to hearing from you.

Dominic Sykes
Creative Director

Dominic Sykes. A man whose office was devoid of dust, all plate glass and chrome fittings. Numberless clocks ticking on the walls.

***

'Where do you see yourself in five years, Chris?'

Dominic reclines in his matt-black-leather chair, considering me with raised chin. He talks in one of those nondescript transatlantic accents that's part public schoolboy, part movie-learned American.

'I want to do something... meaningful.'

'Riiight, right,' he replies, nodding slowly, 'but I'm talking in terms of what kind of office do you have, who are your clients, what does it say on your door, that sort of bag.'

I look from Dominic to his silent associate, Edward, sitting in the adjacent chair. Edward's tie is knotted small and neat, and ever so slightly too tight.

'I don't really think of it like that. I just think it's important to have a career you believe in.'

'Totally, totally,' agrees Dominic, swivelling from left to right and tapping the desk with his pen, 'but... OK. Tell me what fires you up. What's "meaningful"?'

I finger my CV on the tabletop. Dominic twiddles his pen.

'Music.'

'Huh, sure, sure, sure. Maybe you, er, maybe you should start a rock band.'

He winks at Edward, who agrees with a short laugh that troubles not one of his facial muscles.

'Actually I've already got a band, we've been together for eight years.'

Dominic lifts a hand, shaking his head.

'Sorry, no, you misunderstand – I'm joking. I'm talking about professional goals, not hobbies.'

'Oh, OK. I mean… we've never really seen it as a hobby.'

'Sure, but come on. A band *is* a hobby, unless you're Coldplay. And we can't all be Coldplay, can we? What was that song? That song they do?'

He sticks his teeth over his lower lip and hums the chorus from 'Why Does It Always Rain On Me?'

'…Bloody brilliant.'

'I think that one's Travis.'

'What?'

'No, nothing. I was just saying I think that song's Travis.'

'Same diff, right, Edward?' Edward confirms this. 'But like I was saying, we can't all be Coldplay.'

I study the photo in the top corner of my CV. I'm wearing a blank expression, thin-lipped and flat-eyed.

'Thing is, Chris,' continues Dominic, elbows on the table, 'I like you. You've got a good degree and all that jazz, and I can see you're a guy who's prepared to work hard, which is *great*. But think about it – when did chasing a dream ever buy anyone a timeshare in the Algarve? Yeah?'

He laughs at his joke and click-clicks the end of his pen.

'Edward knows what I mean, don't you Ed?'

Edward confirms this.

'Anyway, look, bottom line is, advertising's a shitstorm. Mega fat shitstorm. You have to really *want* it… know what I mean?'

I nod. Dominic leans back in his chair again, causing the faintest moan from the leather, and runs his tongue around the inside of his mouth.

'What is it that you actually want?'

He watches me, waiting for an answer. I can hear music in my head, pulsing to the beat of the clock hands. Edward makes a note on his pad.

Clouds fly by, and the afternoon dies, and I count to the tick of the numberless clocks.

7

When Our Lord God first begot Mother Earth in all her resplendent glory, and He bestowed upon the rich and fertile soil a forest of tall and mystical trees, and He filled the sky with dew-specked clouds for the harping angels to slumber nightly upon, and He gifted unto the plains and mountains and deserts and wild tundras a congregation of sublime and gentle beasts, He reached the mighty zenith of his task and discovered to his dismay that He had not sufficient materials left in His divine arsenal to build the indie-band rehearsal studios on the A234 to Bickley that He had so majestically planned, and thus was He forced to do a botch job using leftover scraps of heinous primordial sludge He found kicking around the Celestial Workshop.

Hell's Palace, Penge. The last place God built.

'So I listened to the tracks on your website.'

Studio 12, which we have hired for the afternoon, has been painted Hue of Burger Sauce and smells faintly of Stilton. Tony is sitting behind the rickety drum kit foot-tapping a complex rhythm on the hi-hat while spinning a drumstick in a perfect figure-of-eight and, in his spare hand, holding a massive pie from which he periodically takes enormous flakey bites with his unfeasibly large mouth.

'Problem is,' he adds through a mouthful of pastry, 'your music's not really my thing.'

'Oh… right.'

I glance at George, who is sitting on a busted amp on the opposite side of the room, restringing his electric guitar. He doesn't look up.

'Why not?' I ask. Tony swallows a wodge of pie. 'It's chick music.'

A metal fixing drops from my microphone stand and sends it careering down onto the keyboard with a loud thump. The tiny screw bounces from my grasp and hops away across the mustard-yellow carpet.

'Chick music?'

'Yeah, chick music. Music for chicks. It's bedwetter rock, basically. See, you're the band all the wet kids like. The ones that get bullied a lot. They get home from school, drink a cup of milk, stick on your CD and then go to sleep and piss the bed.'

'And that's not a good thing?'

Tony shakes his head gravely and spins his drumstick again. I poke at a random button on my keyboard.

'Everyone needs a niche.'

'Think of your band like a Transit van,' Tony continues, shifting on his stool. 'You need a mechanic to get in there and give it a once-over. Chassis's probably all right, but it'll be something small in the piston, knackered gudgeon pin maybe. Or your harmonic balancer's rusted. You with me?'

'Sort of.'

Tony finishes his pie, screws up the empty packet and lobs it over his shoulder towards the wastepaper bin. It hits the rim and bounces inside.

'So when's the bass player turning up?'

Danger. This could set him off. Just be diplomatic.

'The truth is, vis-à-vis the bass player, is that currently, as it stands right now, we are sort of in bet—'

The door to the studio swings open with a *ssswwwssh-DUD*, and a tiny little man appears in the entrance, holding a Peperami in one hand and pushing a massive wheeled amplifier with the other. He spanks the amp with his tiny palm.

'Give me a hand with this, wouldja?'

I grab the other end of the trolley and we pull it inside the studio. The little man huffing and puffing behind it is small, creepily small, as if someone left him too long in a jar of vinegar, with a mop of long, stringy hair and scrunchy little features arranged randomly about his head. He looks like somebody put a scrawny baby in an Axl Rose wig and then punched it in the face.

'Not convinced that's an SLP-1959 head, mate.'

Tony is scrutinising the equipment, bottom lip poking out.

'Yeah it is,' replies the Scrawny Old Axl Rose Punchface Baby. 'This is the actual one Jimmy Page used on *Led Zepp One*.'

That's right, because if there's one thing the undisputed kings of rock and roll are going to do with their treasured antique equipment, it's donate it to a squalid rehearsal studio in the arse end of Penge.

'No, mate, can't be. Page didn't use a Marshall on that album.'

'Come on,' insists the Scrawny Old Axl Rose Punchface Baby, running a bony hand through his hair, 'everyone knows Page played Les Paul through Marshall. That's schoolboy.'

Tony leans forward on his stool.

'Not in '68 he didn't. First album was recorded on a '58 Telecaster through a Supro Thunderbolt. OK, yeah, he had a triple-humbucker Black Beauty Les Paul with Bigsby vibrato *as well*, which he was using live, but he definitely went through a Supro for *Led Zepp One*.'

Punchface bobs his chin and tugs his T-shirt down over his belt.

'Yeah, well, watch it anyway. Page gave it a proper hammering on tour, so don't turn the gain up any higher than seven or it'll blow your bloody head off.'

Wiping his nose on his sleeve, he takes a wounded bite from the Peperami and clomps out the room. The door slams with a *ssswwwssh-cluk* and silence returns to Studio 12.

'So the bass player?' continues Tony.

'Yes. Right. The bass player.'

Tony tinkles the ride cymbal. I glance again at George, who is fiddling with controls on the amp.

'The truth is… we don't have one.'

Silence from the drum kit.

'You don't have one?'

'Not as such, no.'

Tony spins his stick at me.

'Can't have a band without a bassist.'

'I know.'

'I can introduce you to some session players if you want. There's Big Molly from Woodley Green, used to play bass with me in the Evil Beavers. He was jamming with Jah Wobble until they stuck him in the clink.'

'Right.'

Tony runs his tongue around his mouth.

'You don't know who Jah Wobble is, do you?'

'Yes, *obviously* I do.'

I'm ninety per cent sure he's the barman in *Return of the Jedi*.

'So you want me to get Big Molly on the phone? He's very talented, plays the keys too.'

'It's fine, we'll think of something.'

We can't take an ex-felon on tour with us. He might rob me in my sleep.

'Can we play a song?' suggests George, strumming a crackling chord on his guitar. '"Girl on the Radio"?'

Tony tickles his hi-hat as George steps up to the microphone, and I boost the volume on my keyboard. The opening chord floats out into the room, sustained and melancholy, from the ancient guitar amp.

'*Dark night, driving home…*'

George's voice is submerged by the song as my piano surges in like a tide, moving under, over and around the guitar. The song begins to swell and breathe, and the words wash and tumble through the slowly building soundscape.

'*I see silhouettes on the dash, in my eyes, and the lights in the rain…*'

Fragments of rhythm float into the song, a tomb-like tom-tom, a careful wash of splash cymbal, a brittle rimshot. I watch Tony working the drums, subtly dropping in different textures, some rough, some smooth, some wide, some narrow. The song sounds different, deeper somehow, as George drifts into the chorus.

'*Sing out, the voice on the radio over again...*'

Suddenly, the drum kit explodes into a complicated, jagged beat. It's heavy, and aggressive. The rhythm doesn't work. He's doing it all wrong, and the song soon buckles under mechanical noise. I pull my hands off the keys. George steps off the microphone. The room goes quiet.

'Tony...?'

'Yes, mate.'

'What was the, um... what was... er, with the drums there?'

From a pocket in his combat trousers, Tony has produced what looks like a large slice of cold broccoli quiche.

'Just laying down a fat breakbeat.'

A fat breakbeat? Perhaps someone ought to tell him we're not the Wu-Tang Clan.

'What this song's missing,' he continues, taking a huge bite of food, 'is a little bit of cheeky drum 'n' bass.'

'But it's an acoustic ballad,' protests George.

'Yeah, exactly. And what's the last thing anyone expects in an acoustic ballad?'

He tears another chunk out of the quiche and points at George.

'A big nasty breakbeat, that's what. I mean, think about the Prodigy. What would the Prodigy do?'

'But we're nothing like the Prodigy.'

'Exactly why you need to start thinking like them,' he says, whacking the snare drum, hard. 'See, problem with you lads is you're just not... very...'

He searches for the word.

'What?'

'You're just not very rock 'n' roll.'

My hands navigate to my hips.

'That's not necessarily true.'

Chewing patiently on his quiche, Tony gives this some thought.

'Back in the nineties,' he says, eventually, 'when everyone else was at illegal raves taking ecstasy, what were you boys doing?'

I look at George. He shrugs.

'Jigsaws,' I reply.

From across the corridor, the angry sound of a punk band murdering their guitars bulldozes through the thin studio walls.

'This is why,' continues Tony, 'I thought we could chuck in a bit of electric guitar, give it some edge, find your own sound. No point doing what everyone else does, otherwise you end up sounding like Coldplay.'

But I want to sound like Coldplay.

'It doesn't matter whether our music's different,' says George, removing his guitar and dumping it on a nearby stand. 'It just has to be *good*.'

'Being different is the same as being good.'

'Not if it's crap it isn't.'

Ssswwwssh-DUD. The door swings open again and the punk-band racket vomits through the entrance, filling the room. The Scrawny Old Axl Rose Punchface Baby is standing in the entrance holding a limp sausage roll and a can of Tizer.

'Any of you lot bring a car?'

George sticks up his hand.

'Yeah, some geezer's about to clamp you.'

'Mum'll kill me!' blurts George, grabbing his keys and rushing out the door. Punchface laughs to himself, shakes his head, swigs a fizz of Tizer and points towards the guitar amp.

'That Marshall working out all right…? Yeah? Yeah, I was chatting to Dan, our engineer, and turns out what actually happened was Page didn't use that on the first album. He didn't have a Marshall on the first album.'

Tony frowns at him.

'I know, mate. That's what I said.'

'Yeeeeah, they're great blokes, those blokes out of Led Zepp. My cousin's best mate met Robert Plant's son down the Crown once, so I'm pretty good mates with all that lot. Yeeeeah. Crazy times.'

The band across the corridor relent for a moment. A fragile silence hovers in the air.

'I'm going for a wazz,' announces Tony, disappearing out the door. Punchface rocks back and forth on his feet, whistling a tune.

'Want some Tizer?' he asks, doing a little burp.

'No thanks.'

'Hope the lads in Studio 10 aren't disturbing you lot. Lesbian Funk Academy, here every Saturday. Bunch of mentalists.'

'It's fine.'

Before the words have left my mouth, Lesbian Funk Academy thunder into the opening chords of 'Right Next Door To Hell' by Guns N' Roses.

'So what kinda band you got?' says Punchface, picking a long, greasy hair off his sausage roll.

'*Our* band? Um... well, it's sort of Ben Folds Five-ish, I suppose? Bit of Crowded House, with the harmonies and so on, and then it's basically the pop sensibility of early Beatles, but with the emotional depth of, you know. Late Beatles.'

George crashes in through the door.

'Christoph, good news is we haven't been clamped. But we have been fined. Sixty quid.'

He shoves the crumpled penalty notice into his bag. From the Lesbians' rehearsal room comes the sound of somebody screeching into the mic.

'Gutted,' offers Punchface. 'That is well annoying.'

Tony thunders into the room, his left shoe dripping with brownish liquid.

'Bloody toilets have flooded. There's piss everywhere!'

'Not again!' laments Punchface, scampering away down the corridor.

'Shall we get something done?' I ask, beginning to understand why they call this place Hell's Palace.

'Hang on,' replies Tony, abandoning his dripping shoe. 'Before we do... try this.'

Reaching underneath the drum kit, Tony reappears with a small metal box and throws it in a looping arc towards George, who stumbles to catch it.

'I brought you this old delay pedal,' says Tony. 'Think of it as a make-good button.'

'What's a make-good button?' asks George.

'You'll see.'

George kneels down and sets about plugging it in. This time, when he strums that same opening chord, everything changes. Through the delay pedal, one chord becomes hundreds, a never-ending sonic hall of mirrors. Notes fill the room, dashing and diving, surrounding us all like a storm in a snow globe.

'*Spotlight, riding on…*'

Carefully, expertly, Tony releases ice-cold droplets of rhythm into the song and, as we move through the verse, he brings in a full and driving beat, opening us out into the soar and swell of the chorus.

'*Sing out, the voice on the radio over again… and show me… the voice that I know, sing to me…*'

With the climax of the song looming, the sound seems to multiply, burst wide open, and I realise Tony is singing long, high notes across the top. Gradually, the tide of the music ebbs and slowly flows before coming to a gentle stop, and calm returns.

Tiny pinpricks of nervous excitement are swarming through me.

'That was… really good.'

Tony spins a drumstick.

'Can't go wrong with a twelve/eight groove.'

The room breathes like an unclenching fist, and George gives me a smile.

'Song needs hacking up of course,' adds Tony, peeling the smile off George's face.

'What do you mean?'

'It's way too long.'

'No it isn't.'

'You have to cut the third verse, at least. Track's nearly six minutes long. If you're not careful, you'll turn into Bon Jovi.'

George and I share a guilty glance.

'You can't… I mean, you can't just take bits ou—'

'Look,' interrupts Tony, sliding a massive spring roll from his trousers, 'if we're going to be in this band together, we've got to be a unit. Work together.'

He takes a big, crispy bite.

Be in this band together?

'Sorry... are you saying... in *this* band?'

'Yeah, you want me?'

The Rock Viking is going to be our Drummer. OUR. DRUMMER.

'YES!'

Think I might have shouted that. 'I mean... yes.'

George sits down on top of his amp.

'I thought it wasn't your thing.'

'I'm up for anything, me. So what do we call ourselves?'

'Satellite,' answers George, retuning. Tony pounds the snare.

'Yeah, but that name's rubbish.'

'Our name's Satellite.'

Tony ignores this and taps at his chin for a few moments.

'How about... Sponge?'

Sponge?

'That's not... very us,' I suggest, quietly.

'Doesn't matter.'

'It does matter,' says George. 'It matters a lot.'

'Why?'

'Because our name's an artistic statement. It has to reflect our music.'

Tony finishes the spring roll, reaches back into his trousers, conducts a short rummage and pulls out a packet of scampi-flavoured Nik Naks.

'Balls. A band name only has one purpose.'

'And that is...?'

'Festival posters.'

George folds his arms.

'What do you mean?'

'You're playing Glastonbury, say, and there's a ton of bands on the bill, and nobody knows who you are, but they see your name leaping off the page and BAM, they're at your gig faster than you can say Gregorian acid jazz.'

'People aren't that shallow.'

'Nah, they are.'

65

Carefully, George suppresses a sigh.

'So what do you suggest?'

Tony closes one eye and feeds a Nik Nak into his mouth.

'Penalty Shoot-Out.'

George's face drops open.

'If you saw that on a poster, you'd definitely go to the gig,' adds Tony.

'No, I wouldn't.'

'Or how about…' His eyes wander around the room for a few seconds. 'Bum Chums.'

'This is ridiculous.'

'You would *go out of your way* to watch a band called the Bum Chums.'

'I really wouldn't.'

'Guys, guys…' I step out from behind my keyboard. 'Shall we figure this out another time, maybe? I think we've got more pressing things to discuss.'

'What's that?' asks Tony, thudding the bass drum.

'Well, I was thinking… if this is official now, then you might be up for… playing our next gig?'

'Count me in. Can't do it without a bass player, though.'

'We'll find someone.'

'I'll call Big Molly if you like.'

Big Molly the pistol-toting scar-faced gangland pimp? No thanks.

'We'll find someone.'

George sits back down on the amp, in his corner, and twiddles a moody solo. Tony is emptying the final few Nik Naks into his mouth.

'So you cool to be at the Water Rats next Friday at seven?' I ask.

'Next Friday? At the Rats?'

'You know it?'

'Yeah, sure, was heading down there anyway.'

'Really?'

Ssswwwssh-DUD. The door swings open and the stale air is filled with the lesser-spotted reggae version of Enya's 'Sail Away', courtesy of Lesbian Funk Academy. Punchface stands breathless in the doorway and slaps a tiny hand to his forehead.

'Ah, bugger, sorry. Wrong room. I was looking for the Plastered Bastards.'

He slams the door behind him.

'The Plastered Bastards,' echoes Tony, pointing a drumstick at the door. 'Now *that* is a great band name.'

8

The Round Reading Room at King's College library is bathed in a cathedral-like silence. The only sounds are the occasional turning of ancient pages and the delicate pitter-patter of spring showers on the glass ceiling. We are talking in strained whispers.

'I'm not sure I understand why we're here.'

'He's around somewhere,' insists George, 'I know it. He always is.'

'This is a library.'

George nods in sage agreement.

'See, this is why I like you, Christoph. You notice things regular humans wouldn't.'

A librarian at a nearby desk flicks us the briefest of glances.

'Where are we going?'

'You can normally find him somewhere between Dialectical Materialism and Pre-Socratic Philosophy...'

We are edging carefully around the octagonal space, the sound of our breathing thunderous in the warm silence. Two tiers of balconied bookshelves soar upwards into the roof above our heads and, all around, tousle-haired students scribble away on cherry-wood writing desks. In the distance, Big Ben calls to its subjects.

'Pre-Socratic Philosophy?'

George nods.

Sighing, I point at a long, narrow bookcase on the far side of the room.

'That's over there, isn't it?'

George squints.

'No, that's Deontological Ethics.'

'Shhhhhh.'

The librarian's silvery hair is tied back from her temples with such severity that her face looks like it's trying to escape backwards off her head.

'Sorry!' I mouth back. She holds eye contact for a loaded second, then returns to her work.

'Can you fill me in here?' I whisper, tapping George on the shoulder.

'What did I say, Cultural Relativism?'

'You said Diametrical Nominalism, but—'

'Cripes, I've forgotten.'

'*Shhhhhhh!* This is a library.'

The librarian gestures to the many, many books stacked in rows behind her tightly stretched skull, thus proving rather effectively that this is, indeed, a library.

'Sorry!' I whisper again, gingerly approaching her desk. Her long nose twitches at me.

'Afternoon, ma'am' – *ma'am?!* – 'you wouldn't happen to know wh—'

'Quiet!'

'... where we could find the Deconstruc—'

'Keep your voice down, please. People are trying to work.'

This miniature commotion prompts one or two scholars to look up from their papers. A boy in a wheelchair adjusts his spectacles and shakes his head at me. I mouth *Sorry* again.

'*George.*'

George has completely disappeared, and so I slip away into the nearby silence of Chinese Legalism. All around, the room is a pin-drop haven of tranquillity, the dusky afternoon calm disturbed only by thoughtful scribbling and the soft *shhwa-dum* of hardback books sliding onto shelves.

'Chris?'

Somebody has touched a hand to my shoulder. Turning round, I meet a familiar pair of sky-blue eyes.

'Oh. Hello there.'

69

'What are you doing in the library?' John replies, his face drifting into curious concern. I peer through the maze of bookshelves.

'I'm not entirely sure. I mean, he said it was something to do with unlocking the mysteries of rock 'n' roll...' John thinks for a moment.

'George, right?'

'Yep.'

His eyes narrow.

'George drove you all the way from Berkshire to Fleet Street without telling you why?'

'You know what he's like.'

John smiles.

'He's one of a kind, my brother.'

An enthusiastic laugh, somewhere between a toddler and a coyote, vaults up towards to the ceiling and bounces playfully around the high walls of the Round Reading Room.

'OK. There you go.'

George is sitting on a stranger's table on the far side of the building, chatting enthusiastically and making a theatrical gesture best translated as *and then he pulled huge cucumbers from his ears*.

'What's he doing in Contemporary Iranian Philosophy?'

'Talking to a Buddhist monk, by the looks of it,' replies John. 'I'd better go and see what he's up to. Meet me behind Immanuel Kant.'

George has now developed the cucumber gesture into a full-body mime that appears to say *sit on my shoulders and I'll do the Robot*. The monk looks very, very confused. Leaving Chinese Legalism, I glide past towering shelves of medical tomes towards the refuge of Immanuel Kant, tracing my fingers along textbook spines.

'Are you a student at this university?'

Drat. She's back.

'Hello again.'

The librarian fixes me with a terror-stare. Far away in some night-stalked forest, Transylvanian bloodhounds whimper into bushes, the moonlight dancing cold fear in their eyes.

'Are you studying at King's?'

'Ha! Am I...? Of cour—... I mean, would I be here if I wasn't?'

I slide a random book off the shelf and open it with scholarly intent.

'I suppose not,' she muses. 'What are you studying?'

What *am* I studying?

'We-ell. I. Am. A. Student. Of...'

I close the book and inspect its cover.

'Holistic Midwifery,' I reply, displaying the textbook as evidence.

'I'm not familiar with that course.'

'It's very new. Started this morning. Professor, um, Stephen...'

Don't stay Hawking. Do not say Stephen Hawking.

'Hawking.'

That's bad. Very bad. '...-ton.'

Her escaping face tightens. She's going to snap like an elastic band.

'Professor Stephen Hawkington?'

'Yes, that's right... Old Hawky McHawking. Lovely bloke. Very tall.'

PLEASE DON'T KILL ME AND FEAST ON MY REMAINS.

'I have to go now,' I continue, frantically searching the building for my comrades. Where's that Immanuel Kant when you need him?

There!

Offering the librarian an awkward parting nod, I flee towards John's table, where he is surrounded on all sides by huge textbooks and dog-eared piles of notes. George is perched on the tabletop leafing absently through a book called *Postmodernism, or The Cultural Logic of Late Capitalism*.

'Ah, Christoph. Where've you been?'

'Why have you brought me to a library to talk to a Buddhist monk?'

'Huh?'

Back over in Contemporary Iranian Philosophy, the monk is busying himself returning books to shelves.

'What does a monk know about rock 'n' roll?'

'Nothing,' he replies, looking at me as if I'm the crazy one here. 'I just liked his hair.'

'He doesn't have any hair.'

'Exactly. So what's new, little brother?'

John is tracing a pencil along a complex-looking philosophy article written in extremely small type.

'Just, er, working on an essay.'

George turns the postmodernism book upside down and a little shower of notes slide out and scatter onto the table.

'Have you read the new *Harry Potter*?'

'No, I… haven't got round to it yet,' replies John, collecting the notes and stacking them patiently into a pile.

'You should, it's wicked.'

John sets his pen down and looks at us, calmly.

'Don't take this the wrong way, but… why are you here?'

'We're looking for a bassist,' beams George. John looks at me, then back at his brother.

'That's… good. I think that's a good idea.'

George continues to beam. John touches a hand to his chest.

'Are you asking *me*?'

'Oh yes.'

'You know I don't really play any more.'

'It's like riding a bike, bro.'

John takes two seconds to gather his thoughts.

'And it's not that I don't like your music, but…'

What's wrong with our music?

'…I've only ever played in jazz bands.'

George shuffles on his behind and fights back a small frown.

'Plus I've got my finals in May. I haven't got time to join a band at the moment.'

All right, I think that's enough reasons now.

'Don't the Easter holidays start next week?' asks George.

'I've got this big overdraft to shift. I'm spending Easter in a call centre.'

George shakes his head.

'Bleak.'

John nods, and returns to examining his miniature text. George looks at me with a determined expression on his face.

Above our heads, the rain pitter-patters on the glass ceiling.

'Johnny, listen,' he continues, shifting across the table and knocking a book called *Being and Nothingness* onto the carpet. 'It's dead simple, you already know most of our songs. We only need you for *one gig*.'

John, sensing defeat, closes his work folder.

'All we need is someone to turn up on time and play the chords in the right order. After that we'll leave you alone. Scout's honour.'

John reaches down to retrieve *Being and Nothingness* from the floor.

'You were never in the Scouts.'

'Beaver's honour then.'

'Beavers don't have honour.'

'OK,' continues George, leaning in towards him, 'remember when we were kids, you were about six, and you smashed Mum's favourite painting with that miniature football, and I took the blame?'

A reluctant but handsome smile grows slowly across John's face.

'I did that for you, little brother.'

'OK, OK. Fine. I'll do it.' John looks at us both with his bright, keen eyes. 'But just one gig. And then I'm done.'

'Hello Wembley!' laughs George, clapping at quite extraordinary volume. Almost immediately, the librarian with the escaping face rises like a sword through canvas and begins advancing in our direction.

'Uh-oh. I think we're done for.'

As the librarian is leading us out towards the main doors, a fierce grip on each of our arms, the people of King's College library heap their silent judgement upon us. The boy in the wheelchair is watching me like a hawk.

'Thrown out of a library, Christoph,' whispers George into my ear, as the crisp London air meets our faces once more. 'Let the rock 'n' roll commence.'

9

He's late.

The Drummer's late.

It's a chilly spring evening on the Gray's Inn Road, and crowds are already gathering outside the venue. Sirens wail in the distance.

'He said he'd be here twenty minutes ago.'

I scan the full length of the road for a glimpse of Tony.

Dark figures walk the streets, hands stuffed in pockets. 'Tony's a loose cannon, Christoph. He doesn't want to be tied down. Besides, don't we have to wait for the Water Rats to finish their soundcheck?'

'The Black Cats.'

'That's them.'

Inside the venue, the din of feedback, angry guitars and the thrashing of drums rumbles on beneath Heidi's unmistakable half-rap.

'You said he's a professional,' replies John, hitching his bass guitar onto his shoulder. 'So he'll be here.'

'And if he doesn't turn up,' adds George, 'we'll just play anyway. Easy.'

'This isn't Unplugged and Intimate at Windsor Arts Centre, George. It's a rock gig. Without drums, we're—'

'It's still only a gig. It's not like this one night was going to change our lives forever.'

And that's when I see him.

Making his way along the winding queue, past the waiting fans, and walking straight up to the doorman.

'Yeah, hi. I'm on the guest list.'

The doorman consults his notepad.

'Name?'

'City Records. Yeah, that's me. Cheers, mate.'

The main door opens, the racket of laughter and guitars and riotous drinking spills out onto the streets, and Paul from City Records disappears inside the building.

***

The Water Rats is a hot pit of noise, a seething inferno of sweaty, grabbing arms, cackling laughter and booze-guzzling teeth. We're squeezing through the dark, battling bodies, tugging our instruments through tangles of limbs, and as we struggle past the metre-thick queue at the bar, I spot him.

'I'll catch you up,' I say to John and George, breaking away and heading for the bar.

'Excuse me, hi.'

City Records is picking his teeth while the barmaid serves a rival customer.

'Hi there,' I repeat, doing a sort of casual lean on the end of my upturned keyboard. He turns and looks at me.

'D'I know you?'

'Yes. Well, I mean no. I'm a musician,' I reply, gesturing at my instrument.

'Wha'?'

He scratches his ribs, chewing at me. What on earth am I supposed to say now?

'I play keyboards in the greatest pop combo since The Beatles, a band so stupendously pivotal in the history of rock 'n' roll that, upon hearing just the first five seconds of our demo, your brain will immediately liquefy and pour freely from your ears in a spontaneous rampage of aural ecstasy.'

No. Obviously I didn't say that.

'Fancy going ten-pin bowling after this?'

Or that. No, try something low-key. Unobtrusive. 'I'm in a band... called Satellite.'

No reaction.

'We're up for Best New Act at the LIMAs. We played at the launch night last week...?'

'Oh, right. Yeah. Yeah.' He leans forward on the bar to attract attention. 'I didn't see it.'

'And Shawn didn't mention us?'

'Who? What? Nah.'

Danger. You're losing him.

You need to do something bold. But something that doesn't involve stripping, or starting a conga line.

What would George do in this situation?

'We've just booked a European tour.'

Nice move. That's a really excellent move. Well done, that man.

'Wha'? Really?'

I find myself nodding, eagerly.

'But... you're unsigned, right?' he asks, looking me up and down.

'Mm-hmm.'

'And you're touring Europe?'

'Ye-ep,' I reply, slapping the bar top. I'm in this now, may as well milk it. 'We be Europe bound. Yooo-rope, capital of...'

I started that sentence with no clear view of the end. I wonder what I'll say.

'...cheese.'

His head is nodding, but his eyes are the eyes of a man watching the neighbour's dog to see if it's going to crap on his lawn.

'What kind of music?'

'Well, it's acoustic ballady kind of stuff, I suppose, so you *could* say it's a bit Simon and Garfunkel? But I don't know, really it's more of a new type of, you know, *sound*, that does this kind of acoustic-pop-upbeat-rock-harmony-led... *thing*. Does that make sense? So, OK, imagine if The Beatles were born now, well not now, I mean, in the eighties, and John Lennon wasn't

76

shot, but they were all still around, and they listened to loads of Crowded House and Phil Collins and stuff. So it's basically that.'

The barmaid indicates by means of a desperately deep sigh that she's ready for his order. City Records clicks his fingers and points at the Guinness tap.

'Right, but what's your angle?' he replies, dumping his gum into an ashtray. 'And some nuts, darling.'

'Our angle…?'

'Yeah. Like, has one of you got a famous dad, or do you work in a zoo, or is someone in the band terminally ill, or whatever.'

The barmaid tosses a bag of peanuts across the counter, and City Records tears it open.

'Nobody's… terminally ill, no.'

'Bret Michaels: diabetes. Freddie Mercury: AIDS. Mike Nolan out of Bucks Fizz: epilepticism. Bish bash bosh, hundred million records in the bank.'

Munching nuts, he has a conspiratorial look over his shoulder and then leans in close towards me.

'I just signed this band right, called Air Biscuit, drummer's only got six months to live. Absolute genius. First single's called 'Cancer Romancer', it's about how he uses his melanoma to get laid. KA-POW. Angle City. *NME* are filling their pants.'

Slipping my hand into my back pocket, I thumb the top of our CD sleeve. This is it. This is that moment you hear about on VH1's *Behind the Music*. The moment everything changed.

> *I suppose the moment everything changed was when Paul from City Records got hold of our demo after a gig at, oh, where was it? The Water Rats. Man, that old place…*

'I've got a demo here, if you're… you know.'

City Records points right into my face. 'Listen, Craig, was it?'

'Chris.'

'Truth is, mate, industry's buggered up the arse at the moment. Bands have to stand out, right, 'cos this isn't the seventies, you can't just screw around growing a beard and expect to get a deal anymore. Knowhatimean?'

'Exactly! My thoughts exactly. In fact, that's why this nomination is so...'

I trail off, waiting for him to agree with me.

'This nomination i... um. You do *know* about the LIMAs, right?'

He scoffs at me.

'Know about them? Mate, I'm one of the judges.'

He devours another fistful of nuts. My eyes go wide.

'Yep, your fate in my hands. Just call me Simon Cowell. Except I'm not a twat.'

The CD is still quivering in my outstretched hand. City Records collects his pint, winks at the barmaid and takes a big slug of his Guinness. Heidi and the Black Cats thrash on in the other room.

'That for me?' he says, eyeing my demo.

I nod. He sniffs, loudly, and takes it off me.

'Cheers, Craig. I'll give it a spin.'

***

In the dim and dingy performance room at the back of the Water Rats we find Heidi standing behind the microphone, surrounded by her band, wearing a midnight-blue dress with a plunging neckline and heavy, highwayman-style boots. Her hair is piled haphazardly on top of her head, rebellious locks cascading down her face.

She looks fantastic.

Noticing us, she signals to the rest of the band, and the music slows to a stop. Two guitarists, one bass, one lead, slope away into another room.

Silence.

'All right lads,' says Tony, from behind the drum kit. 'How's it going?'

Nobody speaks for a few moments. I point hesitantly at Tony, then at Heidi, who frowns back at me, unimpressed. Tony, meanwhile, spins a battered drumstick and returns our confused looks with an apparently innocent smile.

George breaks the deadlock.

'What are you doing?'

'Soundchecking,' says Tony.

'I think you have to let their drummer do his own soundcheck,' replies George, with a nervous laugh.

'But I *am* their drummer.'

'Whose drummer?' I ask. A horribly pointless question.

'You boys know each other?' says Heidi, still standing at the mic, one leg raised slightly against the metal stand.

'Know each other? Tony's our drummer.'

She snorts at me.

'No, he's not. He's our drummer.'

'We hired him last week.'

'Yeah, and we hired him last month. Finders keepers.'

Tony stands up from the drum stool and, navigating past an engineer poking listlessly at a guitar amp, he walks out into the light, waving a calming hand.

'Nobody panic! I'm playing both sets tonight. Happens all the time.'

Heidi crosses her arms and flicks her chin at us.

'I'm not sharing a drummer with The Proclaimers.'

'Y'what?'

'They're the support band, we can't have the same drummer.'

Tony hesitates.

'Why not?'

'It doesn't matter why not, *I'm telling you* we can't have the same drummer. And we found you first, so... know what I mean?'

Heidi cocks her head, robotically. Tony blows air out from between his lips.

'I have no idea what your problem is.'

'My problem,' she says, her grip on the microphone tightening, 'is that you're either *in* my band, or you're *out* of it.'

Tony still seems vaguely amused.

'You're kidding, right?'

She almost smiles at this, but the smile soon fades.

'It's either us…' she concludes, fixing us with those fierce, dark-chocolate eyes, '… or them.'

Tony scoffs in response, but as silence falls, it's clear she means every word. He runs a hand through his hair, shaking his head in disbelief. Behind him, the sound engineer curses at the misbehaving amp.

Through closed doors, beer-fuelled revelry fills the Water Rats from table to ceiling. The fans are warming up, lining their bellies, numbing their brains and sharpening their claws for a night of hot, sticky rock 'n' roll. A sell-out crowd, thirsting for a party.

Time seems to stumble and slow as we await Tony's move.

'I still think you're over-reacting,' he says, eventually, hands in his pockets.

Pausing, Heidi stares directly at George, John and me, a lingering, smouldering stare, and then turns back towards Tony.

'The Black Cats, *mate*, aren't some piss-poor Sunday-afternoon pub-rock act. We're gonna be the biggest band in the country by the end of the year, so you'll forgive me if I'm not crazy about sharing a drummer with a bunch of cheesy nice boys who look like they cry themselves to sleep listening to The Lighthouse Family.'

How dare she? That has only happened once.

'And that's non-negotiable, is it?' asks Tony, his normal laid-back demeanour now stained with irritation. My heart sinks. We've only just found our drummer, and now we're losing him before we've even played one gig.

'Non. Negotiable.'

As Heidi waits with crossed arms, Tony shakes his head and takes a step back. Away from Heidi. *Towards us.* Suddenly, we are standing as four for the very first time, and Heidi takes us in, one by one, stranded alone in her pool of red light.

Her mouth twitches almost imperceptibly.

'Fine. You've got ten minutes to soundcheck,' she says, shouldering her handbag and walking off the stage.

Without looking back, she calls: 'Then we're opening the doors.'

***

The network of backstage corridors at the Water Rats is like a run for rodents: cramped, badly ventilated and littered with plastic bags, beer cans and guitars. I am sitting on a bucket in a small, closet-like room off the main passageway, with Tony perched opposite me on the corner of a drum case. He is peeling splinters from his drumstick.

'So John seems like a good bloke…'

'He is, yeah.'

'Can he handle the tunes?'

'He used to share a room with George. He could probably play them in his sleep.'

Tony laughs. In the bar, someone shouts, 'Tequila!'

'Tony.'

'Yip.'

'Thanks for choosing us.'

His face breaks into a smile.

'That's all right, mate.'

'I am a bit confused though…'

'Oh yeah?' he replies, tearing open a cold pie.

'Why didn't you tell us you were drumming for the Black Cats?'

He shrugs, and bites into the pastry.

'You never asked.'

'Weel, if it isnae the dutty Unglish…!'

Standing in the doorway, and casting a black shadow right across us, is a broad, huge-handed man with a shock of curly hair and a face you wouldn't want to meet down a dark alley (or any alley, for that matter). An elbow on each side of the door frame, he fills the space entirely, a half-spent cigarette hanging from the corner of his mouth.

Heidi's bass player.

He grins at me, the wide, crazy grin of an escaped clown in the rain, and ash tumbles to the floor.

'Plescha to meek yer acqueentunce, wee man.'

I stand up and offer my hand. Forearms still clamped to the door frame, he looks down at my puny wrist with an expression that's both confused and grazed with disgust. I sit back down on my bucket.

'Everything all right, Duffy?' asks Tony, wearily.

'Ah don't know, Tony. Is. Ev'rything. Oh-kee?'

Tony crosses his arms, and leans back against the shelving. Duffy shakes his head and sniffs.

'He's comin'.'

This voice came from behind Duffy, out of the barely moving mouth of the guitarist, the short, stocky guy from the Rock Garden with the military buzz cut. His eyes are square and suspicious, locked permanently into the narrow, letterbox gaze of a soldier on patrol.

'D'ye hear tha', boys?' adds Duffy, eyebrows raised. 'D'ye hear THA'? Mishy says *he's comin'*.'

Tony shrugs this off and returns to his pie. I attempt a casual tone.

'Who's coming?'

'Crazy Wee Willy,' explains Mishy in a low, gravelly voice.

'Crazy... Willy?' I echo, suddenly painfully aware of my Home Counties accent.

'Aye, y'see, sum *jawker* stole our drummer aff us aboot twenty minutes agoh, so we goes, rayght, shit's hit the fan, only one thing for it, Crazy Wee Willy. Used to drum fer us afore he got busted fer smack up his copper crack.'

'Oh... OK. Lovely.'

There's a commotion in the corridor outside, the approaching clatter of booted feet, and Duffy spins on his heels to meet the noise. A frantic figure crashes into him.

'Heh-*hey*, Crazy Wee Willy! Gimme a kiss, yer big bawbag.'

Crazy Wee Willy is half Duffy's size, with eyes like hot little stones and hands clenched permanently into fists. Breaking away from the embrace, he gawps into the room, looks up at Duffy, and points straight at me. 'Hoozat?' he says, in an unexpectedly high voice.

'Support band,' replies Duffy, dropping his cigarette to the floor and crushing it. 'The boys from Satellite...'

'Hello folks,' comes a familiar voice from the corridor.

'Weel, sook me aff wi' a hosepipe. It's Jon Bon Jovi.'

George laughs heartily at this, peers into the room at me and Tony, and then returns his attention to the Scots.

'I'm George – who are you?'

'Ahm Duffy, an' this is Hamish… an' Crazy Wee Willy.'

'Wicked name,' replies George.

'So yoose are all country boys, isnae tha' rayght?' continues Duffy, nudging another cigarette from his packet. 'Ah mean, yoose all *look* like village people to me, if yoose ken what ah mean.'

'We're from Goring,' confirms George. 'On the Thames. Where d'you chaps come from?'

'Ibrox,' replies Duffy, scratching his stubble. 'On the dole.'

'What's going on?'

Heidi's voice this time, emerging from the corridor. Duffy steps back and she moves inside the doorway, completing the quartet. The four of them stand together, Wee Willy with his clenched fists, Hamish with his shaved head and letterbox gaze, Duffy grinning wildly and Heidi with her savage hair, black make-up and intense, ferocious eyes. This band look twisted, armed and dangerous.

'Ah wis just gin tae know yer wee pals here, Heids,' explains Duffy, staring straight at me. 'Crackin' fellas.'

On the other side of the wall, the room is filling with people and sweat and excitement. Heidi aims a sharpened glance at Tony.

'You're on in five, Judas.'

Standing from my perch, I touch a steadying hand to the wall and my fingers meet the fat buzz of deep, rising vibrations. Unless I'm imagining it, the whole place seems to be moving.

***

Clutching the end of my piano, I stare out into the black of the Water Rats. The room is filling up by the second, the dirty noise growing and seething and spitting and spilling as if someone were turning up the volume, notch by notch, on a telly with busted speakers. And from the back, all the while, we're being watched by Heidi and her gang of Black Cats.

Onstage, Tony sits at the drum kit, eyes steely, hands steady. George grapples with his mic stand, guitar slung behind his back, and John waits silently on the far side of the stage, concentrating hard, probably running chords inside his head. I grip my piano, peering out into the tangled mess of people, the jagged haircuts, the red leather, the cigarette smoke, the black eyes and the torn jeans and the rum and vodka shots, and my heart is beating like a punctured drum. And I curse myself. Curse my *stupidity*. Because it seems so obvious to me now.

This was a mistake.

A terrible, terrible mistake.

10

The face in the crowd is flat, white and small-eyed, like a bull terrier.

It's a face that watches mine, in silent provocation. A shaved head, pierced brow and thin, pale lips. There's a cagey emptiness in the exchange, like two animals sensing threat. Breaking gaze, it returns to the herd, and beers are clinked in salute.

These aren't Satellite fans… they're *Black Cats fans*.

Beneath the noisy brawl filling the room, our music begins to rise. George strums out the brooding guitar intro to 'Fine', his powder-blue delay pedal sending endless sound-shapes out into the cosmos. Tony flicks a cymbal-edge in response, and John waits in the dark at the side of the stage. I catch his eye and he gives me a smile, which I fail to return.

'*We're just fine, don't be afraid…*' sings George, barely audible above the clamour. To his left, the Bull Terrier sets down his drink and observes us through small, black eyes. He nudges a friend, and points at the stage.

'*Something else is bothering me…*'

As George walks cautiously through the second verse, my gaze drifts back into the room. We've never been ignored like this before. An entire crowd acting as if we weren't even here, our music nothing more than a magnolia background hum. There's a clattering beside me, and at my feet I find what looks like a scrunched-up beer mat soaked in alcohol, rolling away from the guitar amp. It leaks a droplet onto the floor. In the dark, the Bull Terrier shares a joke.

The song drifts by and I pad on autopilot through the music, scanning the audience for a familiar face or a friendly pair of eyes. And I find one. It's the Noise, standing by the cigarette machine clutching her gig bag, its familiar strap dotted with badges. Home-made Satellite T-shirt, hair everywhere. Our eyes meet and I wait for that grin, the huge beaming smile she always wears to our gigs.

But it's not there.

'There's a picture in my head… of all that I want you to be…'

She's trying to smile, trying really hard, but it's just her facial muscles sending a signal to her cheeks. She looks anxiously around the room.

'Should I just think or speak on this? I don't know…'

We could leave. We could just sack this off, stop dead in our tracks and leave the stage. No one would care. We could scratch it from the record, pretend it never happened. Start again tomorrow.

But of course we can't.

Because another familiar face, this one not so friendly, is standing a few heads to her right. It's Paul, the Man From City Records, his eyelids lowered, taking an occasional swig from a bottle of beer.

'I just want to know that I am still alive…'

The song ends, two or three people clap, and another projectile clatters into our midst, this time grazing the crash cymbal. A few people in the audience notice, and a ripple of amusement travels around.

'Yeah, thanks, cheers,' says Tony, coldly, glancing over his shoulder at the soggy missile. A group at the back of the room jeers in response, and I watch Paul for his reaction. He checks his watch.

We struggle through the set, unsteady on our feet, while the room slowly fills to capacity. John and Tony do an admirable job, but the tightness we're used to has gone. We're concentrating on our parts, not playing together, and the monitoring is poor and I can't hear the band. The Noise shuffles uncomfortably during song breaks. Paul yawns and finishes his beer. The Bull Terrier knocks back endless black shots.

We reach our final song, and George walks over to my keyboard.

'No more ballads – this is the wrong crowd. Let's finish on a cover.'

Before I can reply, he steps back to the mic and launches into 'A Little Respect', the Erasure song we learnt once for a friend's wedding. Tony is beaming behind the drum kit. At the sound of a familiar track, the energy in the venue shifts, and people soon turn back round, returning phones to pockets. A scatter of rowdy whoops fill the air, and an insistent bark starts up in a dark recess of the room. Somebody is shouting a single word at us.

And that's when I remember.

'Gay!'

This song is a gay anthem.

'GAAAY!'

It's the Bull Terrier, calling in our direction. He stands up from the table, his hands cupped to his mouth.

'You're all *gays!*'

We're barrelling through the song now, and my fingers are skipping across the keys, but I'm distracted by George, who has stopped playing and is returning the Terrier's eye contact. The drums rumble on, the bass thunders and I try to keep up, but I'm mesmerised by George, swinging his guitar behind his back and stepping to the front of the stage, one foot on the monitor. He is staring straight at the guy.

The Terrier takes a step forward.

The song clatters on, a guitar-less mess of drums and piano and stumbling bass, taunting calls crying out over the top, and the Terrier's at the stage, squaring up to George. George stands his ground, buoyed by the height advantage, his band at his back like an army. That same old curious smile spreading slowly across his face.

'*Gay-boy.*'

The Terrier grabs a fistful of George's T-shirt and yanks him forward, causing the guitar neck to swing violently round and jab him in the ribs. This angers him more and he pulls George off the stage, instrument and all, and onto the floor. People scatter, drinks spill and the lead from George's guitar pulls taut like a tightrope. In seconds, Tony is on his feet, clambering over the drums and flying towards the Terrier, shoving him hard in the back. Taken by surprise, the man stumbles forward into a table, losing his footing, and sends several pints crashing across the tabletop.

A hush descends on the room.

The only sound is the gentle fizzing of spilt lager.

The Terrier straightens up, turns round and finds Tony waiting for him. Face flat, white and small-eyed, he examines each of us in turn.

Then, dragging a tattooed arm across his mouth, he flicks a single raised digit and saunters off into the dark.

***

'I could have taken him.'

Through the walls, the Black Cats are tearing through a song that's half AC/DC, half Beastie Boys. George is rubbing at a grazed elbow.

'We know,' agrees John, zipping up his bass case, 'but you're the frontman. You need a full set of teeth.'

I look at George, concerned.

'You sure you're OK?'

He punches me playfully in the arm.

'Always, mate.'

The door to the main room swings open and a hunched sound engineer slopes through. Guitars roar and spit through the gap, then dampen again as it shuts.

'I don't know how we fix this,' I say. George is fiddling with his sleeve.

'It's just a T-shirt, I can sew it back up.'

'No, not that. The awards, Paul… everything. Between tonight and our made-up tour, I think we might've blown it.'

Tony is bouncing a rolled-up ball of elastic bands against the ceiling. He pauses for a moment.

'Did you say tour?'

'Yeah, I made up a tour onstage,' explains George, talking about himself as if he were a mischievous two-year-old. Tony looks at me, puzzled, then goes back to bouncing. 'There's an A and R guy out there tonight, looking for a new signing, and he also happens to be judging the LIMAs. He thinks we're about to tour Europe, and right now that's just about the only thing keeping us in the running. When they all realise we made it up, we'll look like…'

An almighty cheer erupts through the walls.

'… we'll look like fakes.'

'I can get us a European tour.'

Tony's elastic-band ball ricochets off a nearby shelf and rolls into a crevice. He curses quietly to himself.

'What did you say?'

'Yeah, ten days in the French Alps.' He sniffs. 'If you want.'

'But… how?'

'Mostly covers gigs, but y'know. Should be a laugh. Through this agent I did some work for once, couple of lounge-core trance festivals out in the Crimean Peninsula with Angry Salad. He mentioned it to me the other week, actually, but I had stuff going on with the Black Cats. Besides, before I met you boys, none of my bands were right for it. Butt Trumpet can't even tie their own shoelaces.'

John looks at me, a smile grazing his lips, and mouths *Butt Trumpet?*

'Definitely,' I reply, turning back to Tony. 'I mean… we should do it. Let's do it. That's amazing.'

'You're on. I'll give him a bell.'

'Why'd you wait until now to tell us though?' I ask, thinking about how I'd lied to City Records. 'We could've used this last week.'

Tony spots his lost ball, and scoops it from the floor.

'You never asked.'

'So where do we sign?' asks George, pulling an ever-increasing thread from the tear in his T-shirt.

'Well, steady on, there'll be an audition first. But we'll storm it after tonight.'

After *tonight*? Was Tony at the same gig *I* was?

'You'll have to find another bass player.'

All eyes turn to John, and he raises both hands, smiling handsomely.

'I mean, as fun as tonight was…'

'*Please*, little bro, just one more gig. We're screwed otherwise. We'll pay you whatever you want. We'll pay you in philosophy if you like. Aristotle audiobooks. Read by the man himself.'

John's eyes are trying to say no, but his brother has played this game before. He shakes his head and looks at the ceiling.

'One more gig.'

'Hello Wembley!' laughs George, grabbing John by the shoulders and ruffling his hair.

'Big Molly's still free…' offers Tony, but it falls on deaf ears.

***

The bodies in the gathering crowd twitch and pulse under hot, fizzing lights. Shoulder bones thud, feet scuffle and scratch through spilt beer and shards of broken glass. The room throbs with body heat. Sweat drips from the ceiling.

'How you doing, twats?!' spits Heidi into the microphone, to a jeering roar from the crowd. Next to her, Duffy stands with his legs apart, bass guitar swinging low between his hips. Half-spent bottles of Jack Daniel's litter the stage, and Hamish and his black Les Paul guitar are masked behind a fog of cigarette smoke. Crazy Wee Willy, meanwhile, pushes a beanie up his forehead with a splintered drumstick.

'We're Heidi and the Black Cats, yeah? This next one's called "Stick It To Me".'

The tension crackles and spits, the guitar moans, and Duffy leans in to whisper in Heidi's ear. The burn of whiskey breath on skin, like a thousand tiny needles. Heidi smiles, her eyes on the audience. Crazy Wee Willy clicks one, stage lights flicker and spin, he clicks two, feedback howls, he clicks three, fists are forming in the crowd and then on four the bodies break apart and the Black Cats plummet into a new song, thunder-crack and battering rams, a freight train hitting a woodshack at six hundred miles an hour, and the fans lose it. Bodies thud and collide, bones bend back and screech, and the room explodes into sound.

I shout into Tony's ear.

'You really think we're ready for our first audition… after *tonight?*'

'You kidding me?' he yells back over the screaming guitars. 'Tonight was the perfect opener. After this, nothing'll faze us.'

He looks at me seriously for a moment, his lips pursed together, then leans in closer.

'There's a reason you have shitty gigs, you know.'

'I s'pose. But… George and I… we're just not used to it.' Tony rolls his tongue around his mouth, thinking.

'I once played a gig so bad, the owner stopped us in the middle of the set and paid us an extra fifty quid just so we'd shut up and go away.'

'Really?'

'Yep. Mind you, Crapulous were pretty dire. I tried telling them you can't mix liquid funk with German space rock, but they're stubborn buggers. Another beer?'

He drains his drink and points back towards the bar.

'Yeah, sure.'

As I watch Tony power away through the crowd, my ribcage vibrates with the sound of the band, thumping to the beat of the bass drum. Hemmed inside this beer-soaked backroom, I take a long look around, studying all the faces, swept up in the magic of someone else's rock 'n' roll.

I suddenly feel very small.

***

The countryside, 2 a.m. Four bedroom walls. My anglepoise lamp casts a quiet yellow glow across the desktop, discarded Water Rats wristband curled up in the corner.

The fantastic racket of the Black Cats is still ringing in my ears.

Open on my desk is the letter, typed on plush, cream-coloured paper, its austere grey logo staring back up at me. The Harley Bourne Group. And the sign-off underneath: *We look forward to hearing from you.*

Tonight, we stood onstage in a room full of strangers and poured out our hearts. Laid bare the secrets of our souls, our hopes and our fears, and waited as a hundred silhouettes ignored every beat, scorned every sound. The hours of rehearsal, the sleepless nights, the years of sweat and tears… and nothing. We might just as well have been bar staff clearing away their empty pints, except of course those guys got paid.

I could change everything. I could change it all, in an instant, by simply writing a letter. I could choose money, acceptance and security, reject the hardship, cast aside the uncertainty, turn my back on the ever-present threat of humiliation. I could choose simplicity, and live a normal life, under the radar. Wouldn't that just be so much… *easier?*

No more stinking backstage hellholes, no more bitter sound engineers, no more picking fights with psychos.

No more faking it.

It would be that easy.

As easy as reaching for a pen and writing a few words.

The moon looking down on me from a silent black sky, I spread out the paper face down on my desk. Then I pick up a biro and begin to write.

> *Pick a dream*
> *And fire the machinery*
> *Remember being fast and free, when we were young?*
>
> *We said we'd take it all*
> *We'd start by never growing old*

But there's another story told
So boy, you'd better run

I am alone, in the embrace of many

I read the lyrics back to myself, slowly crafting a melody inside my head. I can hear George's voice turning the words over and over, making them soar, making them sing.

I keep scribbling, and the minutes fall away in the dark.

Finally, with the clock on my desk blinking 3:58, I fold up the letter and hide it away in a drawer.

11

The brilliant April sunshine glints off the windows of approaching high-rises, fluffy white clouds reflected huge across the glass. It's a crisp spring afternoon and the Tour Bus is cruising into London with the windows wide open, the city sprawling in every direction around us, cranes and skyscrapers, stadiums and towers, synagogues and spires.

'It's a fine day, Christoph,' George is saying as he surveys the vista ahead. 'I mean, look at us. Our own drummer, a European tour, the world is our oyster.' He drums a quick rhythm on the steering wheel. 'Only it's an oyster playing a DOUBLE-NECK GUITAR.'

I cast an eye across the rooftops of the city.

'You really think it'll still work?'

'Whassat?'

'The band. Will it still work with, like… other people in it?'

'Why wouldn't it?'

'Because… I was thinking about that time at school, you know, when we asked Karen Braithwaite to join Pro Mori, and… well. It was pretty weird.'

'Karen Braithwaite played the flugelhorn. That's the main reason she never pursued a career in rock music.'

George reaches into the glovebox, locates his shades and slips them on. He flicks a switch on the stereo and Def Leppard blares from the speakers.

'George.'

'Yes, old fruit.'

'Do you ever think about… doing anything else?' He wrinkles his nose at the traffic ahead.

'I suppose we could take the Hammersmith Flyover, but it's an absolute nightmare at the moment.'

'No, not that. I mean… in life.'

He turns the music down and half-smirks at me.

'Like what?'

I stare through the window at the passing office blocks.

'Like… I don't know, something that isn't the band. Something normal.'

He looks at me, oddly.

'No. Course not.'

I shift in my seat.

'Yeah… me neither.'

George slows down at an oncoming set of traffic lights, and the engine gurgles as pedestrians cross.

'Are you all right, Christoph?'

'Uh-huh, course.'

He revs the engine, and I turn and talk to the window.

'I just think, some people… some people might find being in a band difficult, don't you think? The insecurity, the rejection. Not knowing whether it's going to work out.'

'That may be true, but those are also the kind of people who say things like "That's a nice ottoman", or "I'd hate to live in London, it's full of people".'

'Yeah… I s'pose.'

He turns to face me.

'Did somebody spike your porridge this morning?'

'No, I'm just… I guess I've been thinking a bit about our lives.'

George tuts at me and jabs a finger into my cheek.

'You know what I've told you about thinking, old sport. It's not good for you. It gives you the willies.'

I stare at my shoes in the footwell for a while. George beefs up the volume on the stereo again and pats me hard on the thigh.

'The thing about this band, my sexy floppy-haired friend, is that *we couldn't do anything else.* You and me, we *are* this band, and it *is* us. That's gospel. Am I right?'

I nod, tight-lipped.

'Sure.'

'Everything's about to change, Christoph, as of today,' he yells at me above Def Leppard. 'In fact, I'd say there's a very strong chance our lives will never be the same again...'

His foot to the floor, George whips the wheels into motion, dives into a new lane, and we fly towards London.

***

The door creaks open and, with all eyes glued to it, a thick, wide hand clamps around the side of the frame. The hand is soon joined by a startlingly large, moustachioed head.

''Ow do.'

There follows the shoulders, arms and legs of a hugely tall and broad man in a diamond-patterned tank top and coffee-coloured slacks, carrying a ring-bound folder that reads 'Worldwide Gigs'. He slowly fills the room.

'Oh, hello. Jeff, is it?

Suite 2, Shepherd's Bush Studios. Another mustard-yellow rehearsal room.

'No, it's Geoffrey. Wi' a G,' he replies, in a thick Yorkshire accent. I extend my hand.

'Chris,' I say, waiting for the reciprocal handshake, which doesn't arrive. Geoffrey is eyeing me blankly, so I give him a jaunty smile. 'With a C.'

I laugh, but his face remains rigidly deadlocked.

'You're a wee bit early,' I add, checking the time.

'Aye, six minutes early. Can't abide tardiness.'

Geoffrey lowers his mighty frame into a seat in the corner of the studio. Somehow this doesn't seem to make him any smaller.

'Tony,' he says, with a nod but no look.

'Geoffrey, how're things, mate?'

'What's this new band, then, any good?'

He opens his folder and flicks through some papers. Clearly this is a man with little interest in pleasantries.

'Uh, yeah, we're quite new, but we're… ready for action.'

Geoffrey clears his throat gruffly into his chest.

'I see a lotter crap in this job, you know.'

Silently, John raises his eyebrows at me, and I shrug back at him. Unfortunately Geoffrey spots this.

'Y'all right?' he asks, nodding at my shoulder. I point theatrically at myself.

'Who, me?'

He nods again, clicking the end of a pen.

'Yep, absolutely. I'm fine. Just got a spot of the old… shoulder spasm. Think I need to eat more oily fish.'

A horribly long pause.

'Better gerron, then, eh?' says Geoffrey, finally. I throw a glance at Tony, who gives me the go-ahead. John and George strap on their guitars.

'Right. So… we're planning to do two covers, and one of ours, if that's…?'

Geoffrey scribbles something angry-looking into his folder.

'… sooo, OK. This is "Great Balls of Fire".'

John and Tony nod at each other across the drum kit. George plucks his plectrum out from between his teeth and winks at me.

Somewhere, out in the cosmos, a dark light begins to shine.

Tony clicks four into his microphone and we're off, a fireball of energy railroading into the room, walloping into the drum kit at sixty million lightyears an hour and sending shards of rhythm and crash careering into the walls and ceiling. The bass guitar powers down into the core of the drum kit like a pneumatic drill, pulsing and rumbling, while on top George's guitar jangles and splatters and my piano notes clatter and ricochet off the rising heat of the music. We're a runaway train, terrifying, unpredictable, almost deranged as we hurtle and swerve through the jagged landscape of the music. Two and a half minutes pass and they could have been forty seconds as we tumble and plummet towards the climax of the track and sparks are flying and wires fusing and fires igniting as we hammer out the closing chord in a cacophony of sound and when the final lightning bolt strikes, Geoffrey spontaneously combusts into a raging human inferno of white-hot flame.

Finally, calm returns. Tony's ride cymbal shimmers quietly to rest in the corner.

I look over at Geoffrey. Steam is rising off his singed hair.

Amazing the difference a little rehearsal can make. 'Next.'

We all exchange curious looks. George shrugs, and I fiddle with the settings on my keyboard.

Geoffrey caresses his moustache.

Tony raises his sticks, and click click click click *bang* we jangle back into action, the guitar riff from 'I Saw Her Standing There' leaping out through the amplifier as the drums shatter and dive around it, thumping and wrestling with the rhythm in the bass. The vocals tumble and call and rise and fall across each other, energy firing up, down, backwards and forwards, guitar solo rasping, piano chords vaulting, the song twisting and spiralling in a tangle of power and sound until we end with a flourish, and the walls cease their vibrating, and once again silence descends.

At first, Geoffrey doesn't react. He doesn't move or speak, in fact, for quite some time. Outside in the corridor somebody is on the phone, shouting at a late band member.

'Aye,' Geoffrey says eventually, allowing himself the briefest of upward glances. 'Last one, then.'

He goes back to grooming his 'tache.

'Right, boys,' replies Tony, picking a splinter from his drumstick. '"Girl on the Radio"?'

We all nod. Tony clicks his fingers and points at us.

'Oh yeah, and no third verse. Just cut it right out.'

I catch George's eye, and raise a calming hand at him. He shakes his head, sighs and steps up to the microphone.

'*Dark night, driving home…*'

Four minutes later, as our audition draws to a close and the shimmering melodies of 'Girl on the Radio' fade slowly into memory, Geoffrey crosses his thick arms over his tank top. They look like a stack of felled tree trunks. He sniffs in a gallon of air, and my lungs tighten.

'You got yerown car?'

'Um… sure, yeah.'

'And yerown gear?'

Tony gives me the thumbs-up.

'Absolutely we do.'

'Then tour's yours.'

I resist the temptation to jump up and down on the spot. George does too. All eyes return to Geoffrey, who appears to be filling in a form.

'Satellite. It is Satellite, in't it?'

'Yes.'

'No,' interrupts Tony. Geoffrey's huge eyebrows meet in confusion.

'Is that yer name or in't it?'

I squeeze out a little cough.

'We're… in between names right now. We'll keep you in the loop.'

'Aye, best yer do, needs to go ont posters. Now, we'll send details in due course, but int meantime, cash.'

What? We don't have to *pay* him, do we?

'It won't exactly cover yer pensions, but yer looking at summat like three hundred and fifty euro a gig, so once you knock off travel and board, you oughter come back wi' at least fifteen 'undred pound each, if yer sensible.'

Fifteen hundred pounds? For playing my *keyboard*?

'Did you say one and a half grand?' asks John, thoughts flooding his face.

'Aye.'

John scratches the back of his head. His big brother smiles at me.

'That's me done. See you lot in two days, I'm flying tomorrow. Don't do anything daft ont way down, mind, it's a bloody long way.'

With that, he snaps his folder shut, casts us all one final weary look and then shrinks his massive frame out through the door. For a few seconds, nobody speaks.

John is deep in thought in the corner.

'So, Johnny,' says George, dropping his guitar into its stand. 'Fifteen hundred quid. I mean… that's really rather a lot of money, isn't it, Christoph? Almost the same as a… student overdraft.'

George joins his brother on the edge of the amp.

'Fancy being our bass player?'

John holds his hands up, surprised at himself.

'OK. OK, temporarily, yes. You've got me until the end of April. But I'm bringing my books.' He smiles. 'And I only do international tours.'

'Boom shake the room!' concludes George, flicking his guitar pick into the air, ducking to catch it and missing entirely. 'Looks like we have a band, then. What do you say we celebrate in the pub with a round of Eggy Benders?'

'I think I'll stick to beer,' suggests John, zipping up his coat. Tony points a drumstick at him.

'Now you're talking my language.'

We slip into a comfortable quiet, de-rigging stands, coiling leads and clipping up cases. Other bands make awkward, muted noise around us, the sirens and car horns of Shepherd's Bush wail and honk in the distance and, fifty miles west, the hills of home wait under slowly purpling skies.

Standing at the open door, George breaks the silence.

'Tony?'

'Yes, mate.'

'I've been thinking,' he says, deliberately, as Tony joins him in the doorway, 'and… you might have been right.'

'About what?'

'About "Girl on the Radio". The third verse. Cutting it… actually works.'

Tony sticks out his bottom lip in appreciation, and pats George on the shoulder. They nod silently at each other, and the room seems to warm, imperceptibly.

'Anyway, nuffa that bollocks,' continues Tony, leading the way out into the corridor. 'We have to talk transport. My van's on the blink, so we'll need a vehicle.'

'We'll just take the Tour Bus, right?' I say to George as we stop at the main entrance and I reach for the handle. Tony stares at me in amazement.

'Did you say *tour bus?*'

'Um…'

'You two've got a bus? Bloody hell, lads.'

I clear my throat.

'Well, bus is sort of a… term of endearment. Really it's more of a…'

'What?'

The door opens to reveal George's mum's peach-coloured hatchback, jauntily reverse-parked and sporting an impressive dent from the time we accidentally backed it into Little Stoke Primary School.

'… Skoda.'

'Classy,' replies Tony with a laugh. 'Bit small for a band, though.'

'Maybe Dad'll lend us the Omega?' suggests John. 'He hardly uses it anymore.'

'Really you need a transit van for my PA system. S'all about packing space in this business.'

'Plenty of space in the Omega,' replies George. 'I'll ask Dad tonight.'

As we stand together outside the studio, a tiny gang gathered beneath the railway bridge, the light slowly fades across our backs and the sun dips its brow behind the skyline of London. The day disappears.

'Tell you what, though, lads,' says Tony, sliding a huge carrot from his rucksack. 'You know what all this means?'

'What?'

Sniffing the end, Tony takes an enormous bite from the carrot, chews for a while and then points it straight at us.

'It means that we, my boys, are going on tour.'

And things will never be the same again.

12

Dominic reaches across his desk to shake my hand.

'I'm glad we got this chance to meet, Chris.'

'Thanks,' I reply, returning the handshake. 'Me too.'

'And hey, win some, lose some, right? Right? Yeah, but things change, people change. I have a feeling this won't be the last time we meet.'

Behind Dominic's head, a plate-glass sign reads *Harley Bourne Group: imagine the future.* His army of numberless clocks tick their monotone tocks on the wall.

'So, yeeeeah,' he continues, as I'm gathering up my little folder of notes. 'The ol' *pop-rock music.* You know, I saw Toploader once in concert. Bloody fantastic. You like Toploader?'

I look up.

'Uh-huh.'

'Toploader's my go-to party music, Chris.' (He pronounces it 'pardy'.) 'Ease them in with "Dancing in the Moonlight", pump it up with some serious Nickelback and then BAM!'

The BAM is quite loud in my face.

'BAM! Hit the bastards with disc one of *Driving Anthems.* By the time they're knee-deep in REO Speedwagon they'll have forgotten their own names.'

He fires an imaginary gun at me. And blows away the smoke.

'But anyway. Where were we? Oh yeah, life goals. So think about what I said. Hobbies on the weekend, *focus on your goals.* In the meantime, we'll give you a bell if anything suitable comes up.'

Sliding my CV from the table, I give Dominic a little nod and follow Edward from the room. As we're leaving, the phone rings and Dominic grabs it from the cradle.

'Yep? Yup? Totally, beer o'clock, meet me in the Crown…'

Edward walks me to the lift, where we wait in silence for the gentle hum of the elevator. The little red LED display reads '1'.

'I was in a band once.'

Edward is looking straight ahead at the lift doors, his tight lips fidgeting.

'Oh…?'

'Yes. Sort of a university thing. We were called Firefly.'

The LED reads '2'. Edward quietly straightens the knot of his tie.

'We were quite good, actually. Not Bruce Springsteen or anything, but quite good, and we had a management deal on the table, and a tour of the States. Of course, I was offered the job here, and… the other guys… I mean, it's probably a good thing. This career is much more… you know.' He looks down at his feet, tucked together. 'Stable.'

The LED changes again: '3' – *bing*. 'That's true.'

'We all have our decisions, though. In life.'

'Yep.'

The doors open, and Edward makes a mild gesture. I step inside.

'Good luck,' he says, solemnly, straightening the corners of his suit jacket.

The lift doors close between us.

***

My letter from the Harley Bourne group is lying face down on the bed, the reverse side graffitied with scruffy black scrawlings. Fragments of a new song, snatches of lyrics and half-formed ideas. Most importantly, one rhyming couplet that won't leave me alone.

Over the fields and beyond
Where will I be when you're gone?

Folding it carefully, I slip the lyrics into the front pocket of my suitcase and zip it up. Then, pulling open the small door by my bed that leads into the eaves, I drop to my hands and knees and shuffle inside. Somewhere in this labyrinth of spidery dark crawlways, snuggled between my bedroom and the roof arches, is a bag of clothes containing my old school fleece and a warm winter jacket. Perfect for weathering the snowy French Alps.

The first bag I find has my name written on it in marker pen, so I drag it out, heave it onto the bed and zip it open. Inside, instead of clothes, I find a long-undisturbed treasure trove of school memorabilia wrapped inside a tartan blanket. Crayon-streaked notebooks, corner-browned swimming certificates, a button-nosed, one-eared teddy bear. Inside, too, is a pile of papers and birthday cards, strapped together by elastic bands, on top of which sits a strangely familiar, hand-stapled village pamphlet: *The Parish Church of St Thomas Gazette*.

One of the pages is bookmarked with a Post-it:

> *July 1st, 1999. Local band Pro Mori play at St Thomas' Church, Goring…*

I skim through the review, written, it would appear, by the vicar's wife.

> *What was apparent about Pro Mori, besides their obvious musical ability, was their dedicated professionalism – including helping us to clear up at the end. We are most indebted to the boys, who managed to raise £167 for the church organ appeal…*

If only it was so easy to earn such glowing press in the real world. Mind you, I guess 'clearing up at the end' isn't quite so important to the Water Rats as it was to the folk of St Thomas' Church.

Underneath the pamphlet is a birthday card with a cartoon aardvark on the front. The aardvark is saying 'Pro Mori rule!' inside a scribbled speech bubble. I open it, and a musty scent escapes into the air.

Dear Christoph
HAPPY BIRTHDAY!! Having fun at 16? I hope you are! Keep
on rocking, keep on rolling, keep the faith and just ROCK ON!
I hope you like the card.
With love from your ever-best mate, George
PS. We should make an album.

Reading and rereading the words, their fountain-pen blue turned a yellowy aquamarine over the years, I notice something has dropped from inside the card and landed on the bed. It's a small rectangular token, cut from a cereal packet, with a loop of string threaded through a hole in the top. Computer-printed text on the front.

LB96
ACCESS ALL AREAS
Pro Mori Backstage Pass
GEORGE

Lower Basildon Village Hall, summer of '96. Our first proper gig, complete with dressing room, groupies, and even a paying audience. We harangued every friend and family member we had into attending, and played a three-hour set (because that's what Bon Jovi did) involving several encores and at least four costume changes. Diving back into the bag, I rifle through the mess of random keepsakes and knick-knacks and locate a second cereal-packet rectangle, identical in every way, except for the name.

This one says 'CHRIS'.

Downstairs, the doorbell rings. I'm running late.

Stowing both passes in my inside coat pocket, I take one last look at my room, flick the light switch and walk out the door.

***

'I dunno about this. We're supposed to be in a rock 'n' roll band.'

The four members of soon-to-be-international beat combo Satellite are standing in a crooked semicircle around an ageing

Vauxhall Omega estate car, musical equipment scattered about on all sides, each privately assessing to what extent driving around in a plum-coloured Dadwagon is likely to result directly in sexual contact with a lady.

A sticker in the back window reads 'Baby on board'.

'I don't think it's that bad,' reflects George.

Tony folds his arms, wrinkles his nose and leans over to inspect the exhaust pipe.

'It looks like the kind of car my old man used to drive around in the early nineties.'

John squats down on the gravel and starts tightening one of the hubcaps.

'That's probably because our dad actually *did* drive this around in the early nineties.'

'I don't wanna go on about it,' Tony continues, whipping a slice of cold pizza from his trouser pocket, 'but touring without a Transit is pretty much a crime against music.'

The Drummer's right, of course. The Omega doesn't so much say 'rock and roll freewheelers' as 'Sunday afternoon at Furniture Village', but it's not as if we have a choice. I leaf through the documents on my clipboard and double-check the details of our ferry crossing.

Buying a clipboard, I thought, would make everything run on time.

I was wrong.

'We're running pretty late, guys. We have to be in Dover for eleven o'clock.'

'Calm your boots, mate,' replies Tony, rolling up his sleeves. 'This is the fun part. *The Pack*.'

Lit only by the waning evening sun and the harsh glare from the outside light, we begin silently comparing the open boot of the car with the enormous pile of musical equipment stacked outside the front door. Geometrically speaking, it is basically impossible to fit two large speakers, a stage piano, bass guitar, electric guitar, six-piece drum kit, hundreds of leads, mic stands, keyboard stands, guitar pedals, guitar amp, bass amp, microphones, speaker stands, acoustic guitar, monitors, mixing desk, snow chains, first-aid kit, road maps, philosophy textbooks, clothes to last two weeks and four fully grown men into a Vauxhall Omega. Even the most optimistic of packers would have to admit that.

'I think we'll be all right,' says George.

'Nah,' sniffs Tony. 'We're buggered. We'll have to lose some gear.'

'I've got an idea,' adds John, disappearing inside. Tony, meanwhile, is circling the mountain of equipment, gravel crunching beneath his feet. In the distance, a train rumbles through the valley. It's 7:37 p.m.

'Why don't you bring a smaller keyboard?' Tony suggests, looking into the car boot but pointing at me.

'He's right,' agrees George, stroking his chin. 'That would definitely do it.'

This is some sort of musical apartheid.

'Can we not... take out a drum or two?'

'Nah, mate, all that kit's essential. I'm a drummer, I've got special needs.'

George and Tony are standing together in silence, waiting for me to respond.

'I can't bring a smaller keyboard with me. I don't have one.'

'Let me tell you a little something about the music industry, Chris,' says Tony, lobbing the last gob of pizza into his mouth. 'There's a mystical rock hierarchy, right, sort of like a musical food chain, that we all have to respect if we want this thing to work. You don't talk about it, it's just there.'

'OK.'

'Drummers at the top, keyboard players at the bottom.'

A bird squawks above our heads.

'That doesn't sound very fair.'

'Look, mate,' he continues, 'I'm not being funny or anything, but it's just one of those things.'

'What is?'

Tony looks at George, then back at me.

'Everybody hates keyboard players.'

'Everybody what?'

'Don't get me wrong, it's nothing against you. You're clearly a top bloke. But you are also a keyboard player.'

'Problem solved,' comes John's voice from the hallway. He has appeared at the front door holding a large plastic container. 'Dad's lending us the roof box.'

'Always trust a bassist,' grins Tony, as John sets the box down on the driveway, opens it up and sets about filling it with microphone stands.

'You pass, I'll load,' adds George, climbing into the boot. Tony starts plunging gear into the car, and I check my watch again. 7:39. The final shreds of light are beginning to fade. Picking up the guitar amp, I heave it onto the bumper.

'George, I've got the amp here, shall I—'

'No, I don't want that yet.'

'What then?'

He pops his head back out of the boot, hair dishevelled, and shares a private glance with Tony.

'I don't think you really understand how this works, Christoph. Maybe you should leave it to us.'

'I can help.'

'Our job's planning the route and packing the Tour Bus, yours is…' His face struggles with an answer. 'Clipboard stuff.'

They return to their work, leaving me standing alone on the driveway. For a minute or so, I watch the two of them manoeuvring equipment into the boot together and sharing a joke.

The evening is turning cold.

Over the fields and beyond
Where will I be when you're gone?

'What…? Yeah, this is Tony.'

Tony is half hidden on the far side of the Omega. His shoulders are hunched, phone clamped tight to his ear.

'Oh, hullo mate… Yep… all good thanks. Abroad? Um… yeah, maybe. What? Well, I'm sort of busy…' He throws a brief glance over his shoulder. 'Look, text me your email address, I'll get back to you in a few days. I'll be in France anyway with this new ba—… what?'

I move carefully towards him, clipboard clutched to my chest, and lurk behind the boot of the car.

'Sure, yeah. That's good money.'

George has pulled his electric guitar from its case and is sitting in the front seat with the door open, twiddling tiny tunes. John is grappling with the fastenings on the roof box. Tony, meanwhile, clears his throat and runs a hand through his hair.

'No… yeah. Appreciate the thought, but… sure, if you want. You've got my number. Cheers, no worries. Bye.'

Tony turns back towards the house and I step out from behind the car, blocking his path.

'What was that?'

His eyes widen a little. I don't move.

'Nothing.'

'Sounded important.'

'Nah, just some guy calling me up about insurance.'

I nod at him, very slowly.

'George,' calls Tony, suddenly. George pops his head up over the roof of the car, like a meercat.

'Word up, blood.'

Tony claps his hands together.

'Let's pack this mother.'

With renewed gusto, the two of them return to packing the car, Tony launching into a story about touring with the Hurdy-Gurdy Verdi Orchestra, George laughing at every detail. Above our heads, the skies darken and the evening soon turns bitter around us.

We have just two and a half hours before the ferry doors close.

'We nearly done yet?' I call into the boot, struggling to wedge a bag of clothes into a narrow gap between drum cases. Despite my best efforts, the bag sticks out of the boot like a fat tongue.

'Don't panic, Christoph,' replies George from inside the car. 'We miss it, we'll just get the next one.'

'Didn't you read Geoffrey's contract?'

George re-emerges into the fresh air, holding a guitar stand.

'Well,' he replies, one finger to his mouth, 'if by "read" you mean watched that scene in *Wayne's World* where they meet Alice Cooper, then yes.'

He beams at me.

'It says "excessive lateness will be treated as a no-show, and may jeopardise payment and/or your place on the tour".'

'Yeah, but who cares about contracts? We're a rock 'n' roll band. When was the last time you saw the keyboard player out of Shed Seven reading a contract?'

'I know, but—'

'When?'

I let out a sigh.

'Never. I have never seen the keyboard player out of Shed Seven reading a contract.'

'Chris has a point, though,' cuts in Tony. 'Geoffrey's a moody bugger. He threw some band off the Crimean tour just for accidentally bringing half an old joint with them. Reckons he's got bands coming out his arse and doesn't need to take any crap.'

George considers this for a moment, and then shrugs.

'Roger that,' he concedes. 'I'm all over it. Keyboard next.'

Tony hoists my stage piano in through the side door of the car like a Scotsman about to toss the caber. I take a step towards him.

'Tony, be careful with that…'

'Relax, mate,' he replies, his face turning red. 'I did this every night for six weeks when I was touring Turkmenistan with Steeleye Span. We're golden.'

As he struggles to wedge the keyboard in behind the driver's seat, I watch the other end lurching clumsily through the interior of the car.

'It's coming your way,' Tony shouts over the roof. Cupping both hands against the rear window, I lean right in so my nose is touching the cool surface of the glass.

'You're getting a bit close to the window back here, Tony…'

He can't hear me. He is, instead, talking to the keyboard.

'Come *o-o-on*, you tinker! Get in there.'

'I really wouldn't shove it in any further if I were you...'

As Tony wrangles with the bottom end and George tumbles about inside the boot, the keyboard comes at me fast, a black shape looming like a shark in the deep, advancing with unstoppable momentum towards the back passenger window.

I step back.

It keeps coming.

The nose nudges the glass.

And the window bows, bends, splinters, cracks and then smashes noisily into a thousand tiny, angry pieces, George simultaneously crying out from inside. I jump back, my shoes suddenly showered in winking shards of glass.

The keyboard hangs out through the gaping hole in the rear of the car, heavy and useless like a beached battleship. George clambers out of the boot, eyes wild, gripping his wrist and holding his arm aloft. Dark rivulets of blood are travelling down his palm and streaming towards his elbow.

'That's my strumming hand,' he says, as the colour drains from his face.

13

The vacant, blotchy woman in the diarrhoea-green smock is picking her nose.

She's doing it very slowly.

Very slowly indeed.

In fact, she's not just doing it slowly, she's doing it brazenly. She actually *wants* me to watch.

This is a spectator sport for her.

> 'Ladies and gentlemen, we're here at the BetterGlass Window Repair Centre just off the B416 to Stoke Poges and you join us at a very exciting stage in the competition, local girl Smocky McFatnBlotchy on the verge of smashing the record she herself set this time last year in Beijing. She's confident, she's poised, she's a woman right on top of her game, Alan.'
>
> 'Aye, Kenneth, that she is.'
>
> 'Shapely index finger extended almost to its full length – but with that trademark half-moon curve at the knuckle, shoulders relaxed but ready for action, you just know she'll tease out every last sliver of mucus from that well-greased nostril. And the concentration on her face, just look at her, it doesn't falter for a second. The mark of a true athlete. Wouldn't you agree, Alan?'
>
> 'That I would, Kenneth. That I would.'

Oh God. I'm *so* tired. She keeps picking her nose, and I just keep on watching.

I need to change the channel.

In the car park outside, a tubby man in greasy overalls is doing the Shag Mime, the one where you pump your pelvis past two clenched fists. Picking up speed, he spanks an imaginary behind, much to the delight of his coworkers, and I let out a sigh. At what point is all of this going to turn into platinum albums and *Top of the Pops*?

'*Baaaby you're the wa-hun… you still turn me ah-hon… you can make my hole again…*'

Blotchy Smock Lady is mumble-singing the chorus from an Atomic Kitten song. She coughs up a little phlegm, and my stomach twitches.

It is 6:03 in the morning at the BetterGlass Window Repair Centre. We are sitting in a plastic and lino purgatory, porridge-grey, musak dribbling through tinny speakers and pocks of drizzle clinging to the window like pimples. The waiting room is empty, save the band, and so far we have spent precisely zero per cent of the tour hanging tough with Eddie Van Halen and pissing out of hotel windows. I mean, I suppose in one sense there is something *kind of* rock 'n' roll about smashing up your Tour Bus, just not when you smashed it up by accident, your Tour Bus is actually your dad's J-reg estate car and you have to pay to get it fixed yourself. In Slough.

'I'm going to find out what's happening,' I say to no one in particular, leaving my bandmates in the waiting area and heading for the main desk. Above Blotchy Smock Lady's head is the wall-mounted screen that tells you how far away you are from being served by (if the advertising outside is to be believed) the company's flawless team of faster-than-light-speed grinning window-replacing ninjas.

'C'elp you?'

Blotchy Smock Lady isn't looking at me. She is picking her nose and idling over a magazine.

'Sorry?'

She raises her lumpish, rectangular skull.

'Can I… *help* you?' she repeats laboriously, as if helping me was literally the most strenuous thing any human being in history has ever had to do.

'Ah. Well, yes, actually…'

I peer at her name badge. It reads: *Hello! My name is Audrey!*

'… I was just wondering when we're likely to be done here? The screen says nearly an hour, but we're in a bit of a rush.'

'Yeah, well, we're all in a rush, sir,' she replies, yawning like a hippo and flicking over the page in her magazine. The clock above her head, which depicts two cherub-faced BetterGlass employees laughing at each other with a labrador, reminds me that not only did we miss our designated ferry last night, but we're getting perilously close to a repeat performance. And I for one have no interest in driving the entire length of France only to be thrown off the tour.

'Aww, come on, toots! I know this ol' world's been mean t'us these past two years, but I still love ya, baby. Will ya marry me, Audrey, ya crazy, beautiful peach?'

Yep. I didn't say that.

'I know, and I do understand how busy you must be, but we've got a ferry to catch, and I'm just a bit worried—'

'There's nuffink I can do,' she interrupts, her eyes returning to the magazine. I follow her gaze down. The headline reads 'MY DAUGHTER MARRIED AN ALSATIAN'.

'Are you sure? It's just we've been here for ages and there's hardly anyone else around, so…'

'C'ou sit down, sir? There's nuffink I can do.'

Jon Bon Jovi wouldn't stand for this. If this was happening to Joe Elliott out of Def Leppard, he would kick off right now.

'Can't you speak to the chap in the garage and maybe just… um…'

She has given up on her magazine and fixed me with a gridlock stare. It's a face only a mother could love. Imagine a bulldog chewing on a bag of pinecones.

'There's nuffink I can do.'

I open my mouth to speak.

'Sir.'

I am defeated.

'Any joy?' asks George, as I slump back into my horrid plastic chair. Next to us, Tony is spread across five seats with his belt

114

undone and a magazine called *Sound on Sound* open over his face, snoozing noisily and clutching a half-eaten naan bread.

'Nope. None at all. Audrey isn't having any of it. Audrey is the big fat fly in our rock ointment.'

'What?'

'Nothing.'

Four months pass. We grow old, empires crumble and Audrey's desolate countenance of existential gloom turns from fallow brown to ashen grey. It is 6:41 a.m., and our rescheduled ferry leaves Dover at nine o'clock. Tony is still miles away in slumber, John is studying *The Nicomachean Ethics* and George is engrossed in the closing pages of *The Hitchhiker's Guide to the Galaxy*.

I have nothing to read.

6:45 a.m. A deflated woman with eyes like overcooked boiled eggs is parked behind the shop counter. On my way past the magazine shelves, something brash and colourful catches my eye.

13 AMAZING TRACKS THAT MADE NIRVANA

It's this week's *NME*, commemorating the ten-year anniversary of Kurt Cobain's suicide. Kurt stares back at me from the cover, half bored, half confrontational, goading me from beyond the grave. *So you think you're cut out for rock 'n' roll, boy? Think again.*

Above his head, those three iconic letters: N... M... E. A memory stirs inside my mind.

> *... What's your angle? ... hundred million records in the bank...*
> *I signed this band last month... Angle City. NME are filling*
> *their pants...*

The Man From City Records. The Arbiter of Cool.

A man who knows when, why and by exactly how much *NME* are filling their proverbial underpants.

'Erm... *what's that*, Christoph?'

Back in the waiting room, George is fiddling with his makeshift bandage. It's bloodstained and loose at the seams.

'The *NME*,' I reply, holding it up for evidence.

'I can see that. But what's it doing on you?'

'I needed something to read.'

'You hate the *NME*.'

'Maybe I don't. Maybe it's my thing now.'

He shifts round to face me.

'Last time we went on holiday, you sat in the tent all day reading medieval literature.'

'Well, we're not on holiday now, we're on tour. And I thought I might learn something. A million people buy this every year.'

George tightens his bandage, sucking in breath at a sudden twinge of pain.

'Maybe, but then a million people also bought that Vanilla Ice autobiography. You need to watch out for people.'

I open the *NME* to its contents page, and a mess of zany headlines scream up at me.

> *Top Ten Bass Players With Moustaches – revealed!*
> *Week 11 of our Morrissey Retrospective*
> *Are bowler hats the new trilbies?*

And then, nestled in the bottom corner, a name catches my eye.

> *THE GENIUS BAND: From living with their mums to major label success in just under a year*

Flicking through the pages, I toy with the name in my head. The Genius Band. I'm sure I've heard that somewhere before. I'm sure... *Shawn* mentioned it to me...

> *This time last year, The Genius Band were living with their parents, driving to gigs in a crappy Transit van and scratching around for a record deal. Then, in May 2003, they won Best New Act at the London Independent Music Awards and everything changed. A record label scrum saw them signing with Virgin, and now their first single is steadily climbing the*

indie charts. We met the boys at RAK Studios in St John's Wood during the recording of their debut album, Her Majesty.

Hungrily, I lap up the article, reading about how winning a LIMA created an industry buzz around the band, how they negotiated a big advance with Virgin, and then toured with Franz Ferdinand. And when I reach the closing sentence, my heart leaps into my throat.

This year's LIMA Ceremony is coming up on 29 April at the Astoria on Charing Cross Road. We caught some of the nominated acts at a recent London gig, so check out page 48 for our review—

'Satellite…? We got a Mr Satellite in here?'

The tubby Shag Mime man from earlier is standing above me. He has a cigarette stashed behind his ear.

'Oh, yes. Hello, that's me.'

'Sign here, mate.'

He passes me an ink-spattered biro and an oil-stained clipboard. The big red number at the bottom reads £178.15.

'A hundred and *what*?'

'Everything all right, Christoph?'

George rubs his eyes and drapes a bandaged arm around my neck.

'This is costing us nearly two hundred pounds.'

'Yeah, we-e-ell,' he yawns, blithely. 'It's cool. We're Living the Dream.'

That may be true, but my version of the Dream focused a little more on reclining on a lilo in the keyboard-shaped swimming pool of my almost insultingly palatial stately home and shooting the breeze with the cryogenically-resurrected corpses of Freddie Mercury and Jim Morrison while drinking champagne from the beaks of swans, and a little less on being financially pillaged by a fat Cockney in a denim onesie.

'There you go,' I say, passing my credit card to Shag Mime.

'Cheap at twice the price, eh, mate?' he chuckles, doffing an imaginary cap and waddling off to the desk. As he arrives at the counter, Blotchy Smock Lady gives him a lascivious look, licks her lips and then bites into a pasty. Baked beans burst from the end and drop onto the pages of her magazine. She picks them up and shovels them into her mouth.

'Right, then,' says George, as his little brother arrives behind him with a yawn. 'John and I'll fetch the car, you wake up Tony.'

We all lock eyes on the Drummer, fast asleep and stretched out across a row of plastic chairs, belt loosened. His snoring sounds like somebody dragging a heavy wooden table across a stone floor.

'I don't want to.'

'Someone's got to do it,' says George, 'and I already bagsied.'

'What?'

'Bagsy not me.'

'Or me,' adds John. And before I can protest, the brothers have left for the main door.

Clutching my magazine, I cautiously approach our snoozing drummer. Something tells me that waking Tony up before he's ready is probably a bit like opening your statement from the Student Loans Company. Never, ever, ever a good idea.

I watch him sleeping for a few seconds. With his wild mane of blond hair, his enormous mouth and his belly slowly rising and falling, he looks like a sleeping lion. And you don't wake a sleeping lion, everybody knows that. Especially if you're built like a gazelle.

'Tony? Tony…?'

No response. He's sleeping too deeply. Kneeling down beside him, I reach into his rucksack, pull out a drumstick and poke him with it.

'What the… who…? Argh, Jesus!' he splutters, clamping a hand to his spine. 'Christ, my back.'

I drop awkwardly onto my bum, and Tony steadies himself on the back of the chair. He looks down at me, a clump of hair on the back of his head sticking out like a paintbrush.

'What are you doing down there?'

My head is directly level with his crotch.

'It's nothing weird.'

'What time is it? Where are we?'

'Slough, I'm afraid.'

'What are you doing waking me up like that?'

I point to the clock on the wall.

'It's gone seven o'clock. The ferry company won't let us onboard after eight thirty. We need to get moving.'

Tony's eyes bulge out of his skull and he sits bolt upright.

'*What?* An hour and a half to get to Dover? Are you having a laugh?'

He begins scrabbling around for his possessions, then looks through the window and suddenly stops. I follow his gaze and find him transfixed by a mother and father stepping out of their car. The back seat is rammed with children.

'Those kids aren't in school.'

I squint at him.

'Are you feeling all right?'

'They've got bags in the boot. And a windbreaker. And a coolbox. That's bad.'

'What are you talking about?'

'It's April, right?'

'Yep.'

'This is bad news.'

'Tony, I really don't—'

'Today,' he interrupts, checking his watch, 'is the first day of the school holidays. Dover's gonna be crawling. I did this once with Pressgang, we were supposed to co-headline with Tudor Groove at a bagpipe and beetroot festival and we missed the ferry 'cos Cliff forgot his passport… and that was it. Booked up all day. We had to cancel the first half of the tour. Ruined our reputation in Azerbaijan.'

'Um, guys… I don't think I can drive. My hand's killing me.'

George is standing in the doorway, holding up his bandaged arm. Behind him, the sky slowly darkens, and the rain turns insistent.

'I'll drive,' says Tony, doing up his trousers.

'We'll have to call the insurance company,' I reply, searching my clipboard for the details.

'No time, mate. This is happening now.'

'Why doesn't John drive this leg then?'

'No offence to John, but he reads books for a living. You need someone with balls. We're up against it here.'

'But you're not insured.'

'Insurance? I don't need insurance.' He holds up both hands, and gives us a wink. '*These* are my insurance.'

Grabbing his rucksack, Tony strides out of the exit and pulls open the car door. As I watch him twist the ignition and tug at the rear-view mirror, insistently revving the engine, a tiny little man inside my head wearing a tiny little neat suit climbs a tiny little ladder up through my Eustachian tube, cups his hands over my cochlea and whispers:

> *Be afraid.*
> *Be very afraid.*

***

'Come *o-o-on*, you donkeys!'

Tony is bent forward in the driving seat, foot to the floor, left hand aggressively changing gear, right hand clamping half a curry sandwich to the steering wheel.

'What's this joker playing at? He's driving like my gran!'

We've been on the motorway for just over an hour now and at no point have I stopped fearing for my life.

'Tell you what, boys,' Tony continues through a mouthful of sandwich, 'this reminds me of the time we supported Fairport Convention at the Käsefestival in München. We're late for the show, right, and we're caning it down the *Autobahn* in this crappy old Transit with no windows, and the whole van starts smelling of fish…'

He laughs, lost in the memory.

'... Turns out the lampie had whacked an old fish inside the engine for a laugh. Faster we drove, more it stank. We called out roadside assistance, and we're stuck on the side of the *autobahn* when this mechanic bloke turns up and starts talking in German and he opens the bonnet and reaches right in and pulls out this bloody great big Atlantic halibut. Classic.'

8:12 a.m.

'Best of all, we made it to the Bierkeller on time and played an absolute blinder of a gig.'

Tony shakes his head and grins, swerving out into the fast lane to overtake a middle-aged couple in a slow-moving Metro. The driver lurches out the way.

'Sorry, mate!'

As we speed past the Metro, I spin round in my seat and watch the two white-haired occupants of the car shrink away behind us, their eyes gripped in mortal fear. The clock ticks into a new minute.

Behind us, John is buried in a textbook and George is fiddling with a pair of headphones. In the boot, a mountain of equipment is piled high, every available nook filled to bursting. Tony produces an orange from the plastic bag at his feet and, resting it on the steering wheel, tears off the peel in three strokes. Little juicy geysers spray out in all directions.

'So that window set you back a few quid, then?'

'Just a few.'

My fingers tap-tap-tap on the clipboard.

'I reckon we could have winged it, stuck a bit of perspex in there. Nobody'd know the difference.'

'Sounds a bit illegal.'

'Naah, it's kosher. When I was in Sweden with Collective Discharge, I knocked up a replacement window for Del Amitri out of gaffer tape, cling film and an old Frank Zappa LP. But you're the boss, boss.'

George leans forward against the back of my seat.

'How many bands have you been in, Tony?'

'Including this one?'

Tony takes his attention off the road and squints out of one eye. The car veers across lanes.

'Erm… not too many. Fifty-eight, maybe.'

'Wow,' replies George, dropping his headphones. Even John closes his book and sits up.

'Yep. Fifty-eight,' repeats Tony, winding down the window and spitting a collection of fruit pips onto the fast lane. 'Give or take.'

'Any of them any good?'

As we pass underneath an archway of road signs, I clock a reference to Dover. Twenty-two miles away.

'We-e-ell, some of them. Pressgang were signed, we were big in north-east Germany, and before that there was Solo in Soho, Robin and the Goblins, Folk Octopus and a pagan heavy-metal twelve-piece called the Chicken Charmers. Then I spent a while drumming for Wumbachumba.'

'Wumbachumba?'

'Chumbawumba tribute act. Not a lot of mileage in that, though, original band only had one hit. So I drifted into the East Surrey Jazz Orchestra for a while, and when they split up – drugs and that – I ended up playing bongos for Die Toten Ausfahrt, which was a bit of a low point.'

He strokes his stubble.

'Then a couple of years with the Kickshins, playing barn dances, and after that I got asked to join Echobelly, but I didn't think they were going anywhere so I turned it down. Oh, and then I hooked up with the Piss Wizards, who did a pretty cool line in post-hardcore acoustic jungle.'

George laughs from the back seat.

'The Piss Wizards? Nice name.'

'You'd go and see them at a festival, though, eh? More than you can say for Satellite.'

John shakes his head and opens his book again.

'The Piss Wizards is *not* a better name than Satellite.'

'We agreed on this, it doesn't matter what we're called as long as it sounds good.'

Did we agree on that?

'It's an artistic statement,' insists George.

'Naah, it's not.'

'Either way,' I interrupt, my grip on the clipboard tightening, 'we have to decide today. Geoffrey's calling me at lunchtime and we need an answer.'

A loaded silence fills the car.

'I still like Bum Chums,' says Tony, under his breath, flicking on the radio.

I rub my eyes and double-triple-check the boarding details for the ferry: '... If any Passenger arrives later than 30 minutes before departure he or she will not be allowed to board the Vessel'. My phone says 8:18, which means we have a mere twelve minutes left to check in. Down the hill ahead of us, the famous white cliffs are emerging from behind a huddle of squat, grey buildings. Great brooding rainclouds stretch out over a choppy, freezing ocean.

'Tony?'

Tony is drumming a lively rhythm on top of the steering wheel.

'Yes, mate.'

'I think you might need to step on it again. We've got eleven minutes.'

'I thought you'd never ask.'

The next seven minutes pass in a blur. Cutting up an Eddie Stobart lorry driver, then a huge BP tanker, ducking into the underpass and flying back out again, the Limekiln Roundabout, the Seafarers Centre, boarded-up buildings, abandoned warehouses, the gateway to Britain, the white cliffs, the heavy black sky and then we're thundering into the Port of Dover Ferry Terminal at breakneck speed and into the queue for boarding behind a stream of people and—

BAM.

The car stops.

8:25 a.m.

We've made it, five minutes to spare. Around us, a sea of cars, a veritable ocean of families on the first day of their holidays. In back seat after back seat, children are screaming, fighting, biting each other, kicking and wriggling and scrapping over biscuits.

'BUGGER IT.'

'What? What's happened?'

Tony's face is contorted as he surveys the lines of vehicles surrounding us on all sides.

'We're in the wrong line. I forgot we're not driving a van.'

'Is that a problem?'

'Yeah, it is. They won't let us in here. It's trucks and lorries only.'

My head thuds back against the headrest.

'Remind me what happens if we miss this ferry...?' asks Tony, peering across the queuing vehicles.

'We won't make the gig, there's not enough time. And then we're in breach of contract, on the first day, which means we don't get paid, and maybe even thr—'

'Only one thing for it, then,' replies Tony, releasing the handbrake. 'Don't try this at home, kids.'

He wrenches the car into reverse, jolts it backwards in a quarter-circle and starts driving across the lanes into the queueing traffic. As he weaves through the impossibly small spaces between vehicles, a rash of angry fathers lean out of windows to yell abuse at us.

'Is this... OK?' I ask, sinking down in my seat.

'You see a sign telling us not to do it?'

I shake my head.

'Exactly. Plus this is important. This is – yes, that's right dear, move out the way – our tour. I'm doing this for you boys.'

Tony flashes me a winning grin. I think he might actually be enjoying this.

'Hey! What the hell d'you think you're doing, pal?'

Tony leans out of the open window.

'We're a band! We're on tour.'

'I don't care if you're the Rolling Stones, this is ridic—'

'OK, I'm rolling the window up now, thanks mate!'

Tony closes the window and shakes his head despairingly. I turn round and throw an alarmed glance at George and John, both of whom reciprocate with their own alarmed glances. The car engine groans.

'Sorry, sorry. Sorry! Yep, sorry. Sorry about this. Coming through. Sorry!'

Finally, we roll to a stop, Tony muttering under his breath. Sitting directly in our path is a battered navy-blue people carrier. Behind the wheel cowers a small Korean man, his face suspended in wide-eyed fear. There are cars behind and in front of him. He is trapped. Tony is gesticulating wildly at him. It is 8:27.

'Love a duck,' says Tony, winding the window back down. 'Some people have no idea…'

He sticks his head out of the window.

'Er, yep. I need you to move. No? Oh, come on. I. Need. You. To. Move.'

He leans back inside the car.

'How can they not understand what I'm saying?'

'They're Korean,' offers John, from the back seat.

'Mate. Yeah, mate. Can you…? Oh, sod it.'

Sitting behind the hapless driver are what appear to be his entire extended family. Uncles, aunts, brothers, sisters, parents, children, grandchildren, all staring open-mouthed out the window. Row upon row of neatly lined-up Koreans, faces frozen in mortification, helpless inside their metal prison. A tiny baby gazes agog at the oncoming threat. Mother covers its eyes.

'That's it, I'm going in,' says Tony, nudging the car forward towards the people carrier. It's 8:29… one minute left.

Then, as our front headlight barely misses his bumper, the driver starts frantically reversing, causing the cars behind him to honk in protest. Forced into action, the queue nudges slowly backwards, bumpers kissing, horns raging. Tony edges through.

'Good morning and welcome to SeaFrance how are you today can I see your boarding pass.'

8:30 a.m. A rotund, balding man is standing in the ticket booth. Dead-eyed, his thick arms hang motionless by his side. He looks like a gorilla in a human suit.

'Coming up,' replies Tony, cheerfully, as I quickly unclip our boarding pass and send it over. Tony slides it into the booth, and the man sighs wearily in an attempt to shift the weight of all the terrible things that have happened anywhere, ever, off his shoulders.

He glances at the pass and nudges it back towards us.

'You're too late. Shut.'

My heart rate quickens.

'What?'

'Ferry's shut. No more space till three.'

In the distance, the boat sounds its horn.

14

'You can't be shut, it's eight thirty. Look.'

I point my phone at the man in the booth, and we both clock the time. It says 8:31.

'Too late.'

'Can't you just squeeze us on? It's really important.'

He gawks blankly at me.

'Could book you onto the 3 p.m. Twenty-five pound surcharge.'

My cheeks are starting to flush, my pulse galloping. Tony looks back at me, drumming my fingers on the clipboard and humming a little tune, and, leaning out of the window again, speaks to the ticket man in a low, confidential voice. Listening, the man's face shifts into an expression first of vague concern, then mild fear. He leans slowly over on one foot and aims a furtive glance at me. After another few seconds, Tony says 'Thanks!', moves back inside the car and winds up the window. The barrier lifts and he drives right through.

'What's going on?'

'We're getting on the ferry.'

'But… how? What did you say?'

Tony produces a bag of peanuts from the car door, stuffs it in between his legs and tears it open with one hand while steering us towards the ramp.

'I told him you were unhinged.'

'What?'

He lobs a fistful of nuts into his mouth.

'Unhinged.'

'You told him I was *unhinged*?'

'Yeah, you know. Said you were wrong in the head. Said you were about to have one of your fits. Said it starts with the fidgeting, and the humming, then sometimes you just lose it and fill your pants. Said I didn't want him taken to court for professional neglect. And that's when he let us on.'

***

As the mighty engines of the SeaFrance *Cézanne* roar to life beneath me, I shake off a shiver. The deck of the ferry is speckled with the occasional passenger braving the chill wind, while inside the main lounge, ugly strip-lighting casts everyone in a pallid white glow.

I open up the *NME* and flick through towards page forty-eight. The magazine whips and quivers in the breeze.

My phone starts ringing – a London number. Maybe the booking agent? After staring at the screen for a few seconds, I close the *NME* again and answer the call.

'Hello?'

'Hey, that Chris?'

The voice is strangely familiar.

'Speaking.'

'Chris, Dom here. Harley Bourne.'

I glance back over my shoulder.

'Oh. Hi Dom. Great to hear from you, I… er…'

'I'm really just calling to check you received our letter, Chris. The job offer.'

'Yes, yes… absolutely. Sorry I haven't come back to you yet, I've been, er…'

'We're keen on having you, Chris, I'll be honest. But you're not the only dude on the backburner for this one, so… y'know.'

'Yeah. Yeah, sure.'

A pause.

'I'm actually just leaving the country for a while, Dom, so—'

'Look, we don't have to fill the position for another couple of weeks, but we won't hang around either. The guys in the office put you high up the list. Edward in particular was very keen…'

'Christoph.'

George has appeared from the main lounge. I turn back round to face the ocean.

'I have to go. I'll give you a call soon.'

'Who was that?' asks George, fiddling with his bandage.

'Erm… wrong number,' I reply, stowing my phone.

George frowns and smiles at the same time.

'You said you'd call them back soon.'

'Yeah. I mean, it was the right number, wrong time.'

'Are you all right, old bean?'

I nod my head vigorously.

'Yeah. Course. Course. It's just… I don't know, I'm wondering whether we're actually ready for this tour, aren't you? We don't really know what we're doing.'

George moves in next to me, and leans his elbows on the barrier.

'Course we're ready. This is all we've ever wanted, isn't it? Life on the road, international tours, chicks all over the place.'

A chill wind pricks up the hairs on our bare arms, and the ferry sounds its horn again.

'Yeah… I s'pose so.'

I suck in a deep breath of cold, salty air and it stings my lungs. On the coast, plucky waves smash against the towering cliffs.

'I've been thinking, though.'

'Dangerous,' replies George, with a smile.

'Ten years ago, we sat up in my bedroom with that little red guitar and we decided to form a band, be famous musicians. Tour the world.'

'We sure did.'

'And the truth is, now we're actually doing it, I'm not sure that selling a million records, or getting a private jet, or any of that stuff is really all that important. It's just… I want someone to look at us, a label, or another band, or whoever, I don't care, just once, and go… those guys… are *rockstars*…'

The ship begins pulling out from the harbour.

'… instead of always being boys next door.'

George slings an arm around my shoulder.

'Just you wait, Christoph. This tour will change everything.' He points at my magazine. 'Heck, I bet the next time you buy the *NME*, we'll be in it.'

He spanks me on the bum.

'See you inside. I'll buy you a beer.'

He strolls away, hands in pockets, singing Dire Straits' 'Walk of Life' to himself. A strip of bandage is hanging off his right hand, and it flaps in the wind.

Turning back to sea, I open the *NME* again and sift through to page forty-eight, where I find a vibrant, brightly coloured half-page feature headed by an enormous photo of four familiar faces.

NME PRESENTS
COULD THIS BE YOUR NEW FAVOURITE BAND?

*

Shoreditch hipsters Heidi & the Black Cats have burst onto the scene this year like a rock 'n' roll hand grenade in the war against boring music. We talked to über-stylish frontwoman Heidi about the new single, her turbulent childhood and the band's recent award nomination…

You've made no secret in the press about the violence you suffered as a child. Has this fed into your music?
Yeah, sure. I used to get beat up all the time, man, my dad was basically a Nazi. That's what our new single 'Tank' is all about. I used to imagine I'd come home from school one day in a tank and blow him to pieces.

And the LIMA nomination. You excited about that?
We don't need an award to tell us we're the best band in Britain. But yeah, it'll be cool when we win it.

You're pretty confident about that…
Have you seen the competition? That band Satellite, they're basically The Osmonds. Sounds like the kind of crap my dad listens to.

You're not a fan, then?

Gimme a break, mate. It's music for bedwetters...

My heart thumping against my ribcage, I skim down to the bottom of the page, where a single block of text sits beside a photo of Heidi onstage at the Water Rats.

> *We caught the Black Cats live at the Water Rats last Friday night, and it seems all the hype isn't for nothing. The band played a storming set of thrilling new wave punk rock, totally owning this small, sweaty North London venue. It's tempting to compare mesmeric frontwoman Heidi to other quirky female artists like Björk, Tori Amos or Kate Bush, but really she's in a class of her own. On the strength of this gig, the Black Cats may well be our New Favourite Band. As for fellow LIMA nominees Satellite, however, who for some reason—*

I reach the end of the page, fingering the thin, tissuey paper. My chest tightens and the second I turn over, I know. I finally understand.

They knew this was going to happen, all the way along. It was all part of the plan. The Black Cats opened up the lion's den, and we just wandered right on in.

> *... Satellite... who for some reason were opening the show, this MOR four-piece seemed hopelessly out of place. Their friendly pop sound sat somewhere between Killers-lite and Travis, and the punk-rock crowd were not best pleased. Satellite actually had some pretty decent tunes but, at the end of the day, these white-bread boys next door are about as cool as Ann Widdecombe jiving at a wedding.*

The pages of the magazine flapping in the bitter wind, I steady myself on the barrier as the ferry lurches out to sea. Inside the lounge, the rest of the band clink beers, Tony whispering something into George's ear, George exploding with laughter. Freezing-cold raindrops cling to the windows between us.

Slotting the *NME* into my back pocket, I turn to watch the stern of the boat begin its slow crawl off the windswept coast of Dover. The familiar white cliffs of home are slipping gradually away, dry land giving way to black, choppy sea. Behind us there's England, and the world we know, while ahead there's nothing but a vast expanse of dark, cloudy ocean, waiting to swallow us whole.

15

'That's it. I've had enough of this. We're sorting it out *now*.'

Châlons-en-Champagne, north-east France. The featureless grey *autoroute* stretches on ahead of us into infinity, the endless winding spinal cord of a five-hundred-mile country. We are flanked on both sides by field after field of neatly kept crops watered by giant mechanical sprinklers, their long, spindly arms reaching out over the ploughed earth to spill fresh water into the soil. Ancient tumble-down barns drift past, all empty, all frozen in time from centuries long forgotten. Ghost towns dot the countryside, shutters closed tight.

'Before the next service station,' continues Tony, 'we're deciding on a band name. I've made a shortlist.'

John is sitting next to me in the back with Plato's *Symposium* open on his lap. He sets the pen down between the pages and rubs his face.

'What do people think,' he begins, from behind his hands, 'about a change of subject?'

'I've brought *The Gormenghast Trilogy* on audiobook,' suggests George, fishing his iPod from his pocket.

'Or,' says Tony, 'if you want, I could tell you about the time I played Cropredy with Folk Octopus and woke up in a bathtub with Chas and Dave.'

'Forget I mentioned it,' sighs John, closing his eyes for a snooze.

My phone begins to ring: an unrecognised number. The word UNKNOWN flashes angrily at me, which means it's either

Geoffrey calling about the band name, or Dominic trying to finish our chat from this morning.

I slip it back into my pocket.

'Chris, mate?'

Tony is peering at me in the rear-view mirror.

'Yes?'

'You ready for my list?'

So far, we have Sponge and Penalty Shoot-out. There's definitely a case for suggesting that things can't get much worse.

'Um… OK.'

'So the *NME* think we're bland?' Tony continues, fishing an old quiche packet from the glovebox. 'You wait till they hear these bad boys.'

One eye on the road, he begins to read from the list he has scrawled across what was once a red pepper and Roquefort tartlet. The car veers between lanes.

'Bumgravy.'

An excellent start.

'That's not… *quite* right.'

'Buy One Get One Free.'

'It's not very… I mean, I don't think it's quite… *us*…'

Tony bites the lid off his chunky black marker, crosses the top two names off his list and shifts up a gear.

'Lung Mustard.'

'That sounds a bit like a disease.'

'Ting Tings.'

This is making my fingers twitch.

'I'm not really sure what that means.'

'Nah, me neither. I just made it up.'

He crosses off Ting Tings.

'Midget Sperm Bank.'

'Sounds like a terrifying porno.'

'Meat and Two Veg.'

'That one could also be a porno.'

'OK, OK. Fine. This is my ace card.'

He allows himself a ceremonial pause.

'Phlegm Fatale.'

George boils over in the front passenger seat.

'Tony, we've talked about this, our name's an artistic statement. I don't think you understand how important it is.'

'Course I understand how important it is, I just spent hours coming up with a list! What are your ideas?'

'Well… I don't have any yet. I'm just saying it's important.'

An itchy silence creeps into the car. In a nearby field, a little flock of pigeons are hopping all over each other, fighting for the same food. George clears his throat and stares out the window.

'Trust me,' continues Tony, 'I've been in loads of bands, and we need a name to make us stand out. And a unique selling point, like all dressing up in wetsuits or growing handlebar moustaches.'

The pigeons scatter as a tractor approaches. I turn back to face the front.

'Is having a moustache a unique selling point?'

'Course it is. Worked for The Beatles on *Sergeant Pepper*.'

'The Beatles were the greatest songwriters of all time,' says George. 'I think that might have been why they were successful.'

'Nah,' replies Tony, sniffing loudly. 'Definitely their moustaches.'

He returns to fiddling irritably with the dial on the stereo. Since crossing the Channel, Tony has been engaged in a lengthy but futile endeavour to find a French station that isn't playing wall-to-wall Europop by bands called Poo-Poo and Le Click. He also ran out of miniature Scotch eggs somewhere near Paris and as such his temper has been short for quite some time.

My phone resumes its ringing – again the unknown number.

'This is it,' says Tony, steering into a service station. 'Band name pit-stop.'

I take a deep breath and answer the call.

'Hello?'

'Alloh,' comes the voice from the other end, a thick Yorkshire burr. 'Geoffrey here, Worldwide Gigs.'

Just remain calm and try not to lie to him. But also, under no circumstances tell him the truth.

'Greeeat, hi Geoffrey! How's it, er… hanging?'

As Tony brings the car to a stop, everyone opens their doors and steps out into the cool spring day, stretching aching limbs.

'D'you boys have a name yet?'

Looks like we're not doing small talk, then.

'A band name, you mean?'

Tony looks back over his shoulder at me.

'Aye, that's right,' replies Geoffrey.

'Well, as it stands, we're kind of exploring options, because—'

'Bum Chums!' calls Tony from a few feet away.

'… because we want to make sure we get it ri—'

'Bum Chums!'

'Did somebody just say Bum Chums?' asks Geoffrey. I can virtually hear him frowning down the phone.

'Yes, yes he did. But he's just… larking around. We're not… I mean, we're still working on the name.'

'And yer not going to be late now, are yer?'

What would Axl Rose do at this point? Probably lie. Just outright lie, and worry about it later.

'Oh no no no, no no no, no. No. No. It's – no. We're good. We are *runnin' on time.*'

I say these last three words in a Texan accent. I have no idea why.

'Glad t'hear it. We'll be seeing yer later, then. Bye.'

With that, he hangs up.

I stare at my phone.

A Frenchman honks his horn at me.

***

Tony is driving with one hand and twiddling the tuning knob with the other, tutting as the stereo pops and crackles through a series of dubious-sounding radio stations. Then he reaches into his paper bag for a croissant, and the car lurches to the left.

Oh my god, c'est le Rock Show! Avec moi, Pipi Le Popo. Nous avons beaucoup de musique super-cool pour vous aujourd'hui,

136

alors, voila le SMASH HIT par Kaugummi, 'I Want Your Sex Time'. Et après ça, le NUMBER ONE par DJ Spinkee-Minx, 'Come And Live In My Pants Please'. C'est formidable. Let's go!

The corner of the *NME* is well-thumbed, newsprint smudged. Kurt Cobain is glaring up at me from the front cover through tousled hair, daring me to creep back in. I can't read it again, can I? More than five times an hour is probably overdoing it.

'Anyone for cheese?'

Tony is waving a fat triangle of cheese at us, and a pungent, curdy twang slowly fills the car.

'What is it?' asks George, sniffing the air. Tony squints at the label.

'More Beer.'

I think he means Morbier.

'If you ask me,' continues Tony with his mouth full, 'while they know a thing or two about cheese, there are two major things wrong with the French. A, they make you crap into holes, and two, they don't have Radio Four. How can a country not have Radio Four?'

Tony clicks off the stereo and, for a few moments, there's calm. Then, outside the car, the sky begins to blacken and churn and fat, juicy raindrops slap noisily against the windscreen. I return to the view from my window, scrawling a curly doodle in the condensation, watching rural France fly by behind a sheer cascade of quivering rain. Soon the car is resonating with the pitter-patter of precipitation, and the steady hum of the engine lulls me towards sleep. In the midst of a heady pre-sleep reverie, fragments of lyrics swim through my subconscious…

> *Now we sit alone in the dark*
> *Fist full of fear in our hearts*
> *Wondering if we broke apart*
> *Who'd guide us home?*
>
> *In one thousand miles we'll be saved*
> *Now we quiver like bats in a cave*

And the lights by the road seem to say

We used to be closer…

The orchestra of raindrops sings a symphony against the roof, and my heavy lids threaten to close, a slumber overcoming me like a dark wave lapping at the shore. My eyelids wink once, twice, and I go under…

***

'Hey, French fella! Vooze in the hat!'

Where am I…? Am I in bed? I can't be. It's freezing cold in here, and it smells of cheese.

'Voolay-vooze, erm, you know, oo-ay le ski-town mer-see?'

A twisted dart of pain shoots up through my back as I shift in the seat. Tony blots into focus.

'Nooze sweeze un petty lost.'

Next to me, Tony is leaning out of the window and talking at a wrinkled Frenchman in a flat cloth cap.

'Nooze. Sweeze. Trair trair lost.'

The Frenchman shrugs and sucks on his droopy little cigarette. Tony turns back into the car.

'How can he not understand what I'm saying?'

'He's French, Tony.'

'Oo-ay… parlay… *longlay*, fella?' continues Tony, elbow on the window frame. The Frenchman shrugs again, and puffs of wispy smoke escape his nostrils.

'*Nous cherchons Méribel, s'il vous plaît?*' I ask, leaning towards the window. Suddenly, his craggy face breaks into a smile and he chuckles huskily.

'*Méribel, c'est ici!*'

'YEAH, MATE,' Tony replies, throwing a weary glance back at me. 'It might be easy for you, but you live here.'

'*Non. C'est… ici.*'

'Yeah, like I said, easy for you, but *do vooze know where Méribel is?*'

'No, Tony, he says it's here. We've arrived.'

'Oh, right. Well, he could've bloody said.'

Beyond Tony's window, the roadside is lined with a thick wall of trees and, beyond the canopy, silent in the darkness, an armada of black mountains dominate the horizon.

'*Ou, s'il vous plaît?*'

The Wrinkled Frenchman gestures for us to drive forward. In response, Tony inches the car on a few feet and, as we creep past a break in the trees, bright lights flicker and wink and soon gloriously fill the windscreen. Below us, nestled within a sweeping, snow-kissed valley, is a fairy-tale Alpine village, illuminated like a Christmas tree and bathed in a festival of twinkling lights. The centre of the village glows orange at the foot of the snowy hills, surrounded on all sides by luxury chalets dotting their way up the flanks of the valley like vines up a garden wall.

'We're… actually… here…' I murmur, mainly to myself.

Then I check my watch. '*Christ*, we're an hour late!'

George awakes with a bolt in the back of the car, startling his brother from sleep.

'Uh. Urgh. Where are we?'

'We're here, and we're *very* late. This is not good.'

I wave through the open window at the Frenchman.

'*Merci beaucoup, bonne soirée*! Step on it, Tony.'

'Yep… cheers mate, Bon Jovi!' adds Tony, releasing the handbrake and flooring the accelerator. Stones crunch beneath the tyres as he speeds off, and in the wing mirror I watch the Frenchman shrink away into the distance, shaking his head and stubbing out his fag.

As we begin the descent into town, I peer out through Tony's window. There are no barriers or fences at the roadside, and we are mere feet away from a sheer drop of many hundreds of metres. All that stands between us and certain death is a scattered pile of rocks and a few quivering shrubs.

'Shouldn't these roads have barriers…?'

'We'll be fi-i-ine,' replies Tony, tearing open a packet of Rolos and chucking a handful into his mouth. 'I've driven mountain roads tons of times. Did I tell you about the time I was on tour with Milky Dwarf in the Balkans and we were skudding up this huge hill and the van was a bit dodgy so I had to fix the exhaust pipe with a bass guitar string and then we turn the corner, right, and we only pile into this enormous great *ostrich*, and the guitarist was going absolutely m—'

'Tony, look out!'

A jet-black Range Rover has appeared from around the corner, hogging the centre of the road, its bright lights bearing down on us like the headlamps of a mighty locomotive. Tony piledrives the car horn.

'Watch yourself, cowboy!'

The screech of tyres meets the blast of two horns, and a shower of Rolos scatter across the dashboard. As the car flies past I catch another hair-raising glimpse of the cliff edge, a chasm of black, unforgiving forest staring back up at me, and for just a fleeting moment feel distinctly homesick. Behind us, the Range Rover disappears into the dark, its 'YUMMI MUMMI' numberplate fading gradually to black.

Tony follows the winding mountain road down into the valley, and we pass a decorative sign welcoming us to Méribel. As we descend, the village wraps us in a warm embrace, the sound of music, laughter and merriment cascading from the many bars and restaurants clustered along the main street. Young, attractive couples in pink and blue ski gear stroll past boutique shops in the village centre, wrapped up warm in woolly scarves and bobble hats. The town buzzes and throngs with fanfare and festivity and, as we glide through the snow-blown streets, staring out the frosty windows, the music and merriment grow louder.

'There it is,' says John, pointing down the road. 'Le Rond Point.'

Ahead, a collection of triangular-roofed buildings lead out onto a decked terrace at the foot of a long, steep ski slope. The terrace is dotted with glowing outdoor heaters and snow-topped picnic benches, and a cluster of friends in puffy ski-suits are leaning on the terrace banister, smoking and admiring the view. The tiny orange specks of their cigarette tips dance in the darkness.

'I'm going to see how close I can get,' says Tony. 'This load-in's a nightmare.'

As Tony squeezes through a space between two parked Freelanders and mounts the kerb outside the venue, I clutch my clipboard and stare into the building. Le Rond Point is absolutely pumping. The muffled cacophony of people shouting at each other over loud music spills out down the street, and butterflies collect in my gut.

'Right then, lads, here we go. Last one onstage is a jazz trombonist.'

We all pile out of the car and make our way round to the boot. As John clicks it open, a hand-painted sign above the pub entrance snatches my attention, and I find myself stumbling towards the doors, clipboard in hand, snow crunching like biscuits beneath my feet. Inside the bar, somebody drops a tray of drinks and the resultant crash is greeted with a boisterous cheer.

Reading the sign once, twice and a third time, I blink in the darkness and rub my tired eyes.

'Oh... my... God.'

Above the main doors, hand-painted in enormous red block capitals, the sign reads:

TONIGHT, ALL THE WAY FROM THE UK...
THE BUM CHUMS!

16

Inside Le Rond Point, 'Cotton-Eyed Joe' starts up to a boozy hurrah from the crowd. From behind me comes the sound of hysterical laughter.

'Tony.'

He is doubled up by the Omega, choking, actually weeping, with mirth.

'Tony, this isn't funny.'

He rests a steadying hand on the bonnet, his eyes streaming with tears.

'It is. It's *really* funny.'

I run both hands through my hair and listen to the stamping of feet inside the venue. Tony stomps towards me through the snow, and clamps a blacksmith's hand on my shoulder.

'Look at it this way, mate,' he says, pointing towards the doors. 'If you were walking past and saw that sign, you'd definitely go inside to check it out.'

'Maybe, but you'd be expecting some kind of erotic burlesque act, which, by the way, I have no interest in being in.'

John pokes his head out from the open boot.

'Guys, we're already late. Let's get inside.'

Two minutes later we are hobbling like a decrepit, overladen centipede through the main doors of Le Rond Point, each carrying several items of tattered equipment. As we emerge into the room, the deafening roar of merriment spanks me hard in the face.

'Bum Chums.'

My path has been blocked by a diamond-patterned tank top and coffee-coloured slacks.

'Yer late,' he adds, in his thick Yorkshire accent.

'Hi Geoffrey! Yes, sorry, we are a teeny bit late… although as I mentioned earlier, we're not actually called the Bum Chums.'

His moustache twitches.

'Y'are now.'

'Right. I see.'

I struggle to set the heavy amp down at my feet. Slipping from my fingers, it drops to the ground and sends my clipboard tumbling onto the wooden floor with a slap. The biro is jettisoned from its holder, and rolls underneath the bar.

'Can't abide tardiness.'

I'm on my hands and knees, scratching about for the pen.

'Yes, I know…' I raise my head and bang it on a brass railing. 'Ouch. Sorry about that. Thing is, though, it wasn't really our fault, y'see, we were driving into the mountains and we hit… um…'

What lives in mountains?

'An ostrich.'

Geoffrey stares down at me, huge arms folded.

'Get yer gear set up ont stage. S'over there.'

He gestures at a wooden platform in the corner of the room, raised about six inches off the floor. After ten weary, sweaty minutes spent lugging equipment through narrow passageways, we find ourselves standing onstage among a scrapheap of instruments, all crammed into a space about the size of a double bed.

'You boys do leads, I'll mark up channels,' commands Tony, steadying the mixing desk on a small wooden table. He begins spinning knobs and faders, and clicking buttons, while the rest of us pull endless cables from bags.

'Oi, mate, are you the Bum Chums?'

A tall, hairy man in a babydoll negligee is standing by the stage, pointing his beer at me.

'Um… well, no, we're—'

'Nice name, mate.'

'You any good?' adds an associate of his, appearing from behind. Like his friend, he is dressed from head to toe in women's underwear. 'Um, well—'

'BUM CHUMS,' shouts the first one.

'You better be good,' adds the second, with a burp. 'The band in here last night were a pile of shite.'

'Oh.'

Behind the bar, I notice that Geoffrey is eyeing me like a grizzly bear. I busy myself with a lead.

'Oi, mate, d'you know any Metallica?'

'Metallica's not really our style.'

'I love Metallica.'

'OK.'

'Anyway, more drinks for us. Ten more drinks for the lads in pink! Ha. Later, Bum Chums.'

The drunken pair stagger away and I follow their uneven course back into the main space, taking in our surroundings properly for the first time. The room yells back at me from a hundred open mouths, most of them poorly lipsticked and gulping pints. In the centre of the building, hanging from a pillar, is a chalkboard scrawled with dates.

COMING UP...
16th April: 2-4-1 Drink-Till-You-Puke Night
21st April: END-OF-SEASON BLOWOUT
24th April: Méribel Music Festival

TONIGHT!!!
CROSS-DRESSER NIGHT!

Next to 'Cross-Dresser Night!' somebody has sketched a bra, a pair of frilly knickers and an enormous dildo, and spilling out from the central pillar in noisy ripples is a congregation of oak-tree-necked rugby-player types in tight-fitting women's clothing, pouring pints over each other's heads. By the bar, four beefy men in purple feather boas knock back a round of tequilas. The mostly male bar staff wear short skirts, beehive wigs and garish make-up. A bald chap with a sunburnt neck who is almost as wide as he is tall stands at the fruit machine with his back to the room, chugging coins into the slot. He is wearing a very, very tiny G-string. And nothing else.

It is 8:17 p.m.

'You all right, Christoph?'

George is standing next to me, unravelling an extension cable.

'I think so, yeah.'

He looks at me, right into my eyes, like we were thirteen years old again.

'We started this, you know,' he says, blue eyes gleaming, and I nod. Ten years ago, on a cheap Fender Strat with the top string missing.

'You lot nearly ready?'

Geoffrey has moored his huge frame by the side of the stage, moustache twitching.

'We're past ready,' replies George, 'we destroyed it. We ate ready for breakfast.'

Geoffrey shakes his head, wearily, and taps at his watch. 'I want you started in ten minutes. That's eight thirty ont dot, Bum Chums.'

Groaning back round, Geoffrey gunders off to the bar, and George salutes him as he goes.

Ten minutes race past in a frenzy of unzip, plug in, turn on and tap-tap, and come 8:29 p.m. we are stationed at our instruments like soldiers of war, a scattered crowd of big, belchy boozers gathering in front of us. Watching them from behind my piano, I lean into the microphone to speak and feel the nervous ghost of stage fever, ashen-leather black, creeping quietly upon me. A dying bat along my spine, it's all quiver-and-twitch, whispering dark, tangled word-sounds into my ear. I shake it off and it flutters into a ceiling corner.

'We're Satellite. This is "Great Balls Of Fire".'

Tony raises his sticks, crossing them above his head. Onlookers let out a few mistimed whoops. I catch John's eye, and he nods.

Click, click, click, ba-ba-ba-BAM and George is pressed against the microphone, heart-punching the opening lines, his bandage half unravelled. Pockets of mini-skirted beefcakes are memory-stirred into the song, they know this one, they can *move* to this. And they do, drunkenly, and the crowd shifts, rise and fall, fizzle and splash, laughter firing in cannons from corners.

But I can't hear anything. The sound is like fudge. It's too loud in here, and we aren't together. I can't hear George. It's just mess.

We're not playing together, and I call to Tony, but he can't make me out. The song stumbles to an end. The beefcakes shout out for more and so we keep going, but it's not right. 'I Saw Her Standing There'. 'Tutti Frutti'. My hands aren't working. We brave one of our own, 'Sleepless'. Normally a crowd-pleaser. And then we lose each other again. Still I hear only noise.

It wasn't supposed to be like this.

'Sleepless' marches on, and Tony hits the drums hard and solid, but the sound is thick – it doesn't have a shape. The room is dark and I think people are moving in the crowd, but I can't see faces. Songs happen. We struggle to get them right. We throw in one more of ours, 'Emily', one of the classics, 'Video Killed the Radio Star'. The bar is noisy and busy and careless. Nothing works. Nothing makes sense.

This was supposed to be…

…*different*.

Then it goes quiet. George has approached my keyboard, a troubled look on his face. He lifts his arm, a dark stream of blood snaking downwards from a tear in the bandage.

'Are you OK?'

'It's all these guitar solos, Christoph. We have to play something slow.'

I brave a glance at the swaying mob of burly cross-dressers. 'With this crowd?'

He smiles at me, through the pain.

'Trust me.'

I watch George from behind as he returns to the microphone, and the air seems to thin. His eyes are firing, his good hand gripping the guitar neck, knuckle-whites standing proud beneath the glare of hot lamps.

He strums the opening chord to 'Girl on the Radio', shaky but purposeful, and the delay pedal turns it into endless, glassy echoes.

'*Dark night, driving home…*'

Somehow, the energy in the room changes. New faces appear in the gloom and, as the song slowly builds, the band is lifted for the first time tonight, finally connected in the dark. We hit the chorus, and it soars.

The song awakens something in us, harmonies drift and shift, and the music starts to move and breathe beneath the tumbling of lights. An invisible force works the air between us.

But then, before long, it all ends, and the threads soon unravel.

Time stumbles by, and songs stumble by, and the music falls away and the lights fade and die. Ninety minutes have passed, in the heat and the dark, and the gig is finally over.

With 'Summer of '69' flooding in over the in-house speakers, I lean on the end of my piano, chest tight, hair tousled, clothes clingy with sweat. The crowd disperses, chunky bruisers singing rugby songs, bewigged boys balancing empty pint glasses on their heads. We've just made our international debut, to an audience of intoxicated drag queens, and I have no idea how it went.

'See what I mean?'

Tony is standing next to me, leaning casually on the banister, feeding from a bucket of miniature flapjacks.

'What?'

'There,' he replies, pointing across the stage at George, who has been mobbed by a gaggle of blonde girls dressed in pink. His hair is screaming out at ten angles, his clothes wet, his guitar slung round his neck. He is being fawned over from every direction.

'You with me now?' Tony adds.

'Huh?'

'Chick music.'

He looks at me with a half-smile.

'That wasn't bad, mate. It was a start.'

And then he strolls off to the bar, spinning a drumstick and nodding along to his secret drumbeat. I stare at the back of his head as he goes, remembering that I hardly know this man, wondering how we've somehow managed to form an understanding from the earliest seeds of friendship, a threadbare connection in the dark. Then, as I kneel down to zip up my keyboard case, I remember his phone conversation in George's driveway. The fact that he wouldn't talk to me about it. Maybe it's nothing, but—

'Hiiiii…'

An attractive, husky voice pulls me from my thoughts, and I look up to find a fresh-faced blonde girl in Ugg boots, pink leggings and an England rugby shirt with the collar popped standing above me. She is holding an enormous glass of white wine.

'Hiiii, I'm Araminta. Your guitary man told me you're, like, in the band too?'

I stand up, awkwardly, with my keyboard still in my arms.

'Yes, I am.'

'Which one are you?'

'I'm… Chris.'

'No, but, like, which instrument do you play?'

She says it like this: *un*-strument. I look down at the piano in my hands.

'I play the piano.'

'Oh, pi-ah-no, OK, yah. I was just talking to George, over there, and I was… like… literally wondering if he's single?'

George is still surrounded on all sides by pink ladies. Pointing at the ceiling with both hands, he delivers the punchline to a story and the gaggle of flamingos explode into high-pitched giggling. In every one of their eyes is a determined glint that says HE'S MINE.

'Yes… he is.'

'Oh my gosh, because we weren't watching at first, because lots of the bands that come here are, like, *super* gash, but then George did that song, "The Girl and the Radio"…? Made me feel a bit squippy. D'you know what I mean?'

I shake my head, very slowly.

'But anyway, when we were talking, he, like, he did like sometimes get this funny distant look in his eyes, d'you know what I mean? It was quite random. What do you think it means?'

It means he was thinking about chord sequences.

'He was probably, erm...'

Or possibly web domains.

'He was probably thinking about how... hot you are?'

'Oh, shut UP!' she says, pushing me away. 'Is that rah-ly true?'

'Yes, rah-ly. I mean, really. It really is true.'

You owe me one, George. I am setting you up right now.

'*Hohmygod*, that's blissful. He is such a super fitty, don't you think?'

'Well, he's not really my type, to be honest.'

'He really reminds me of, ummm, do you know Hadley Duckworth from Ampleforth College?'

I shake my head, again, very slowly.

'Because he's got cheekbones a bit like Hadley's, and Hadley has a strong jawline like George, which is probably because he's, like, a duke, and they all have that don't they, the blue-bloods? But I don't really talk to Hadley anymore because he won't shop anywhere that isn't a FatFace, and I think that is, like, *so* early noughties. D'you ski?'

'I don't have any skis.'

'Hohmygosh, you *literally* should. We all fly out here in the hols and just get utterly pyjamaed. Are you classically trained?'

I press my fingertips to my eyes. What on earth is she talking about?

'Sorry... what do you mean?'

'On the pi-ah-no, you know. What grades do you have? Because, like, at St Mary's, I got eighty-nine per cent in my Grade Six exam, which was *way* better than Poppy-Mae did, and everybody reckoned she was the best pi-ah-no player in my form, which is SO random, because it's not even true, and anyway, she only had Grade Eight because her family literally *owns* the Royal Academy of Music and everybody in Upper Sixth said her Daddy was bonking the curator anyway so, like, it doesn't rah-ly count.'

She takes a little sip of her Pinot Grigio and flutters her eyelids.

'Um… I don't really have any grades. I've got a yellow belt in Tae Kwon Do though.'

She blinks at me and wrinkles her nose.

'I have to go now. But, like, would you give my number to George?' She hands me a small piece of paper and then leans in close to whisper in my ear. 'Tabby is being SUCH a little bitch and not letting anybody else have a go on him. She, like, *literally* did this with Sebastien Spencer-Betts when we were in year eight and I was on tuck shop and he said he fancied me and wanted to be my BF, then I found out that she, like, touched his willy behind John Lewis.'

I stare at the little piece of paper, then back at Araminta, then back at the piece of paper.

'Bye then!' she says, and disappears. For a moment or two I'm left standing alone, holding my keyboard half inside its case and wondering where the last five minutes of my life went when George bounds over, T-shirt streaked with sweat. He is drying the back of his neck with a pair of pants.

'I see you got some hottie's number there, my friend. Very nice.'

I hold out my hand and pass it to him.

'Yep. She wanted me to give it to you. Apparently Tabby's being a bitch.'

'Oh yeeeah,' he says, pocketing the number and looking back over his shoulder. 'Yeah, she's right. Tabby is a bit of a bitch. Nice bum, though.'

Beside us, the fat slap of paper on wood. We look down to find a thick, white envelope sitting on the table with 'BUM CHUMS' scrawled across it.

'That's yer cash,' explains Geoffrey, pointing a thick finger into the soft wad of the envelope. We both stare at it in awe, an inch-thick wad of cold, crisp cash with *our name* written all over it.

(Well, not our name. But still.)

'… I'll be back wi' yer Chalet Information Pack,' he adds, sloping off towards a door beside the bar marked 'OFFICE'. As he disappears, Tony and John walk over to join us, Tony nursing a pint, John carrying his notes. He gives his brother a smile.

I look at the three of them together and, for the first time, see my band.

'Shall we go then?' I suggest, zipping up my jacket, bracing myself for the trip back out into the cold.

'I think I'll stay here.'

George is looking past me, towards the far corner of the room, giving someone a little wave.

'What do you mean *stay*?'

'I've got a good thing going on with these St Mary's girls,' he explains in hushed tones. 'They're amazing. Apparently they've never met anyone from a state school before.'

'How'll you get home?'

'I'll figure something out.'

I follow his gaze to find Araminta and the Pink Flamingos glugging another bottle of pinot into huge wine glasses. George is transfixed.

'Right then, Bum Chums,' comes Geoffrey's voice again, 'bad news. Since you turned up so late, you'll have to wake up landlady to pick up keys.'

I check my watch. 10:28 p.m.

'Oh… OK. How do we find the chalet? Is it nearby?'

'No room int town. Yer in Saint-Bon.'

I glance at Tony, who lifts his chin in suspicion.

'Where's that?' I ask, certain I'm not going to like the answer.

'Downt hill, about forty-five minutes. Here's yer Chalet Information Pack.'

Geoffrey hands me a single crumpled piece of paper. It is almost entirely blank, aside from a name and address (Mme Dubois, Chemin Du Paradis, Saint-Bon) and a message at the bottom reading 'WEEKLY RENT PAYABLE IN ADVANCE. CASH ONLY.'

'Now, landlady's got only set of keys, so you'll have to knock ont door and wake her up. She goes to bed at six-thirty though, so rather you than me. She will *not* be happy…'

17

The wind-whistled house stares out into the night through two crumbling window frames. Inside, cobweb-ragged curtains hang at a crooked angle. The towering front door seems to shrink at the top and, beneath the doorstep, a row of broken white stones line the road like teeth.

The lodgings of Madame Dubois, our esteemed landlady, sit halfway up the steep mountain road that carves right through the dusty Alpine hamlet of Saint-Bon. Beyond, jagged black forest cuts into the purple-grey night sky and, at the far end of the street, the blue moon peers through the open wounds of an abandoned building.

The street is deserted.

Deserted, that is, apart from three English boys in a rock 'n' roll band, two of whom are wrapped up warm inside an over-laden estate car parked at the side of the road, the engine running, the inside light glowing fireside orange. The third is standing alone on the doorstep of the ancient house, shivering in silence, clutching a clipboard and watching the breath escape his mouth in little clouds of chilly white steam.

I knock on the door and it creaks slowly open, emitting a high-pitched groan. Inside the murky hallway, a narrow set of stairs winds upwards into black. The banister is caked in dust. A single lamp, laced with cobwebs, sheds a lonely glow on the antique wood panelling.

'Hurry up, Chris, it's taters out here.'

Tony has appeared next to me in the dark, rubbing his bare arms.

'It's what?'

'Taters.'

'Taters?'

'Bleedin' taters.'

'Bleeding taters?'

'Let's just wake the old duffer up, eh? It's nearly midnight and this load-in's an absolute nightmare.'

I poke my head through the open doorway.

'*Excusez-moi*?'

The only reply is the hissing of the icy wind through the trees behind us. Tony's feet shuffle on the gravel.

'*Excusez-moi, Madame, êtes-vous éveillé*?'

There is the faintest creaking from the upstairs landing.

Far away in the forest, some accursed creature wails.

'Come on, you old duffer.'

Tony steps past me and throws the door wide open. It slams against the wall and a puff of dust shoots upwards into the ceiling. Then, with one hand on either side of the doorway and his head jutting out into the hallway, he opens his mouth like a lion and roars.

'BON. JAAWWWW!'

The echoes die away into the darkness, and he grins back at me.

'At your service.'

Soon enough, ancient bones can be heard stiffly descending the wooden stairs. It's a curious sound, a sort of wssssh-*clunk*, wsssssh-*clunk*, wssssh-*clunk* and, slowly, wsssh-*clunk*, wssssh-*clunk*, a shadowy figure materialises at the foot of the stairway and begins to scrape across the floor. Wssssh-*clunk*. Wssssh-*clunk*. A withered hand gropes the large, rusting doorknob and I can feel my eyes widening as the moonlight creeps slowly across her skull to reveal a shrivelled, mean-looking face, all mangled chin, hooked nose and crooked grey teeth. A wispy grey beard lurks on her jaw like barbed wire, and her whiskery chin quivers on the brink of speech. I turn to Tony for support.

But he is gone.

The car door slams.

And I am alone.

I watch the woman's chin quiver as she lifts a long, bony finger and points it right into my face. Fear nudges my eyes to the ground and, at the sight of her lower half, the breath escapes my lungs in a short, sudden gasp.

What do you know? She has a wooden leg.

'*Que veux-tu, eh? Que veux-tu? C'est après dix heures, pour l'amour du ciel. J'ai quatre-vingt-douze ans! As-tu vu ma jambe? As-tu vu ma jambe?*'

Now, here's a thinker. When somebody asks whether or not you've been staring at their wooden leg, what's the polite response?

1. 'Get right out of town – *that's* a wooden leg?'
2. 'You must be laughing at pirate fancy dress parties.'
3. 'Did somebody whittle that for you, or do they come flat-packed?'

Hmm. Too insincere.

I'm going to go for: 'You have a very nice wooden leg.'

'*Vous avez une jambe en bois très agréable.*'

'*Twat stupide! Me prends-tu pour un imbécile? Uh? Alors, va te faire foutre!*'

She didn't like that at all.

'Everything all right?'

John has arrived at my side. He slips a scarf around his neck, and the old woman eyes him distastefully.

'Not great. I think she just told me to fuck off.'

'Has she given you the keys yet?'

'No,' I reply, watching her carefully. 'I'm a bit worried she's going to kill me. Or eat me.'

The old woman's mouth puckers into a tight little hole and she bangs on the floor with her peg-leg. A little shower of dust floats down from the top of the doorframe.

'*Que VEUX-tu?*'

'*Nous sommes le groupe de musique, savez-vous?*' I insist, indicating via the medium of John that I'm not operating alone in the hope that this will make me look less like an opportunistic sex pest with a fetish for the aged. '*Geoffrey nous a envoyés.*'

'*Quoi?*' she croaks back, lifting a small brass trumpet to her whiskered earhole.

'Geoffrey!' I shout, holding up my clipboard like a shield. She squints at the piece of paper on the front.

'*Ahhhhhh, Scheff-ree, je connais…*'

She pushes me away, her withered hand yielding against my chest like a cheap plastic bag full of chicken bones. Across the road, the boot opens and John begins unloading equipment from the car.

'… *vous êtes Le Bum Chums?*'

A sigh escapes my mouth in a cloud of steam.

'*Oui. C'est nous.*'

Grumbling like a boiling pot, she wsssh-*clunks* her way down the hallway into the gloom. An old wooden drawer is forced open and she scrapes through a pile of keys. Some minutes later, she returns to the doorway holding a heavy brass key of the sort you might use to open a portcullis.

'*Me donner l'argent, putain.*'

She wants our rent. The fee from tonight sits happy and fat in my back pocket, but, having been relieved of nearly two hundred pounds by our friends at BetterGlass, we need that money to eat.

'*Le week-end, peut-être?*' I suggest, grovellingly. She sniffs me like a turd.

'*Vendredi, au plus tard. Mais si je ne reçois pas le loyer, je vous met à la porte bande de salope.*'

Well, that's nice and clear. If she doesn't get the rent by Friday, she'll throw us bitches out.

'*Avez-vous des articles de literie?*'

Do we have any bedding? What an odd question.

'*Non…*'

'*Ahhhh, mon dieu. Vous serez ce soir à froid.*'

She shoves the key into my hand and slams the door in my face.

I'm in the midst of examining the huge, medieval key when the boys join me outside the chalet. The street has fallen silent, and the moon is casting us all in an eerie blue glow. Tony rips opens a packet of Jaffa Cakes.

'What she say? Couldn't understand a word.'

'You don't want to know.'

'Come on,' says John, a bag of luggage in each hand, 'let's get inside.'

Next door, in the twisted shadow of Madame Dubois' house, cowers our small, tumble-down chalet. Past threadbare curtains, the interior looks shady, neglected and unwelcoming, and evidence of past inhabitants abounds. A dirty dish here, a discarded sock there. Along the window ledge, fingerprints in the dust.

I force the rusting key into the hole and it slides in with a metallic scrape.

'Not a fan of French,' Tony is saying as we step inside. 'Poncey bloody language. Flemish, though, now there's a noble tongue.'

'Flemish?' replies John, surprised.

'Yeah, picked some up when I was touring Flanders with Pressgang. *Laten we nu stap in onze tijdmachine.*'

'What does that mean?'

'And now, let us step into our time machine.'

'Sounds like a useful phrase.'

'Very handy, yeah. Got me out of a ton of scrapes one year in Oudenbosch. We did this gig in a cowshed, right, and the cow escaped in the middle of my drum solo, so I stage-dived onto this farmer and he st—'

'Tony, can we maybe load in first, then do the cow story?'

'You're the boss.'

Fumbling for the light switch, I flick it on and my eyes immediately shrink at the glare of a naked bulb. The room we're standing in is half pig barn, half the abandoned workshop of a domestically negligent serial killer.

'Welcome to Paradise.'

'Right. Let's divvy up the bedrooms.'

156

'Ah. Yes.' Remembering the last thing the old woman said, I turn to Tony with my fingers interlinked, like a politician announcing budget cuts. 'Now, don't get mad, but…'

'What…?'

'The landlady said there isn't any bedding.'

'*WHAT?!*

Tony's tired, bloodshot eyes bulge from his face, while, next door, the old woman bangs on the wall with what I can only presume to be her wooden leg.

'We'll figure something out,' I offer, unconvincingly. 'And I'm sure it'll warm up…'

The ground floor of the chalet, best described as a kitchen-slash-lounge, is littered with a hotchpotch of rickety wooden furniture that looks like it was built by extremely angry inmates at an asylum for the criminally insane. The walls are decorated with a collection of brutal-looking medieval farming implements, washing-up is piled high by the sink, blotches of damp blemish the ceiling like birthmarks and the bare light fitting in the centre of the room paints everything with a sickly yellow hue.

'I'm so glad we turned down those rooms at the Hilton,' grumbles Tony, chucking a bag of leads into a corner.

Half an hour later, silenced by exhaustion, we crawl into our respective beds. I am sharing a room with George, but he's not here, and hasn't replied to my texts. Bedding-less, I lie awake, shivering underneath a makeshift blanket of T-shirts and ragged old towels, staring out of the tiny window at purple clouds creeping over Alpine peaks. My bed, which is about a foot shorter than I am, is meant for a child.

George's bed is empty next to mine.

'… George?'

It's 1995, year nine camping trip. The tent smells of rain and wet mud, and we are lying next to each other in fully zipped-up sleeping bags.

'What do you want to be when you're older?' I ask. George wiggles his feet through the sleeping bag.

'Rockstar. What about you?'

'Rockstar too.' We high-five. 'But, I dunno, I've been thinking. Isn't it... quite hard?'

'No way! Not for us. We're the best band in Goring. And anyway, I wrote twenty songs last week.'

I nod, silently.

'Games should be wicked tomorrow,' says George. 'Will you be my partner?'

Some girls giggle in a nearby tent, and a teacher calls *Sssh*.

'Obviously, yeah.'

'Wicked. Goodnight best buddy.'

'Night.'

I am staring at his empty bed, freezing under damp towels, as the chalet walls rattle. In the window, the moon surrenders its night-arc to fall behind black mountains, and all light fades.

***

Sitting up in bed, my goose-pimpled legs barely covered by a moth-eaten towel, I am scanning through my page of lyrics, humming scraps of melody in my head. The notes on the plush cream sheet are growing daily like a tangled vine, spidery black words crawling over and around each other, song fragments growing, ideas breathing.

There are at least two songs on here, one that I'm calling 'Blinded By Light', the other as yet unnamed. A story's been unfolding piece by piece...

> *Tell me you can hear my cry*
> *'Cos I'm punchdrunk and I don't know why*
> *I need you there when I slip up*
> *To brush me off and pick me up*
> *Because you're the one and only soul*
> *That understands why I lose control*

And underneath that, one exposed line, perhaps for the chorus:

> *You don't know the weight of your heart on my heart*

Across the room, George's bed is empty. And it hasn't been slept in.

'Anyone heard from George?'

Downstairs in the kitchen-slash-lounge, John is sitting quietly in a corner, taking notes from an essay. He glances over his shoulder at me and shakes his head.

'Nope,' adds Tony, who is slumped on the sunken sofa, reading what appears to be a child's hardback book. He is holding a fresh baguette upright like a spear.

'This is weird,' I reply, staring at my phone. 'I haven't heard anything.'

'Weren't we supposed to be rehearsing this morning?'

'Yep.'

'Can't get much done without a singer,' concludes Tony, turning over a fresh page. I examine his book more closely and find that it has a cartoon drawing of a medieval knight on the front and appears to be chew-proof.

'What are you reading?'

'What, this? I always read this on tour. It's *The Ladybird Book of Kings and Queens*.' He tears the head off the baguette with his teeth and, chomping, points the stub at me. 'Did you know that Edward the Second died from a hot poker up the bowels?'

Picking up a stack of crusty, unwashed bowls from the breakfast bar, I transfer them across to the sink, which is still loaded with chipped, rancid crockery.

'Why are you reading that?'

Tony pauses, swallows the bread, and crosses his booted feet on the coffee table. It buckles slightly.

'When the internet breaks, who's the government going to turn to?'

John looks up from his work. Tony taps the side of his head.

'I tell you who. The People with the Knowledge.'

'I don't think the internet's going to break,' I reply, looking for a corner of free space in the dry, browning sink.

'Who says?'

'Well, I don't know, but I'm pretty sure that's not how it works.'

159

'Everything breaks mate. Washing machines, Transit vans. The internet. And when the internet breaks, you'll all be coming to me because you'll need to know, um…'

He studies his book for a moment.

'…you'll need to know what kind of fur the lower-ranking servants in King Edward's court used to wear.'

In the kitchen, I struggle with the stiff cold tap. It groans, coughs, and splutters a puke of powdery water.

'It was budge, in case you're wondering. Lambskin.'

'I see.'

He points his baguette at me again.

'Knowledge is power, mate,' he concludes, nodding sagely. 'Knowledge is power.'

Past my drummer and bassist, through the dusty chalet window, the mountains are just visible between a crack in two buildings. A faint wind creeps up the street, reminding me that we're miles from anywhere.

I check my phone again.

The hours clock by.

***

'ROCK OUT TONIGHT TO THE BEAT OF THE BUM CHUMS' reads the chalk-written sign above the spirits shelves at Scott's Bar, Méribel. I stare up at it, chin on palm, trying to imagine 'Bum Chums' on an album cover. Onstage, Tony is checking microphones while fruit machines blip and twitter in the corner.

Not a word from George, all day. I have spent the afternoon learning all the lyrics to his songs, just in case.

Scott's Bar is a quiet, snow-topped café-bar in the centre of town, complete with a circle of comfy sofas and a steady supply of hot chocolate and marshmallows. The crowd in tonight is thin, a table of rugby types playing cards by the stage, the occasional candlelit couple and a cluster of long-haired snowboarders hanging out by the slot machines. Tony and John are setting up onstage.

'Boys, this town is my new favourite place on earth.'

The door swings open to reveal George, standing in the hard orange glow of the streetlamp.

'Where have you been?' I ask, checking the time. He strolls inside, grinning his valley-wide grin.

'Melton Mowbray.'

He looks enormously pleased with himself.

'I haven't heard from you all day.'

'I told you, I was hanging out with the girls.' His eyes narrow slightly. 'You all right, Christoph?'

'You missed rehearsal.'

He blows air out through his cheeks.

'We'll rehearse tomorrow.'

'That's not the point. The award ceremony's in less than two weeks.'

'We'll walk it, Christoph. We're a touring band now, we make our own rules.'

'We need new songs in the set. We need to rehearse.'

'Aren't you gonna ask me about last night?'

I spin back round on the bar stool, turning away from him.

'Forget it.'

'Fine, I understand,' he says, joining me at the bar. 'You need a drink first. *Coolio*. Boys, who's for a Massive Desperado?'

The evening crawls by, and the room begrudgingly fills. It's still a patchy, uninterested crowd when we take to the stage, and in response our performance is guarded and shaky, fractured, parched of energy. More than once, George steps up to the microphone to sing and forgets his words, which he's never done before. He laughs it off.

An hour and a half in, a rabble of baggy blue shirts in deck shoes tumble into the venue, some scattering to the fruit machines, others staggering drunkenly towards the stage, buoyed by the sight of a band. One makes a beeline for my keyboard and starts yelling at me. His breath smells of pepperoni.

'Hey! I wanna die!'

My mouth hovering over the microphone, I side-eye him as he leans precariously on the end of my keyboard. The band is reaching a crescendo.

'Sorry?'

'I wanna DIE!'

He belches loudly and looks immediately surprised.

'What did you say?'

'"Oh What a NIGHT"! Can you play "Oh What a Night"?'

'Sorry, no,' I reply, finding my gaze drawn back to the main doors, where a familiar face has followed the deck-shoe-blue-shirts into the building. He stops to watch us play.

'Aaaaah, come o-o-on, *everyone* knows it.' Mr Belchy starts to sing. 'Da da daaaa da, it was ninety-three, there's a something… in a monkey tree…' Belch.

'I know the song, we've just never played it.'

'Ah go o-o-on…' Belch. '*Everyone* knows it.'

The familiar face remains at the back of the room, silently observing the action. Mr Belchy smacks the end of my keyboard like a toddler.

'Do it, go on! It's the fricking best song ever.'

The track draws to a close in a thrashing of drums and bass and, finally giving in, Mr Belchy staggers back to his gang, muttering into his neck and smacking himself in the forehead. The crowd cheer, and drinks clink.

'This is our last one. It's called "Girl on the Radio".'

The familiar face watches us for most of our closing song, the occasional slow nod, bottom lip sticking out. With the final chord falling away and applause rising, he moves across to the bar and, leaving my keyboard, I head straight over to join him.

'Christoph.'

George has stopped me, one arm around my shoulder.

'Yep.'

'We OK?'

'Well… not really, you forgot loads of lyrics.'

'Yeah, think I'm still hungover! Last night was mad.'

I try to tug myself from his grip.

'Right.'

'But it won't happen again, OK?' He points into my face, his smile growing. 'One more screw-up and you can chuck me out the band. Deal?'

When I fail to respond to this, George gathers up my hand, slots it into his, and uses his spare arm to initiate a floppy pretend handshake.

'What now, then? Round of Angry Germans?'

'I'm going to talk to someone. I'll see you in a bit.'

Leaving George behind, I head for the bar and weave through the gathering queues. A Europop dance track bounces in over the speaker system, and I can feel him watching me as I go.

Soon I am standing right next to the familiar face.

'Paul?'

City Records is drumming his fingers on his jaw. He looks at me, confused, his mouth halfway open. I wave awkwardly at him.

'How's it going?'

'Uhh… not bad, I s'pose.' He pauses. 'D'I know you?'

'We met at a gig last week. In London.'

'Um… right. Barfly?'

'Water Rats.'

'Oh. Yeah.'

'I just, um… wow. It's good to see you.'

He looks faintly scared.

'Y-yeah.'

'I mean… this is a long way to come! What exactly are you doing here?'

Reaching into his pocket, he hands some money to the bartender.

'Well, y'know. Duty calls. Gotta sign a band sooner or later, or bang goes my Christmas bonus.'

We both laugh at his Christmas joke, and a thrill powers through me. *Got to sign a band sooner or later?*

'Plus, yeeeah, I spent all day skiing with ol' wassisface from Atlantic, bloke who just signed that posh fella, Blunt. Gonna be huge apparently. Can't beat this place for schmoozing.'

'No, you cannot,' I agree, moving to pluck my drink from the bar before remembering I don't have one. 'But anyway, thanks for coming.'

He sniffs.

'Well… my flat's only round the corner.'

While City Records swigs his beer and glances at his watch, the main doors slam open again and a chilly gust of Alpine wind billows inside.

'Eh, wee man! Hae ye *deein'*?!'

An icy feeling comes over me at the sound of that unmistakable Glaswegian accent. Turning round, I find a cluster of twisted figures standing behind us. Three terrifying men, one tall and big-handed, one stocky and emotionless, the third tiny and clench-fisted.

Duffy, Hamish and Crazy Wee Willy.

18

Duffy grins slowly at me, that cracked smile of an escaped clown in the rain. The saloon doors could almost be swinging behind him. Crazy Wee Willy points a tiny finger.

'Hoozat?'

'That, yer crazy bastard, is the boys from Satellite.'

'Says Bum Chums up there,' points out Hamish, indicating the banner above the bar.

'That sign's wrong,' I reply, shaking my head. Hamish fixes me with his letterbox gaze.

'Crackin' neem, Bum Chums.'

'It's not our name.'

'Shud be.'

'It's not our name.'

'So here yoose all are,' says Duffy, arms spread wide, 'hangin' oot in Merry-Bell, playin' a wee gig. Jis like a proppa band.'

What's going on here? Am I dreaming? Is this just a horrible dream?

'So… what are you folks doing here?' I ask, cautiously.

Duffy's mouth drops dumbly open. 'Yoose no' pleased to see me?'

'No, I mean, obviously I—'

'Ahm ON TOUR, wee man.'

I flash a glance at his bandmates.

'But you're supposed to be in Germany.'

'Aye, we dud Germany, an' it wis fulla burds wi' bigger nuts than me. Ah reckon France is more ma style.'

He conducts a quick audit of the girls in the bar.

'But…' My blood feels hot and my skin prickles. 'This is *our* tour.'

Duffy runs his tongue slowly around the inside of his mouth. 'This toon ain't big enuff fer the baith of us, izzatit?'

'Well, no, I didn't mean—'

'You boys wanna beer?'

City Records is standing at the bar, waving his wallet in the air. Duffy sneers at him.

'Hey, it's the Suit.'

'I told you, man, I'm not a suit,' laughs City Records, nervously. 'I'm on your side.'

'Aye, ah've heard tha' before. *Ahm no corporate bloodsucker, ahm one o' yoose guys*. Jis because we're signing a deal wi' yoose, disnae mean ahm yer bitch.'

A record deal? What the…?

'You crack me up, man.'

'Do ah now?'

I turn to City Records, who is currently failing to attract the barmaid's attention.

'So you're here… with the Black Cats?'

'Yeah.' He squints back at me. 'Why?'

'Oh, no! No reason. No, no. No reason.'

ARRRRRRRGGGGGGHHHHHH.

'Oh my god, it's the Piano Man…'

Out of the ladies' toilets strides Heidi, instantly attracting the attention of the deck-shoe-blue-shirts. Her tousled hair tumbles in locks about her face, and she is wearing her high-collared red leather jacket over a faded Ramones T-shirt. She regards me with lazy amusement.

I am surrounded, on all sides, by Black Cats.

'Well, here we all are,' she says with a snarl. By now, the commotion has attracted the rest of my band, who have arrived to join us.

'Look, everyone,' I say, gesturing at the congregation. 'It's *Heidi and the Black Cats*.'

George looks excited, and John nods a quiet hello. Tony's face hardens.

'Weel, hark at this,' says Duffy, leaning back against the bar. 'The whole gang's back taegether again. This calls fer a party, does it no'?'

A party? With the Black Cats? That doesn't sound like a good idea.

'I don't know, dudes,' I reply, ostentatiously checking my watch, 'I think we might have to get home…'

Silence. All eyes are on me.

'I mean… John, don't you need to crack on with *The Communist Manifesto*?'

'It's fine,' John replies, 'you guys go. I'll stay here with the car and pick you up later.'

Duffy, City Records and Heidi are all watching me and waiting. Heidi is chewing gum and winding her hair around one finger.

I clap my hands together.

'Well, that's sorted then. We'll all go off and have a… bloody big party together. You guys and us guys. What could possibly go wrong?'

WHAT COULD POSSIBLY GO WRONG.

***

'Drink! Drink! Drink! Drink!'

We are climbing the fire escape to the Black Cats' top-floor apartment in the centre of Méribel, and there's already a party going on inside. Up ahead, the door has been flung wide open to reveal a large open-plan living space littered with pizza boxes, beer cans and pornography. Drinking games are raging, punk rock blasting from the massive stereo.

'So… it's mad that you guys are out here same time as us, right?' I'm saying to Heidi as we walk along the narrow balcony.

'Not really. We've all got the same agent, Geoff whassisface. Small world, rock 'n' roll.'

'Oh, right! I see. Good old Geoffrey.'

'I think he's bit of a prick.'

'No. Yep.'

We are seventeen storeys up, which means a full panoramic view of the dominating sweep of black mountains to the west. The world doesn't seem that small to me, right now.

'...But hey, the Black Cats are signing to City Records? That's exciting.'

'Yep.'

'I mean, you've got your tour, national press, now a record deal... that ought to impress the judges.'

'Maybe.'

'I, um...' I force out a laugh. '... I read what you said about us in the *NME*. That was pretty funny.'

She smokes at me.

'Wasn't meant to be funny.'

'No, no. Course not.' I pretend to examine my fingernails. 'It wasn't actually that funny.'

'Wait a minute, this is right by Araminta's building!' exclaims George, coming up behind us. 'You chaps mind if I invite some friends?'

Duffy drops his cigarette to the floor and stubs it out.

'Burds?'

'HOT BIRDS.'

He kicks the stub underneath the balcony railings, and it scoots off the edge into snowy oblivion.

'Yoose be ma guest, wee man. Be ma guest.'

Inside the flat, clusters of strangers are drinking and touching and shouting at each other. We all file in and Crazy Wee Willy dashes to the fridge for beers, while Duffy hooks a powerful arm round my neck, pulling me towards him. He points at a group of girls in the corner, his breath all pizza crust and whiskey.

'See the lassies in this toon, right? They are TOTUL HINGOOTS, every one of thum. Most nights it's like shaggin' fish in a barrel. Yoose find that?'

I struggle to free myself from his grip, but he's got me tight like a vice.

'Well... er, a bit. I mean, sort of.'

'Hey, Mishy,' he continues, clicking his fingers at Hamish, who is across the room searching through discarded boxes for a stray slice of pizza. 'Ah dinnae think these lads ken aboot the Ten Minute Rule.'

'Wha'?' calls back Hamish, over the music. Duffy turns back to me and releases his grip on my neck.

'Well, do ye?'

I look to George for support, but he is texting in the corner. I shake my head.

'Yer poor wee bastards. Hey, Mishy! Tell um.'

'Ten Minute Rule? It's deid simple,' begins Hamish, sparking up and blowing a plume of smoke into the ceiling. 'Yoose do a gig, and for ten minutes after leavin' the steege yoose can have *any... burd...* yoose *want*.'

'Chicks,' agrees Duffy, 'are creemin'.'

Heidi is sitting at the dining table, glugging from a bottle of Jack Daniel's. She snorts, and shakes her head.

'But y'only got ten minutes.'

Duffy cups his genitals with both hands.

'We came oot here last year right, an thanks tae the Ten Minute Rule ah spent ninety-five per cent of my time shaggin' fatties. Real burn-yer-arse-on-the-lightbulb kinda burds. Ah mean, yoose shoulda seen the lassie ah winched in here last night, right. She wis totully mad wi' it, boys. Ah must a been hangin' oot the back of her fer three oors. By two a'clock I had a bawsack like a coupla shruvelled greeps in an empty haggis bag.'

'Wit, that lassie frae Wales, ya mean?' replies Hamish, sniffing a furry piece of pizza. 'She wis dodgy, pal. She had a feece like a bagga smacked twats.'

'Mebbe, but ah wisnae lookin at her feece, wis I?'

Duffy parks a cigarette in his mouth and raises a flat, shovel-sized palm. Wee Willy high-fives it.

'So, Bum Chums,' he continues, 'yoose oot here to dae some winchin'?'

'Come again?'

'Yoose lookin' for a shag?'

He doesn't want to shag *me*, does he?

'Well... a bit... I mean, mainly we're just here to hone our sound and perfect our... stage presence...'

The cigarette teeters on the corner of Duffy's mouth.

'Yoose not intae pumpin' lassies then?'

Pumping? Sounds a bit grim. Mind you, when in Rome.

'No no no, of course we are. Love a nice bit of, you know... sex and that.'

There's a sudden lull in the music, and the room goes quiet.

George pipes up.

'Chris has tons of girlfriends back in England, don't you, Christoph?'

I throw him a look.

'Not really, no.'

'He's just being modest. There's this one girl in London, comes to all our gigs, she's mad for him. They went to Melton Mowbray once.'

Duffy is flicking at the wheel of a near-empty lighter. He stops.

'Didya git yer nuts wet?'

'Well... the thing is...' Duffy is in stasis, fag protruding from his mouth. I clear my throat again. 'The thing is, George and I, we um. Well, we have this system, if you will, for when one of us has... been intimate with someone, and your friends ask you about it, but you don't want to embarrass them with actual details.'

Duffy squints at me.

'Do yoo nat *like* yer friends or summat?'

'No, I mean, yes, but... hang on. It's like this. You have to imagine that you're travelling on a metaphorical train, from King's Cross to Glasgow, and Glasgow represents "going all the way"... Does that make sense?'

'We're from Glasgae,' replies Hamish, eyeing me through his letterbox gaze. Crazy Wee Willy nods in frantic agreement. 'You been to Glasgae, Piano Man?'

'Hang on, that's what I'm about to explain.'

Duffy shakes his head and takes a deep drag.

170

'So there I am, I'm stepping onto this imaginary train at King's Cross, and that represents getting into bed with a lady, you see? Then every new town I travel through on the way to Scotland symbolises one further increment in the, erm... sexual process.'

'I dinnae take trains,' says Hamish.

'OK, but just for now, imagine you *are* on a train, or rather that I'm on one, and I'm seeing if I can get all the way to Glasgow, Glasgow being the figurative equivalent of... well. Sexual intercourse.'

Duffy blinks back at me.

'Nah. I dinnae ken wit ya mean.'

'If you want to know what happened in the bedroom, you have to ask me where I got off the train.'

'Suit yaself,' he replies, flicking the briefest of glances at Hamish. 'Where did ya git off the train?'

I pretend to ponder this for a moment.

'Hmm. *Let me see*. I got off the train...'

I emphasise the next bit with a regal sweep of my arm.

'...at Melton Mowbray.'

Silence. Duffy regards me with squint-eyed confusion, as if I were some kind of relic from a time past, a dusty knick-knack in a curio shop; a box of snuff, perhaps, or a clay pipe.

'Melton Mow-*whit*?'

'Melton... um. Mowbray.'

'Whit – the *fuck* – is that?'

'It's, erm. Well, it's a small market town just east of the M1.'

'Eh?'

'Home of the pork pie?'

He curls his lip disdainfully at me.

'Never mind. You follow my general point.'

'Naw, I dinnae. Ah jis wanna know if ya ploughed her.'

I go to cross my arms. For some reason they don't connect and end up flopping past each other like dead eels.

'Erm, no. I didn't... do that.'

'Foot-job?'

'Crikey, no.'

'Weewankanapoke?'

'Um…'

Hamish rests a bottle of beer against the table edge and, wrenching it hard, pops the top and sends bubbling white suds spewing onto the carpet. He points the beer at me.

'Dud she gie y'a gobble?'

'I'm afraid I really have no idea what that means.'

Duffy plants his drink hard on the table.

'Just bloody *tell* us then!'

'I *have* told you.'

'No, ya didnae,' counters Hamish, shaking his chunky head. 'Yoose told us you took a train and ate a pie.'

'Yes, but that was a metaphor.'

Hamish farts, an immensely meaty fart that elicits a snigger of appreciation from Crazy Wee Willy.

'Eh?'

'The train to Glasgow isn't *real*, it's a sort of… conceit. Like, I don't know…'

HELP ME.

'…the concept of blindness in *King Lear*?'

Crazy Wee Willy points at me with both hands.

'Are ye an arse bandit, pal?'

'RIGHT!' proclaims Duffy, sweeping an enormous hairy hand around the room. 'Enuffa this bletherin' – we've been crappin' aboot too lang! *Bring oot the drugs.*'

Like a faithful dog, Crazy Wee Willy flies underneath the table and reappears moments later with an old, frayed rucksack. Duffy flips his beer bottom-up, drains it in one swig and casts it onto the carpet.

A shiver creeps over me.

'Fancy a wee pick-me-up, Bum Chums?'

No fear. I might pass out and get shagged.

'I think I'm probably allergic to, um…'

'To whit?'

'To whatever's in there.'

Duffy leers right into my face, and whiskey breath stings my skin. He speaks low and breathily, as if we were the only two here.

'Nothin' wrang wi' a wee toke after a hard day giggin', isn't that right, Shakespeare?'

Please don't flatten me like a blancmange.

'That's... correct, yes.'

'So,' he continues, aggressively emptying the contents of the bag across the table, 'we got billy-whizz, apple-jacks, Dennis the Menace, burgers, Bin Laden, jellies, juice, junk, rhubarb and custard, astro-turf, shit, uppers, dooners, wobbly eggs, biscuits, Christmas trees, penguins and Sweet Lucy.'

'I don't know what any of those things are.'

'Weel, then,' he replies, sorting through the motley collection of plastic bags, decorative pipes and colourful pills. 'It's dealer's choice.'

While Duffy organises drug bits, Wee Willy cackles with delight across the table.

'Jon Bon Jovi, y'in?'

George points at his phone.

'I'm off to meet the girls,' he replies, slipping on his coat. My blood panics as I realise I'm being left on my own.

'Guid man, guid man. Where's yer drummer, Shakespeare?'

'I don't know.'

I haven't seen Tony since we got here.

'Then yoose'll jis have to toke enough fer the four o' yoose, eh?'

I agree with a low, non-committal sound. Heidi is sitting to my right, still nursing her bottle of Jack Daniel's, and I inadvertently catch her eye. For the first time ever, she almost smiles at me.

'Um, yeah man, yeah,' I add, as gruffly as I can muster. 'Bring on that... bad shit.'

'Take a tan o' that fust,' continues Duffy, passing me a yellow-labelled bottle of a burgundy-coloured drink called Buckfast. Heidi is still watching me, so I glug about half a pint into a nearby glass, and lift it to my lips.

The smell hits me like an angry cat in the face.

Whatever this drink is, its bouquet is something approximating earwax and prunes cooking over a pot of hot Superglue. But it's too late to back out now.

Down the hatch, old boy.

Oh my WOW that's CRIKEY eurgh oh no no no no no. No. NO.

'Behold.'

The boozy fug disperses to reveal Duffy brandishing a small, hot pipe, which he hands ceremonially to me.

'Yoose fust, wee man.'

We cool here. We cool. I'm old hat at this stuff, I smoked weed at university.

Once.

'This looks like some grade A shiz,' I reply for some extraordinary reason, staring intently at the end of the pipe for what is almost certainly an awkwardly long time.

Marijuana can't actually kill you, can it?

'Let's take this baby for a test ride.'

What am I *talking* about?

Pipe to lips. Brace your bones. Have a good suck. Smoke flooding system. Am I feeling anything yet…?

'Woo! Mama!' I proclaim, forgetting for a moment that I am not Little Richard.

I am trying desperately not to choke, as that would not be very street right now.

But we're OK.

This is floaty.

This is rather nice.

I am all OVER this!

This is my new thing!

I am a drug smoker!

Actually, no I'm not.

This is horrible.

I. Am. Going. To. Die.

OH MY GOD.

In one terrifying black instant, my brain floods with a feeling like being crushed inside a trash compactor, and the contents of my skull instantly putrefy into sinewy Angel Delight and start flowing from my nose, and ears, and mouth, and I'm emptying bit by bit, and OH GOD what *is* this? What *is* this?

But after ten dark seconds, the feeling subsides, and cools, and my organs relax, and peace returns, and my heart is still beating.

But *man*. That is some powerful weed.

'Roond too, bitches.'

A second round. Everyone has a go. Duffy, Hamish, Crazy Wee Willy, a gaggle of random corner-strangers. But curiously not Heidi.

And I am feeling very wrong.

The pipe comes to me, I take a big toke, and the darkness fills my brain again. I feel a shudder creeping through me, and a sickness grips my gut.

And then a third round, and a fourth round.

And a fifth.

But I can't take a fifth. I need to get outside. I need to eat the air.

But when I come back, they'll make me smoke more.

AND I CANNOT SMOKE ANY MORE.

Duffy is inhaling next to me, his eyes closed, lids quivering. Got to do it now.

I swipe the little bag from his stash, the one he used for the pipe, and stow it in my pocket.

Ha! I win.

But can I walk?

I can't walk.

Can I walk?

'I'm off to eat some air.'

And I'm up, and away, and through the door, and onto the balcony. And I am leaning, ruined, against the railings. Ahead I can see all of Méribel, the chalets and the bars, the glistening cold ski slopes, and the mighty Alps beyond. The land we must conquer. My head is dropping off. Below, seventeen floors below, is the cold hard ground. The concrete. It shrinks, and then expands, and seems to rise, and then fall, and the snow glows, and my feet aren't touching the ground any more, they're free, they're floating, and this feels amazing, and my body is cooled by the breeze, and my mind is free, and my body is free, because I'm my own man, I'm in charge, I am finally winning… I AM THE KING.

…Because I'm not on the ledge any more.

I'm falling off it.

19

I am falling off a balcony, and I am definitely going to die.

'Christ alive!'

Bolts of electricity fire through me from top to toe as I leave the ledge and slow-motion plummet to the concrete below. The air is cool, crisp and freezing, and the world is bigger than ever before.

I am going to die.

But now something tugs, some invisible force, and a hand is on my sleeve, and I am pulled back, stumbling and grasping, into a warm body, another human, a wrestle on the ledge and a frantic collapse into the chilly brick wall.

Heidi.

We are pinned against the building. She just saved my life.

Our breath mingles, and her eyes are on fire.

She pushes me away.

'Are you *mental*, Piano Man?'

My head is still squashed, vision fuzzy. I try and focus on her beautiful face.

'Nope, not at all. But I am terribly, terribly high.' She looks at me in amazement. 'I fear I may vomit.'

'You need a glass of water, mate. You're a liability.'

Back inside the flat, the party is in full swing. I can hardly make out people, just shapes and the thumping of music. Is that George in the corner, in a sea of pink? Shrill voices hark poshly across the room – Araminta and the Pink Flamingos. Drug smoke clouds everything, beer cans open with a *pssssh*, booze-fuelled boys tell jokes and fart and suck on hot cigarettes.

I slip from the room into the nearby corridor. I'm going to go and stick my head in the shower.

'Yeah, I'm with you, it's just this band… they're only kids, they haven't toured before. They don't really know what they're doing…'

Tony's voice, coming from a darkened room at the end of the corridor. Making my way down, I stop outside the windowless door, slightly ajar. Shadows move in the dark.

'… What? Well, yeah, I can sack all this off if I need to. The money's no good anyway. I just have to find a way out of it, without… huh? Yeah, without causing World War Three.'

Through the sticky black wad of drug-wax in my brain, I remember. When we were packing the car, outside George's house… Tony's phone call… it sounded just like this.

'Yeah, cool, sure. Something has to give… Uh-huh. Give me a few days, I'll do what I can. And let me know when it's official. Cheers, bye.'

Before I can get away, the door opens and Tony is standing in front of me, pocketing his phone. He freezes.

'Oh… hello,' he says.

'Hello.'

Someone is being sick in the kitchen.

'What are you doing?' he asks, looking over my shoulder.

'Me? Nothing. Just… walking around.'

Tony examines my eyes, each one in turn.

'Are you OK?'

'I smoked on a doobie.'

'You look like death, mate.'

He moves to walk past me. I stand my ground.

'Were you talking to someone in there?'

'What?' A pause. 'Naah, just running over my lyrics for "Twist and Shout".'

I nod, slowly and silently, and watch as he heads off down the passageway. He slips round the corner and is gone.

I need to find George.

But first I have to stick my head in the shower.

'Chris, what on earth are you doing?'

With the party still raging on in the living room, John is standing in the bathroom doorway, car keys in hand, head backlit by a bright white light. I am in the bath, fully clothed, holding the showerhead up in the air.

I am very wet.

'I had to have a shower.'

'In your clothes?'

'It was just meant to be my head, but then I had to get in the bath, you know, for health and safety.'

'Are you high?'

Stepping out of the bath, I drop the showerhead to the ground and it spurts a crazy geyser across the wall.

'That is some *dreadfully* strong weed those fellas have got in there.'

'You mean what they're smoking in the kitchen?'

'Uh-huh.'

'Through those little pipes?'

'Uh-huh.'

John has a very serious face on now.

'I don't think that was weed.'

'What do you mean, of course it was, no tobacco's that strong. I know weed when I smoke it, young man.'

Which is of course a lie.

'That wasn't weed, Chris,' John repeats, the contours of his face going gluey in front of me. 'That was crack.'

'Come again?'

'You just smoked crack.'

'Oh dear Lord.'

The upturned shower gurgles feebly in the bath.

'Are you OK?'

Now I am definitely going to puke.

***

George and I are standing on top of the highest mountain in the Alps.

It's night time, the sky dripping its inky blackness into our hair, necks, shoulders. The bluish glow of the moon creeps over our hands and faces in silent ambush, and diamond-white snow twinkles in the dark.

Across the mountain range echoes a steady slam, slam, slam, a distant pounding like a drum in the night. Slam. Slam. Slam. A duel for attention between storm and drum, a terrible rising symphony that rumbles and spits and seethes. Through the noise and the white whipping snow I reach for George, but something has changed. He is different, somehow. Transformed. Mutated.

In fact, he has turned into a goat.

A *mountain goat*.

Oh, I see.

Of course.

This is a dream, isn't it?

I am having a dream.

'He's alive!'

A face is in my face.

'Morning!'

'Holy crap, what are you?'

This is terrifying. Where am I? *What* am I? Who's this? Am I at home? Why does my skull feel like it's been sucked dry by a camel?

Hang on... this is Araminta. I am in the chalet. I am not dead. Everything is going to be OK.

'Do you know, Tris, I've been watching you for twenty minutes now...'

You've been what?! I reach instinctively for my nether regions. I am wearing pants. At least, ladies and gentlemen, I am wearing some pants.

'...and it's been bugging me silly, but you do look rather familiar. Where did you school?'

I straighten my poor, broken body, bones groaning under cold flesh. The potato-sack upholstery of the sofa scratches my thighs.

'Christ *alive*, my head. Why did I sleep down here?'

180

'Was it Radley? You've got Radley written all over you.'

Araminta is still waiting for an answer. I press my fingertips into my temple.

'Sorry, I have no idea what you're talking about.'

She tuts and sighs, as if I've just asked her the world's dumbest question.

'Everyone knows Radley boys are, like, arty and nice and whatnot. I just thought you might have schooled there.'

'Um… no.' I cough, jaggedly. That doesn't sound good. 'Where I schooled, school wasn't a verb.'

She wrinkles her nose at me, confused.

'Place called Langtree,' I continue, trying to sit up but finding the process disconcertingly complex. Araminta's face has gone entirely blank.

'It's a state school,' I add. She gasps and holds a hand to her chest.

'You went to a compy? Oh, Tris, you poor thing.' Why does she keep calling me Tris?

'So… you mean… one of those funny little places with the free school dinners? Oh, that is literal hilarity.'

A look of horror splashes across her face.

'Do you have A-levels?'

Everything hurts. Everything in me hurts.

'Araminta, what are you—'

'Oh nonsense, just call me Minty. Everybody else does.'

'OK, Mi—'

'Or Arry, or Arry-Minty. Or the Mintmeister. But then the Uppingham boys used to call me Fizzy Fanny because of the hoo-hah with the Pimm's at Henley Regats.'

She pauses for breath.

'Right… OK. So where's George?'

'Oh, *George*. Gorgeous George. He was literally so funny last night, I nearly died. But hohmygosh Tris, I am *hanging* this morning, I tell thee. What a classic jollop.'

What's a jollop? Is it something to do with horses?

'Those Scottish boys are so uncouth, especially the big-handed one. He wanted to ravish me behind the bins, it was London

Rankathon. He just *kept* trying to get into my knickers, and he's like yeeeah, and I'm like no-o-o, and it's like, *HELLO*?! You know?'

I FEEL LIKE A CRAZY MONKEY IS RAPING MY FACE.

'Gosh, it was horrid, like when Raggy-T wanted to bonk in the chapel in year ten, and I didn't really fancy him because he's a bit short but then we did it anyway and he could only last, like, two measly minutes and he said it was because he'd been fagging all day and I was, like, *yeeeaaah*, as IF, that is like TT because you don't even fag on Wednesdays if you're at Papplewick's, it's like, duh, *everybody* knows that. You know what I mean?'

Not even one tiny bit.

'This is fun, isn't it Trissy?'

'Yep, sure. But do you know wher—'

'Lapsang souchong?'

I rub my eyes, hoping to disperse the headache.

'Pardon?'

'Cup of lapsang souchong?'

'Yep. I'm still just hearing sounds.'

'Lapsang souchong, *silly*!' she repeats, standing up and sashaying into the kitchen. 'It's lovely Chinese tea, for your naughty hangover. I brought it over because George said you boys only had Monster Munch and ham.'

She busies herself preparing the drinks, grimacing at the state of our crockery. My gaze wanders out of the window at our increasingly familiar panoramic Alpine view. The sky is an unbelievable blue this morning, clean and brilliant against the crisp white of the mountain range.

'So-o-o,' continues Araminta musically, sitting down and passing me a steaming cup of black tea, 'I was thinking. We should chit-chat, you and me. No?'

She is looking right at me now, rather intently. When I breathe, the air scrapes uncomfortably along the inside of my throat. What did I drink last night? PVA glue?

'Oh… sure. We can… chit-chat.'

'Georgeous thought we should spend some quality time together, just the two of us. Like, bonding and such.'

She blinks at me with her big emerald eyes.

'That sounds… fun.'

'I mean, thing is, I'm not totally stupid. You probably think I'm just some silly old boarding-school bozo, don't you?'

She takes a sip of tea while waiting for me to answer. I give it a go, but no actual words come out.

She smiles.

'It's all right if you do. I know I am a bit silly sometimes. I can't help it.'

She pauses, and I spend some time investigating the strange, hot, dark substance in my teacup. It smells pretty heinous, but, oddly, one sip and I already begin to feel better.

'… The truth is,' continues Araminta, 'I really like you boys. And lovely George of course.'

'Well, you're only human. Our George, he's every inch a—'

'Sexpot.'

I let out an involuntary laugh, and she smiles again.

'I was going for charmer,' I cough out, 'but… yeah.'

'You're so clever, all of you, with your music, and I can see how much it means to you, and… I just want you to know that I'm not trying to steal George away from you.'

I shift slightly on my cushion, and Araminta glances momentarily at the floor. She looks a little sad.

'That's… sweet of you.'

'I'd just feel awful if you thought that.'

'Look, it's not really your fault. Bands are weird. And sometimes George just lives in a world of his own, that's all.'

'Word up, homies!' calls George, bursting in through the front door with two fully stuffed grocery bags. Tony is bringing up the rear with an absolutely massive wheel of cheese. 'We've just shopped our buttocks off.'

'What these Frenchies are banging on about half the time, I've got no idea,' adds Tony, chucking his wallet onto a nearby chair. 'I mean, I bought this monster wheel of cheese right, gave the guy a hundred euros, and he only gives me forty back. Nutcase.'

Our bank account is emptying before my very eyes.

'You spent *sixty euros* on cheese?'

'Yep. Belting stuff, though, give it a whiff.'

Tony wafts the cheese wheel at me as he passes, and my gut instantly contracts.

It smells like someone grated a corpse.

'I see you two have been bonding,' says George with a wink, on his way to the kitchen. I cover up my pants with a blanket.

'Um... yep. Little bit. Y'know, Henley Regats. Fagging.'

Araminta gives me a little smile.

'Classic,' replies George. He dumps the bags on the counter, and a pig's trotter rolls out. *A pig's trotter?* 'Tell you what, though, Christoph, when I was looking for the kitty money this morning I found something very revealing in your room.'

He pulls a crumpled piece of paper from his back pocket and waves it at me.

'You must have done this before you went to sleep last night.'

'What...? Done what?'

I am beginning to experience the Fear.

'You've written the same phrase, over and over again, all across it. Look. Twenty or thirty times.'

He passes me the scrap of paper, which turns out to be a flyer for Heidi and the Black Cats. It's absolutely covered in one repeated phrase, scribbled words plastered across the band's faces, obscuring their eyes. I read it afresh, as if from someone else's hand.

The repeated phrase is inescapable: '*the lightyears between us*'.

'I don't remember writing that.'

'I'm not surprised, old sport. You'd spent all night guzzling on your crack pipe.'

'*What?*'

He pulls a nondescript chunk of animal from the bag, dangles it in the air and sniffs it.

'Crack pipe, Christoph.'

Oh my god... of course! *That's* why I feel so wretched. *Because of all the drugs. Because of all the ASTRO-TURF AND WOBBLY EGGS.*

This is really terrible. Maybe I'll get arrested. Is crack illegal? I'm pretty sure it's illegal.

'Hang on, lads, how about that?'

Tony is hacking into the giant cheese wheel with a screwdriver.

'How about what?' asks George.

'How about that for a band name? What you just said?'

Tony is pointing at me with one hand, cheese-tipped screwdriver in the other. I eye him, unconvinced.

'I don't think we can call our band Crack Pipe.'

'No, not that...' he replies, gnawing on a chunk of cheese. 'Lightyears.'

George goes quiet, and stares into the ceiling.

'Huh.'

'You'd want a definite article on the front, though...'

John, as it turns out, has been reading quietly in the corner this whole time.

'... like with *The Iliad*,' he continues, not looking up from his book, 'or *The Symposium*. Otherwise we'll sound like a space programme.'

'The Lightyears,' says George, slowly, a smile growing on his face.

'The Lightyears,' I repeat, under my breath. Tony holds his hands up in triumph.

'That is *brilliant*.'

'I love it!' agrees Araminta, clapping excitedly.

SCHTADDA-TAT-TAT – an angry knock at the door. We all wait, frozen to the spot, Tony pressing a rigid finger against his lips. Seconds later, our landlady's face, that weird old visage like a horrible talking ballbag, presses up against the window. Araminta gasps.

'What is *that*, Georgeous?'

'You'd better get it, Christoph,' says George, with immediate agreement from Tony. 'She likes you.'

The second knock is even angrier than the first.

'OK, fine. But first, do we have a consensus on this? No more Bum Chums?'

'Bum Chums are dead, long live The Lightyears!' sing-songs George, eliciting giggles from Araminta. Tony salutes me, and John offers a silent thumbs-up from his text. Another rap of knuckles on the front door.

'... *est-ce que vous me prenez pour une conne, chien de porc anglais?*' she is saying as I open the door. English pig-dog? That's an encouraging start.

'Um…'

'*Je chie dans tes pantoufles, petite boite à merde attardée!*'

My face is flecked with the old crone's spittle. I wipe it off with my sleeve.

'What's she saying?' asks George from inside.

'She wants to leave a dirty protest in my slippers.'

'Intriguing.'

'And she called me a retarded little shit-box.'

'That's probably a compliment in France.'

'*Pardon, madame, je suis, uuuhhh…*'

She jabs the ground with her peg-leg. Peering past her, I notice an aged goat tied to a post on the opposite side of the road. It is pissing, liberally.

'*Avez-vous l'argent, putain?*'

This is bad, very bad. She wants the rent money, and we're nearly a week behind. Plus I'm not convinced we have any euros left.

'Tony, can I have the petty cash?'

'Ah yeah, there's none left.'

That's right. Because you SPENT IT ALL ON CHEESE.

'*Il y a un petit problème, Madame…*'

I emphasise '*petit*' by making a space between my thumb and forefinger about the size of a pea.

'*Eh? Un problème?*'

'*Parce que… uuuhhh…*'

Just tell her the truth. Cheese is expensive. That's the market round here. Nothing we can do about that.

'*Le fromage est très cher.*'

'*Têtes de bite!*' she spits, kicking me hard on the shin.

186

Well, this is grand. Here I am, still ever so slightly accidentally high on crack, standing in my pants in the freezing cold doorway of a rotting old shack your average tramp would turn his nose up at, watching a goat piss itself while a half-mad senior citizen with a wooden leg opens up a can of whoop-ass on me.

No one can say I'm not living the dream.

'*Je veux mon argent avant la fin de semaine, ou je jette votre petit cul à la rue.*'

'*Absolument, Madame.*'

SLAM.

Silence.

Tony is standing behind me on the doormat, texting.

'Everything all right, boss?'

'She's threatening to evict us. Unless we pay her by the weekend, we'll be homeless…'

I trail off, watching Tony tap away on his mobile. A cluster of memories flood suddenly back to me. A phone call, last night, at the party… *I can sack all this off if I need to… The money's no good anyway… I just have to find a way out of it…*

'Guess we'd better start making some dollar, then, eh?' Tony replies, reaching for his coat. 'I'm leaving, by the way.'

My muscles seize.

'What?'

'Yeah, I'm off.'

'But…' He flicks up his collar and reaches for the door-knob. 'Look, Tony, I think we need to tal—'

'Just a quick walk, won't be long. Back for rehearsal in twenty. Help yourself to cheese.'

And with the harsh Alpine breeze nipping at my bare legs, I watch Tony throw open the door, step out into the cold and disappear down the street.

20

'We're running out of time, George.'

Le Rond Point is gearing up for a massive Saturday night. Endless bar staff are hurrying in and out, stocking up fridges and dinging the till. Tony is testing reverbs through a microphone. George and I are grazing on fries at the bar.

'Time, Christoph? There's always time. I believe it was Gandhi who said *Time is a fish, a fish on a dish, but a slippery one indeed.*'

'What does that even mean?'

'Who knows? Silly old Gandhi.'

Someone flicks on the TV above our heads, and it blares out a pumping pop soundtrack. Babes in bikinis slither onto the screen.

'The ceremony's in one week. This is a big break for us, we can't blow it.'

'One week? That's ages! They built Hemel Hempstead in a week, and look at that place.'

'Everywhere I turn I see the Black Cats. They've got a record deal, national press, everything the judges want. Plus you've seen them walking around here, they act like rockstars. They *look* like rockstars.' I glance at the stage. 'We need to get good… and quick.'

'Look around you, old pal. Tonight is Jägerbomb-Till-You-Vom Night, it's going to be apocalyptic. Not to mention the grand unveiling of The Lightyears… we'll be a whole new band. The bar is about to be raised.'

'I hope so. Because that A and R rep, he's judging the awards, and I'm pretty sure he fancies Heidi. Which means—'

'A-ha, so *that's* what this is all about!' laughs George, pointing right into my face. 'Mr Big is pissing on your lamp post.'

'What lamp post?'

'This is about you trying to cop off with Heidi.'

'I am not trying to cop off with her.'

'No, no, course not. Course not.'

The babes in bikinis make way for an unfeasibly wide rapper in shiny silver trousers. He is listing his possessions while the girls paw at him.

'Fancy a drink, old chum? They do something in here called a Crappy Manhattan, which comes with this massive curly straw—'

'George, how do you talk to girls without sounding like a total arse?'

George pauses for a moment, a curious smile on his lips. Then he yawns and drops an arm around my shoulder.

'It's easy. I just pretend I'm talking to my mum.'

'I don't think that would work for me.'

'Well, then, I suggest you wait until Heidi rocks up at the gig tonight, get your tiny ass on that dance floor and show her what your funk is made of.'

If my funk was made of anything, it would almost certainly be tweed.

'You want me to try and woo her… from the *dance floor*?'

'Yep.'

'I don't think so. I dance like Mr Bean having a coronary.'

'What you mean is, *you have your own style*. She'll take one look at the junk in your trunk and her brain will, I'm not kidding, actually fall out.'

George turns to head back to the stage and I grab the corner of his sleeve, pulling him towards me.

'Before you go, there's something else.'

'Yip?'

I lower my voice.

'I think Tony might want to… quit the band.'

George pulls a face, then peers over at the back of the room where Tony is busy switching around cables at the mixing desk.

'I think you need to cut back on the drugs, old fruitcake.'

'No, seriously. I've heard him on the phone twice now. Talking to someone about leaving the band, about some other job being better paid. I don't know what it is but he keeps saying all he needs to do is figure out how to get out of this. Then we'll lose him.'

'So ask him about it.'

'I don't know. I'm scared. You saw what happened when Heidi confronted him at the Water Rats, he just quit on the spot. Maybe we should keep quiet, at least until after the LIMAs, otherwise—'

'Dudes!'

A blond, blue-eyed snowboarder is standing in front of us, dressed in full ski gear and drinking what looks like snakebite. He is grinning enormously and bobbing his head.

'You dudes are, uhhh… you dudes are *dudes*, man,' he says, exceptionally pleased about something. I look at George.

'Um… thanks.'

He waits for a moment, still grinning, and then play-punches me on the shoulder.

'Seriously, bros, I've been to all your gigs here – you Bum Chums are *sick!*'

'We're The Lightyears now.'

'Huh?'

'We just changed our name.'

'SICK, man! *Lightyears*. I *like* that! So you bros got a CD I can buy?'

'Right, of course. Sure. George, can you grab one from my bag?'

While I rummage through my jacket pocket for change, Snow-Dude stands in front of me, shifting his weight from one foot to the other and saying our new name over and over again. The change in my pocket is buried deep, so I pull out a jumble of miscellaneous rubbish and dump it on the table. Coins, keys and chewing gum scatter in piles.

'Hey, whoa, no waaaaay!'

Snow-Dude is staring in wide-eyed awe at the litter of knick-knacks laid out between us.

'Are you OK?'

'You selling, man?'

He's looking right at me now.

'Am I what?'

'Selling.'

'Um, sure, George is getting you a CD now…'

'*No-o-o*, man,' he insists, leaning towards me, hands in pockets. 'Are you *sell*-ing?'

He reaches down towards the objects on the table and nudges at one with his finger. It's a miniature plastic bag containing a small collection of powdery, yellow-white rocks.

Which can be one of only two things. Either emergency parmesan, or…

'Jesus Christ!'

He *Sssh*-es me and glances back over his shoulder.

'Keep it tight, bro, keep it tight. I'm cool. We… are… cooool.'

This must be the stash I stole from the Black Cats. I'd forgotten it was there. I wave a hand at him.

'These are not my drugs.'

'Whoa, whoa, whoa! Who said anything about drugs?' he replies through gritted teeth. 'This is just an everyday financial transaction, right, bro? And all I wanna know is: how much… *for the CD?*'

Great. First I accidentally smoke crack, now I'm accidentally dealing it.

'Look, you're barking up the wrong tree. I really only want to sell you a CD. They're three pounds. That's all.'

He eyes me sideways, nodding with respect.

'I'm widya, boss, I'm widya. Hush hush. Mix it on the down-low.' Sidling over, he slips the CD and the drugs off the table, then speaks right inside my ear. 'I take this now, and by eleven o'clock tonight there'll be sixty fat ones strapped underneath the purple pool table at Jack's Bar. Yeah?'

I have been stunned into silence.

'*Yeeeeah*,' he repeats, stashing the loot into his big ski-jacket pockets. Then, turning on his heel, he saunters out the door.

'What a lovely bloke,' concludes George, spanking me on the bum.

***

Our music moves, and the whole room is moving with us.

It's a full house tonight at Le Rond Point. We are pounding out the closing chorus to 'Parklife', and the sweat, the beating hearts, the singing and the cheering tell me we've won. We've finally clicked. Tony is that blur of hair and sticks and rhythm from the 12 Bar Club, John's eyes shine bright as he glides through basslines, George grips the microphone while leading the room in chorus. The music swells to a crescendo and a crazed crowd-surfer emerges from the sea of arms, bumping and tumbling across the nest of heads, his feet pressed against ceiling beams.

As he leaps and jolts from one side to another, I notice that the ceiling is layered in faded boot-marks.

'LIGHT-YEARS! LIGHT-YEARS!'

The Lightyears have arrived.

'We started this,' George mouths at me, from centre stage, blue eyes gleaming. Then he turns back to Tony at the kit, thrashing his guitar and laughing.

The hours pass, and we're travelling together on a tide of energy, a churning, soaring wave of sound. It's not perfect yet, but it's thrilling and unpredictable, and for the first time ever I'm not thinking about the chords. I'm not worrying about the shape of the set. I'm not haunted by thoughts of being evicted from our crummy chalet or anxious that the car might just suddenly combust in the snow, or obsessing over whether anyone in the crowd noticed I fluffed the second chorus in 'Bohemian Like You'. I'm cascading, in free-fall, protected by my band.

As the gig draws to a close, and sweaty hands reach into the air calling for more, I spot Heidi striding past the gathered crowds, hair up, eyes down. She is pulling a pack of Marlboros from her pocket and heading for the front doors. With Tony's final cymbals dying away beneath the soundtrack of boozy whooping, I drop off the stage and follow her outside.

It's a cold night, and the streets are all but empty.

'Yo, Heidi.'

It's that familiar look again. The look that a teenage girl gives to her little brother's friends.

'All right, Piano Man.'

I pass a casual hand through my hair. Beyond where she's standing, the mighty black mountains gather in silent judgement, wreathed in purple clouds and specked by the low season's slowly dying snow. A cool breeze freshens the air, raising tiny goosebumps across the back of my neck. The scene is primed for romantic entanglement.

Which means my opening line is of the utmost importance.

OPTION ONE

'So I guess it's just you, me and the stars, eh, kiddo?'

No. Come on. Rein it in. Unless you are prepared to wear a medallion and a chest wig, that's not going to work.

OPTION TWO

'Here's a crazy fact, Heidi. When bees have sex, their balls explode.'

No. Just... no. It's obviously a no.

OPTION THREE

'Beautiful night, isn't it?'

That is weak. Painfully weak.

Only one problem.

I actually said that one.

Which indicates, beyond all reasonable doubt, that *I genuinely believe myself to be David Hasselhoff.*

'What are you on about?' she says, edging a cigarette from the packet, and I watch her roll the tip between finger and thumb. She

193

might be a bit rude, this girl, but my God is she beautiful. Fifties-movie-star beautiful. Beautiful like the softest breeze on the edge of a perfect summer's day in a chocolate advert in the bath.

'Woo! Wild night in there, right?'

She flicks at a lighter and her cigarette tip glows orange.

'Yeah, I guess,' she says, with a crooked smile. 'Your set was all right.'

'*Coolio.*'

I watch her smoke for a few seconds. What do I say now? What's a good icebreaker?

'I've been wondering, Heidi…'

Not that.

'Where did you school?' Tits.

'Wha'?'

You broke the ice all right. You broke the ice with a lacrosse racket, you big posh berk.

'I was just… asking…'

Think of something else. It honestly doesn't matter what it is. I am giving you express permission to say anything you like as long as it isn't *where did you school.*

'Where did you school?' She screws up her face.

'Why d'you care?'

'Ohhh, no, I don't really. Stupid question.'

Silence returns, and she blows white smoke into the purple air. Mouth opening, stupidity marching in…

'I went to Langtree School, in Woodcote.'

OH MY CHRIST STOP TALKING WORDS.

'Huh?'

'Yeah, nothing special, just a little country comp. Excellent OFSTED reports though. Really tremendous geography department, actually.'

Oh, come on. Surely even *you* know that if someone was to write a list of the chat-up lines least likely to entice a woman into bed, the phrase 'really tremendous geography department' would have to be one of them.

'You're so weird.'

194

She flicks ash out into the night, and I take a few steps forward until we're standing in line. I stare at my feet, then out at the mountains.

'Heidi.'

'Yeah.'

'There's a thing happening at that funny wine bar on Friday night, the one down the road? It's just this stupid date-night thing they do, it's really dumb, pizzas and red wine or something, but… do you… maybe…'

She turns to look at me, shocked at first, then perplexed. Finally, her face softens *almost* into a smile, and she starts to reply.

'Oi, you.'

A huge hand has clamped onto my shoulder from behind. Turning to meet its owner, I find Geoffrey towering above me in the doorway, face stern as stone, arms like felled tree trunks.

'Oh… hello Geoffrey.'

After a brief, suspicious glance at Heidi, he nods back over his shoulder and nudges the door open with his elbow.

'Inside, now.'

***

Geoffrey's office is a small, cramped room hidden away behind the Rond Point's main bar. It's uncomfortably warm in here, and the dull thud of revelry soaks through the walls.

'So. Young man. Howdyer say it's going out here fer you lot?'

Geoffrey is sitting behind his desk in a high-backed leather chair, leafing through papers. Dungeon-dark, the office is lit by a single greasy window, set high up behind his head at a crazy angle behind a grille of rusting metal bars. The walls in here are the colour of boiled pig meat, and the carpet feels dank beneath my feet. A cast-iron clock ticks thickly on the wall.

'Well, not bad, really. Chalet's a bit draughty, but—'

'You wouldn't say you've stepped outter line at all, then?'

Something's going on here. Has he been talking to the Aggressive Ballbag next door?

195

'No, not at all, we'd never step outside the line. We love the line. If the line were a human being—'

'Because I've heard summat very different, college boy, and I'd like to know what it all means if you don't mind.'

The hairs on the back of my neck are standing up.

'Okey-dokey.'

'Y'see, we've had problems up here before, problems wi' *troublemakers*, y'know the sort. And sooner or later I have to do summat about it.'

I nod again, more slowly this time, and Geoffrey rises from his chair. His huge frame blocks out the feeble glow from the window and plunges us into semi-darkness.

'Which brings me to the central thrust of my argument,' says his silhouette. 'Namely you, college boy, and yer drug habit.'

An abrupt, surprised laugh shoots out of my face and meets its immediate demise in the air between us. Geoffrey is not amused.

'Look, you've got me totally wrong, I took those drugs by accident. I didn't know what I was doing.'

He steps out from behind his desk, and the feeble beam of light returns, illuminating a tall stack of papers entitled 'DEMANDS FOR PAYMENT'. Perching on the edge of the desk, he crosses his arms and leaves a very, very long pause.

'You telling me you smoked crack cocaine… *by mistake?*'

'Uh-huh, yes sir. Absolutely.'

He shakes his head wearily.

'Well, that's by the by, since what you do on yer own time is actually of no interest to me, daft though it may be. But I will not have you dealing hard drugs on my premises.'

My hands take to the skies in a moment of sudden realisation.

'Right, I see! Sorry, that was a misunderstanding. I'm not a drug dealer, far from it.'

'That's not what the young lad I dragged in here earlier told me. He said you sold him a bag o' crack for sixty quid, just this afternoon.'

'No, that's all wrong. Don't listen to him – I think he was a little slow.'

'Are you taking the piss? D'yer sell him t'drugs or not?'

'Yes, OK, *technically* I did, but that too was, um… that also was a mistake.'

His moustache quivering, Geoffrey extends his arm, opens his vast hand, plucks me from the clammy carpet and crushes me like a clove of garlic, sending my innards gludging through his fingers and dripping into a sloppy jam on the floor.

OK, that didn't happen.

'Typical bloody waste-o'-space musicians, the lotta yer,' he continues, walking back round to his chair.

'But I'm not like the rest of them, Geoffrey. I wish I *was*!'

'Listen to me, college boy,' he says, sitting back down at the desk and producing a long, gnarled fountain pen from the drawer. 'You balls this up again, and you Bum Chums are out of here. Fer good.'

'But this isn't—'

'We're done.'

He plucks the top sheet off the 'DEMANDS FOR PAYMENT' pile and returns to his work. His pen makes a snarling, scratchy sound like scalpel on bone, the jagged tip spurting red ink as he scrawls. I stand my ground for some twenty seconds, but soon Geoffrey's head, huge and sweaty like a lamb shank in the sun, rolls upwards to eyeball me. My heart thumps inside my ears.

'Go on, out of me sight.'

Next door in the Rond Point, the party has ended. Bar staff are sweeping up debris and stacking chairs onto tables, the last of the drinkers have gone home and The Lightyears are nowhere to be seen. At the foot of the stage is a handwritten note.

Christoph, Tony wasn't feeling great so he wanted to get packed up. Meet him in the car park when you're done (dirty dog!!). I'm off for dinner with Minty. See you in the morning old fruit x

Peering out the back doors into the car park, I find John reading in the passenger seat of the Omega, and Tony snoozing behind the steering wheel. He looks rather pale.

But I have unfinished business. Because illegal or otherwise, someone has to pay the rent round here.

I reach Jack's Bar just before the doors close and slip inside. With the last remaining member of staff busy stacking the fridge, I dart into the shadows and quickly run a hand along the underside of the purple pool table.

There's nothing there.

He's hidden it well.

Quietly, carefully, I drop to my knees and scan the length of the table. No package, anywhere. Nothing.

Of course there's nothing.

Sitting on the floor in the dark, I contemplate my current state of affairs. Specifically, it would appear that I am now failing not only as a musician, but also in my new-found career as an accidental crack pimp.

This is a new low.

***

In our bedroom, George's book of lyrics lies open on the desk. He's had this since we were fourteen, stapling in new pages whenever the old ones run out, and these days it's bulging with layer after layer of dry, ageing paper. At the top of the open page, he has written a single lyric: '*this town is anyone's friend*'.

Slipping a pen from my pocket, underneath the line I write one solitary word: '*sometimes*'.

A text message sounds from the bedroom across the hall. Tony's quarters. Judging by the clattering in the kitchen, he's currently preparing his nightly cheese platter, which normally takes at least ten minutes. In the bedroom behind me, John has been sleeping for some time.

Silently, I pad across the hall and into Tony's room.

The screen reads: '1 message received'. I click through and read the text: *Mate, it's on, i need you 2 confirm ASAP*.

I navigate back to Tony's inbox. This is certainly not the first message from this particular contact. There are exchanges going back weeks, months even: *Tony, amazing opportunity for you, buzz me for details… just heard from the promoter, money's great, you need to get out of Méribel!! …you got out of this tour yet big man?*

'All right, mate.'

Tony is standing in the doorway with a plate of food. I am frozen on the spot.

'Hello there.'

'What you up to?' he asks, sighing. He looks terrible. His face is semi-transparent, stretched across his cheekbones like the rubbery skin on a Chinese dumpling.

'No, no, nothing at all. Just… hangin'.'

He nods, absently, sets the food on his bedside table and slowly lowers himself onto the mattress. I retreat backwards towards the doorway.

'You seen my phone? It was in here a second ago.'

This is about to get very sticky.

'Your… telephone? Umm… N-no, I don't *believe* I…'

'Wait,' he interrupts, with a laugh. 'It's there. In your hand.'

I prepare a pantomime of extraordinary proportions. Never before has a human being been quite this surprised to see such an everyday object.

'Oh my god?! That's so weird! I must have been… sleepwalking or—'

'Get out of here.'

'What?'

'Get out of the room. *Now.*'

Standing up, Tony advances towards me, a wild look flooding his eyes like red ink into clear water. Blood rushes to his ghostly grey face and he stumbles, lurches towards me, reaching out for my throat with both hands.

'OK, I can explain, I really just—'

'No, seriously, you need to leave, get out the way.'

This is it: my first proper fight. Time for that Tae Kwon Do yellow belt to finally kick the heck in.

I lift my hands to guard against his advance, but my block is too weak. Just a few inches in front of me his knees buckle and he crashes into me, grabbing at my sleeve. I struggle against him but his body far outweighs mine and I fold like a marionette, lashing out as I go. While the sudden movement throws Tony out towards the bathroom door, I have lost my footing, right at the top of the stairs, and despite a last-minute grab for the banister, it's too late. I am crashing, rolling, pinballing down the wooden staircase, uselessly clutching at passing protrusions for something to break my fall. Picture frames cascade onto my head, one of my shoes is prised off and the flimsy walls shudder with every thud of my limbs until I come finally to an inglorious halt, crumpled at the foot of the stairs.

A quiet descends, leaving only the sound of my breathing, and an owl hooting in the distance.

Seconds tick by.

Then, in the silence, Tony stirs upstairs.

I don't think he's finished with me yet.

21

My feet slip and twist against the frayed wood of the staircase as I struggle to climb back onto my feet. I can't get purchase on anything. My heart thudding, I peer upwards, waiting for Tony's towering silhouette to emerge as he prepares for round two of this frankly one-sided boxing match.

Five seconds pass, and then ten. Eventually, instead of seeing him appear at the top of the stairs, I hear him in the bathroom… being comically, violently, murderously sick.

The noise is truly appalling. Guttural and rich, it's as if his internal organs are launching themselves helter-skelter from his body. And in between the dreadful black retching, Tony can be heard gasping for breath and emitting low moans.

After quite some time, the vomiting subsides. Pulling myself up into a sitting position, I rub at the back of my skull, still throbbing from where it connected with the skirting board.

'Jesus… Chris… you OK?'

Tony's voice.

'Um… I guess…'

He turns on the tap in the sink.

'Christ, I'm so sorry! I thought I was gonna puke on you – I had to make a dash for it. I haven't hurt you, have I?'

What the *heck* is going on?

'Erm… no…'

'Good, good… because *hhurrhhjuggayYEURRLLgeeeueurrrga gak*…'

It's back, and from the sound of it, very much here to stay.

As I squat in a crumpled heap at the foot of the stairs, my brain plays me edited highlights of the last twenty-four hours of my life. This has been a very weird day. And I have to get some sleep.

**

I wake with a start.

Slowly, my eyes adjust to the throbbing dark of the chalet. It is 4:37 a.m. and exhaustion grips me like a fist. Across the room, George's bed is empty and unmade.

Outside, a storm is growing, and the small bedroom window has blown off the latch and is slamming open and shut in the wind. The chalet walls quiver and creak in the freezing cold and, in the bathroom next door, Tony is being viciously sick.

'*BwwulluurrgghhYAKgegakka…*'

It's quite the most disgusting thing I have ever heard. Imagine the sound of a disease-ridden troll reaching sexual ecstasy while simultaneously emptying a bathful of chum into a swamp.

'*HhhurrhhjjgymmeerYAALLLRRRGGHHrrr…*'

Our little world is coming apart at the seams. Something's going on with Tony, but after tonight I think I understand it even less than before. George is elsewhere, as he always seems to be these days. Our landlady wants to throw us out, we barely have enough money to pay our debts and Geoffrey has given us one last chance: if we screw up again, he'll send us packing. And tomorrow… well, tomorrow is a very big day. The Méribel End-Of-Season Blowout, a chance for Geoffrey to squeeze every last euro out of the resort's merry revellers before they fly home next week. Every band on the circuit is playing three gigs in three separate venues. It's an undertaking of marathon proportions, and we need to be rested. Without these gigs, there's no way we can pay our rent.

Eventually, mercifully, an eerie calm descends. The plumbing mumbles and moans, and the window rattles to a stop as the storm relaxes. The drip-drip of the leaky kitchen tap echoes upwards through holes in the floorboards, wind hisses through the leaves in the trees outside, and the goat gently whinnies in its sleep. The street is bathed in night-silence.

But it's an uneasy silence, like the dead air before a firing squad. And seconds later, Tony starts up again.

Only this time, it's coming from the other end.

I strain, I struggle, I *plead* with my poor reluctant brain to take my imagination to a happy place. I'm in the tree. I'm in the silver birch tree in George's garden and we're fourteen years old and we're making dreams and planning futures and we're taking a vow to always stick together, no matter what, because if you work really hard at school, if you do all your homework and follow the gospel according to Jon Bon Jovi and never give up on your dreams then one day you too might be lucky enough to cry yourself to sleep on a child's mattress in a flatpack shed in the middle of French Nowhere listening to your mad cheese-eating drummer slowly shitting and puking himself to death.

I soon slip and slither into a kind of queer delirium. I *ache* from fatigue. After what could be one minute, one hour or ten hours, I wrap the scrapheap of towels and coats around me, my eyes dewy from tears of exhaustion. Water is running in the sink. The sky is beginning to blush as dawn approaches, and I drift, pain free, awash in a state of numbness, floating high above the rooftops in the deep of a distant blue ocean.

By the hypnotic light of the melancholy moon, I watch as gentle snowflakes fall, and listen as the unforgiving north wind begins, once again, to blow.

***

'Is he still alive?'

Tony is huddled on the sofa in a furry shell made of raggedy blankets. His skin is the colour of cooked egg yolk, his eye sockets sunken dunes in the arid desert of his face.

'He just needs to rest.'

I still can't say for sure what happened last night. Did he actually push me, or was it an honest mistake? Does *he* know that *I* know he's going to quit the band? In fact, does he remember even the slightest detail? This morning, from the looks of it, he could barely tell me what day of the week it is.

John arrives from the kitchen with a steaming hot mug and slots it carefully into Tony's hands. I wave an open palm in front of the Drummer's eyes.

'He's gone wrong.'

'Dodgy stomach, I think.'

My stomach walls twitch at the memory of last night.

'You're telling me.'

'Drink up, Tony.'

Tony stirs slightly, both eyes closing and then, one at a time, drowsily opening again. Outside, the snow eddies and swirls along Saint-Bon's steep, potholed streets. The first significant snowfall since we arrived in France. It is 11:34 a.m.

'Where's George? We're running late.'

'He didn't come home last night.'

'I know, but we should have left ten minutes ago.'

'Delhi Belly,' murmurs Tony weakly. We both squint at him.

'Is that one of your bands?' I say loudly into Tony's face.

'No, it's not,' corrects John. 'It's slang for traveller's diarrhoea.'

Tony's head bobs forward with exhaustion, and he attempts a nod. John touches a hand to his temple.

'This isn't good. Delhi Belly's nasty – I caught it once when I was travelling. He'll be knocked out for twenty-four hours, probably more.'

'But we can't… we've got three shows today.'

'You been abroad recently?' asks John, a hand on Tony's shoulder. Tony nods, sleepily.

'On tour, Rajasthan. Nepalese happy hardcore…'

'That'll be it,' concludes John, while Tony stares off into the distance. I run through today's schedule in my head. The timings are tight… very tight.

'I'm glad you boys are here,' comes George's voice from the doorway, 'because I've been meaning to talk to you anyway.'

John and I turn to look. George has left the door wide open, and an icy wind peppered with snowflakes invades the chalet.

'Last night I thought somebody was setting off cluster bombs in my face, you should have seen it.'

'Where have you been? We're running late.'

'Hmm. Let me think. Where *have* I been?' He taps one finger against his lips. 'Penrith, I'd say. And I'd have made it all the way to Glasgow if there hadn't been leaves on the line at Cockup Bottom.'

'You knew we had to leave at eleven thirty.'

He points a thumb back out the doorway.

'Sorry, I lost track of time. Minty just dropped me back.'

I watch through the window as a growling Range Rover crawls away up the freezing mountain road, flattening twigs and frightening the goat.

'Can we keep it down?' says John. 'Tony's been up all night.'

'He's not the only one,' replies George, winking at me. Ignoring him, I concentrate on herding a collection of empty mugs from the coffee table.

'Fine, but you can't make him gig today. He can hardly hold a drumstick.'

'Me and Christoph'll do it as a two-piece,' says George, reaching over to ruffle my hair. I duck past him on my way to the kitchen.

'Exactly,' agrees John, 'or solo. Or whatever you want. But Tony's staying here.'

'Our contract says we don't get paid unless we're a four-piece,' I reply, sliding the mugs onto the breakfast bar with a ceramic clatter. 'And if we don't get paid today, we'll be homeless by tomorrow morning. Plus this End-Of-Season thing is a party – Geoffrey doesn't want Simon and Garfunkel. He's already pretty hacked off wi—'

'I'm coming.'

Tony is standing hunched by the sofa, one eye twitching.

'You don't have to do this,' says John. 'Really.'

Tony shakes his head and wraps the raggedy shell of blankets around his shoulders.

'I do, we're a… band… I'm coming.'

Daring a glance at the growing blizzard, I slide my clipboard from the bar, check the clock and head for the stairs.

'We need to be gone in ten minutes.'

The snow whips and tears in delirious raceways around the frosted windows of the Omega. Equipment is stacked tightly into the boot, obscuring the view through the back window. Snowflakes cling to the glass, quivering in the wind, then lose their grip and fly into the mayhem beyond. The car's air-conditioning system is set to full blast, but with all vents pointing towards Tony in the front seat, the temperature in the back is Antarctic. I zip up my jacket. It's 11:56 a.m. We are perilously short of time to reach Gig Number One, at Méribel's Le Pub. Gigs Two and Three are taking place in venues we've never played before, over an hour's drive away in Val d'Isère.

'Sorry I was late, Christoph,' says George, looking back at me from the driver's seat. My gaze drops into my lap.

'Don't worry about it.'

There is an angry tapping on the car door. The tapping of a wooden peg. Not now. Please, not now.

'*Ouvrez, pouffiasse!*'

She has pressed the bony tip of her nose against the glass, boring a hole in the frosting and sending an icy snowdrop dribbling down the pane.

'*Ouvrez la fenêtre. Vous me devez de l'argent.*'

'I can't guarantee I won't run her over,' says George, revving the engine. It chokes back at him.

'She wants her money. We need to go.'

I lock the car door from the inside, watching the flap of skin beneath her chin quiver in the snow. If only GCSE French taught you the stuff you're actually going to need in situations like this. Fat lot of good 'Do you know of any chemists in La Rochelle?' is going to do me now.

'*Désolé madame! Il faut partir maintenant!*'

She scowls at me.

'Last chance to turn back,' says John, packed in next to me underneath a jagged canopy of microphone stands. The engine gurgles hoarsely.

'*Eh! Eh!*'

She is rapping on the window now, her wiry beard wet with snow.

'*Vous avez un jour, vous branleurs anglais inutiles.*'

'OK, *au revoir*! Go, George, go!'

George releases the handbrake, the tyres screech and crackle over gravel and we sputter into motion, leaving the raging hag behind us in a cloud of dust and snow. She continues to yell obscenities as we speed away up the road.

'Did she just call us useless English wankers?' asks George.

'Sticks and stones, George. Sticks and stones.'

The winding streets leading out of Saint-Bon are neglected and uneven, and the car bounces and judders as we go. With every jolt Tony teeters on the verge of fresh heaving.

'It's so… *cold…*'

'Coats and jumpers off, Lightyears.'

We all remove our upper layers and John donates them to Tony, still wrapped up tightly in his wodge of blankets. His footwell is stuffed with towels and hot water bottles.

Looking up, I adjust the spike of a drum stand poking out over the top of my seat. If we were to crash now, the mess would be horrendous. The press would find us skewered and bloody on the snow-flecked spears of our own instruments, and the coroners would solemnly conclude: 'It was the music that killed them.'

From above our heads comes the industrial fat snap of a thunder crack and, in seconds, the sky darkens under a company of puddle-coloured storm clouds. The frantic snowflakes whipping past the windows seem to thicken, halving visibility, as snowfall becomes blizzard. Meanwhile, on the dashboard, an unassuming orange light has flickered on.

We're running out of petrol.

'Take it easy, George,' says John, as the car skates left and right on a sleety aquaplane. 'Watch your speed.'

George eases off the accelerator and we drop to just thirteen miles an hour. The road ahead is thick with black sludge and, all around, the bruised sky is giving way to the white noise of the snowstorm. Meanwhile, the fifteen-hundred-metre drop on the side of the road is disappearing from view.

'The petrol light's on,' says George, suddenly. 'That's not good.'

It's 12:14 p.m. We are still over half an hour's drive, on a good day, from the venue. We are due onstage at one o'clock.

'We've still got enough fuel, though, right?'

'We should be OK as long as we don't stop before Méribel. It'll be tight.'

I flip open my wallet and count our few remaining notes. Eighteen euros. Until we get paid for these gigs, we're dicing with bankruptcy.

'I'll have to drive faster than this – we'll cane the fuel tank in this gear.'

'Careful, George,' warns John.

George teases the pedal and the car lurches forward in response. Thunder cracks again, louder this time, and the wipers struggle to clear the windscreen of its thick blanket of snow. We're approaching a corner, completely blind and skating from side to side.

'Van...' mumbles Tony, his head lolling.

'It's all right, mate,' says George, patting Tony on the head.

'Van...'

'I agree! This would be much easier in a van.'

Tony nudges his forearm.

'No,' he says more insistently, lifting a pale hand to point at the road ahead. 'Van!'

We all look up to find two yellow headlights bearing down upon us, right in the middle of the road. Whatever it is, it's travelling at speed and heading straight for us.

'George, right-hand down!' calls John as the speeding vehicle hurtles in our direction. George yanks the steering wheel down and we change course just in time to avoid its looming front end, but this leaves us heading directly for a sheer mountain ledge. George slams on the brakes and the back end of the Omega skids on the ice, sending us up onto the grass verge with a scrape and a shudder. We tip, our instruments rattle in the back, the metalwork groans, and finally we come to rest.

Directly outside the window yawns a vast, black chasm, dark and endless like the gaping maw of a deep-sea beast.

Nobody speaks.

In the distance a chorus of cheering can be heard, and we all lean in to Tony's wing mirror to identify its source. A busted-up van, unmistakably that of a band, is speeding away down the hill. The back doors have been flung wide open and, in between them, a naked white arse is gawping back at us through the gloom. Just before it disappears into the mist, the arse spins round to reveal its grinning owner, trousers round his ankles.

We are now all staring at the crazy wee willy... of Crazy Wee Willy.

As the Black Cats' tour bus fades into oblivion, our engine ticks, ticks, ticks and slowly dies. Outside, snow is hammering against the glass.

'Everyone OK?' asks John, undoing his seat belt.

'Think so,' says George, taking a breath. 'What now...?'

John peers out the window.

'We won't get off this verge without the snow chains on. We should have fitted them at the house.'

'Let's do it, then,' I reply, bracing myself for the elements. 'We're running out of time.'

The three of us stumble out of the car into the vicious black wind, whipping and lashing at our skin. The bitter air instantly invades my bones, and I can feel wet sludge seeping through my trainers. George and John are shivering, rubbing at their bare arms.

'Who's getting the snow chains out?' I ask, receiving only blank looks in return.

'I thought you were,' says George.

'I don't know where they are.'

'Neither do I.'

Gritting my teeth against the ferocious gale, I can feel my skin fizzing with the wet dissolve of snow. I am growing light-headed, feverish. Time begins to buckle and slow.

'Tell me we packed the snow chains. *Tell me we did that.*'

'I don't know, Christoph. Might have done.'

'Wha—'

'It's fine, it's fine,' interrupts John, stepping in between us. 'I put them in the car before the first gig, just in case.'

'So where are they now?'

Chunks of wet snow are settling in John's hair.

'They're under the front passenger seat.'

'Underneath Tony?'

George steps back from the group, hands held up in surrender.

'No way, we can't touch the Drummer. No fear.'

'But… we have to.'

We all peer into the car at our slumbering drummer, his head still lolling on a weak, bendy neck. I stride over to his window.

'Chris, what are you doing?'

'We need those chains, or we'll be stuck. Someone has do it.'

I open Tony's door, and he immediately flinches at the sharp Alpine wind. He is staring straight ahead and muttering to himself.

'Tony, can you hear me? I just need you to…'

No response. Instead, he is singing 'Twist and Shout' very, very quietly.

'… Tony?'

Kneeling on the soft, wet ground, I can see the chains wedged behind the metal framework of the seat, but Tony's legs are planted squarely in the way.

'If you could just… move your legs… ever so slightly…' Tony's face has turned an unearthly shade of bluish grey, his eyes still lifeless, sunken black sockets. Straining, I grab his legs with both hands and hoist them out of the way.

'Chris, watch him…'

Reaching underneath the seat, I make a connection with the cold steel of the snow chains. I tug at them, hard, but they're wedged fast inside the framework. Gripping tightly, I start a countdown.

One.

'Be careful, Chris.'

Two.

'He doesn't look good.'

Three.

'Watch out!'

And PULL! *THUD*.

'Oh God!'

Something's dripping down my face.

Something warm and sticky. Is it sick? It's sick, isn't it?

I touch a hand to my nose.

Blood.

Which is marginally better. 'You OK, Christoph?'

Using my T-shirt collar to stem the flow, I feel the hot blood soaking from my nostrils and into the fabric. It dribbles down my arm.

'Just accidentally punched myself in the face somewhat.'

George and John watch me, astonished, as I stand there leaking fluid. Eventually, something in me snaps, and I throw my arms open, spraying a little arc of fresh blood into the air.

'Come on, people! This is *rock 'n' roll, bitches!* Axl Rose wouldn't care about a bit of blood, would he? He'd probably just shoot up a fattie and write a solo album!'

George peers at me through the snow.

'What?'

'Let's just fit these chains,' says John, wearily, 'and get out of here.'

While the brothers get to work on the tyres, I set about washing off the blood with a bottle of water. Minutes later, I stumble round to the bonnet, still half-bloodied, and find them squatting by the front wheel, soaked through and shuddering with cold. They are staring motionless at the snow chains, which are laid out on the ground, collecting snowflakes.

'What's happening?'

'We can't get them on,' says George, confounded.

'Why not?'

'I don't know. I really don't know.'

John points at the near-empty water bottle in my hand. 'What have you done with our water?'

'I'm trying to clean off the blood.'

'What?' John's face is wide open in shock. 'We needed that to hydrate Tony.'

'Hydrate Tony?! You kidding me? I look like a foetus.'

Images of us begging for food outside the Bricomarché begin to flood my brain. There I am, drunk on lighter fluid in a shopping trolley, squeezing out a sad waltz on the accordion while Tony dances a raggedy jig for pocket change and periodically spews into a bucket. This is our future now. This is what's going to happen.

Unless…

At that moment, a lusty, throaty gurgle creeps into my ears from deep within the mountain fog. A car engine… other humans. Seconds later, a pair of fuzzy headlights soak like paint drops through the rolling mist.

'Hey… hey!'

The rhino-like bonnet of a Range Rover emerges majestically from the thick fog, slowly revealing every inch of its gleaming, champagne-gold bodywork. Thick snow crunches beneath snow-chained tyres and, as the car draws alongside us, the driver's tinted window slides silently down. A greying, middle-aged gentleman in a waxed jacket leans his head out. His coiffed wife sits in the passenger seat behind, her neck wrapped in a lavender muffler, her stony face a picture of diffidence beneath a high-stacked grey bun.

'In a bit of a pickle with the old snow chains, eh, chaps?' he asks, pointing to the offending article.

'Yes… yes,' I reply, rubbing at my freezing body. 'B-bit of a pickle.'

'They're a bloody nuisance to fit if you haven't done it before.'

'Do you think you might—'

'Beastly weather we're having, no? Chaps at the Met reckon it hasn't snowed this much late season since '92.'

Small talk? He's doing small talk, and I can't feel my knees.

'I think you might have bumped your nose, old boy.'

I touch a finger to my nose, which is bleeding again.

'I'm f-fine, I'm like Axl Rose, gonna go solo, smoke up a fattie.'

That didn't even make any sense.

'You've got to show those chains who's boss, I always say, because…'

Trailing off at the touch of his wife's hand, Sir Waxed Jacket ducks back inside the car and she whispers something in his ear. She is eyeing me sideways with a you-could-definitely-be-a-rapist kind of a look. Sir Waxed Jacket coughs out a nervous laugh.

'Reminds me of my daughter, you know. Minty couldn't fit a set of snow chains to save her life. Useless girl. Best of luck!'

And the window zips back up.

'Minty…?'

George's eyes are glazing over as the engine hums, and roars, and the car pulls away into the storm.

'Hey, wait! We know your daughter, she's our friend… listen, hey!'

I start to jog after them.

'George just took her to Cockup Bottom! Last night! Come back!'

Actually, that might not be the best angle to open with.

'Hey, wait! Slow down… please…!'

We watch uselessly as the Range Rover's glowing tail-lights are consumed by the swirling white mist, and the low growl of the engine evaporates into the dark.

'Yooooou *bastards*!' I yell after them, actually shaking my fist in the air. But they are gone. I drop my head into my hands.

Come on. Don't give up now.

There's fight in The Lightyears yet.

'This *has* to be possible, come on. Let's just… bloody… *do it*.'

In a frenzy I set about the tyre with the snow chains, my hands red raw with cold, my fingers gnarled with cramp. I force them over the wheel, twisting and turning and shoving and jostling and digging, but nothing works. Nothing. Works.

A creeping despair crawls upon me, and I'm nearly weeping with frustration. I'm not cut out for this. I don't know anything about cars. I'm not an Alpha Male. I've got no idea how to change a spark plug or lubricate the crankshaft, or how to tighten the piston on a Wankel rotary engine.

But wait.

Hang on.

I may not be able to sort my gudgeon pins from my harmonic balancers, but I know somebody who can.

'Tony. Tony.'

John scrambles after me and grabs me by the arm.

'Leave him, he's not well.'

'Tony's the only one in this band with mechanic smarts, and we're out of options. Unless you want to be stuck out here all night getting slowly pecked to death by badgers?'

'Christoph.'

George is pointing at my face.

'You're still bleeding.'

'I don't care. Tony. Tony.'

I'm rapping on the window. Tony looks up at me quizzically, like a caged gibbon. I pull open the door and squat down in front of him.

'We need your help.'

His gaze remains distant, removed.

'What are we doing wrong with these snow chains? They don't fit.'

Tony's head lolls from one side to the other. His eyes close, then open again.

'Have you fitted snow chains before?'

He nods absently.

'Have a look at these.'

I pass him the chains. Blood is dripping onto my trainers, wet snow lashing at my back.

'How do we fit them?'

Tony accepts the chains from me and, setting them on this lap, passes pale fingers around the clasps and fastenings, like a blind man reading Braille.

'These are for… for a Class U vehicle…'

'You beauty! What does that mean?'

An almighty thunder-clap is unleashed from the clouds, and the sky boils red. A rumble rings across the valley.

'Minimum tread-face clearance of… one point nine seven inches…'

'Yes, *and*…?'

'… This is a Vauxhall Omega… Class S… with a one point four six inch… tread-face clearance…'

Sleet and snow and rain and wind are thrashing me witless, but I am now beyond pain. I can hear my heart thumping inside my skull.

'What does that mean, Tony? *What do you mean?*'

He looks at me properly for the first time today.

'Wrong size, mate. We're buggered.'

And I slump, heavy to the ground, and I am done. There's no way back. I am soaked in defeat, despair and destruction. I am staring into the abyss.

'Tony, you all right?' asks George, from behind me. I look up at the Drummer, blood snaking down my chin. His eyes bulge wide, and he seems to surprise himself.

'I think… I'm OK. I think it's passed.'

And it's at this point, at my lowest ebb thus far, when I'm right in the middle of thinking *At least I haven't been puked on*, that I find myself being puked on.

'*Hurlleeuurrrgoruuuhhh!*'

The yellowish-brown torrent of vomit surges predictably into my stupid wet face, coating me in a phlegmy film of hot, viscous body-gum. It's in my hair, up my nose, dripping off my ear and, when it's done, my broken body is left sagging like a rag under the stinking weight of failure. This is like one of those eighties game shows where the contestant ends up in the gunge tank, except there's no chance of me winning a speedboat and I didn't even get to meet Noel Edmonds.

That and I'm being puked on, obviously.

'Might be wrong, though…' adds Tony when he's finished, closing his eyes and shivering. 'Sorry, mate.'

I wave him away, shaking my head. Tony couldn't help this. He couldn't stop any of this, it was inevitable. This catastrophic fall from grace was my preordained, unalterable destiny, a pathetic mini-tragedy of my very own doing, the harbingers of fate laughing right into my tiny, sticky face. I started a band because I actually thought I could be Bon Jovi, and now here I am, sitting in a puddle of sludge on a grassy knoll with a bloody nose and soggy underpants, covered in sick.

'What now?' asks George, wringing sleet from his T-shirt. My eyes are glued to the ground.

'We've lost, haven't we?'

George nods.

'I think you need to give up, Christoph.'

The sky churns angrily above the trees, whipping the snow into a fresh frenzy. George stares at me, right into me, searching my face for answers. His eyes flicker blue against the white of the blizzard.

I look away, skin stinging from the cold.

I never thought it would be this hard.

***

The rest of the afternoon passes in a numb stupor. After climbing back into the car, we call mountain rescue and wait the three hours it takes for them to arrive and tow us away. Gig Two comes and goes in some faraway bar in Val d'Isère, and, at the nearest garage, we are given blankets and hot drinks and asked to sit inside while they find us the correct-sized snow chains. They're awaiting a new delivery, it turns out, around seven o'clock at the earliest. Which means we will miss Gig Three as well.

A hat-trick.

I am sitting in the dreary garage waiting room wrapped in a thin, scratchy blanket and sipping at a cup of tea that tastes like it has been strained four hundred and seventeen times, over a period of many years, through a mossy bog. I consider our options.

Tomorrow morning we will be evicted from our chalet, and become officially homeless. Which means our options are as follows: a) live in the car, or b) form a primitive community with local woodland creatures and hope for the best.

In the corner of the room, an old-fashioned phone rings. A stubbly Frenchman in overalls answers, conducts a brief conversation and then points the receiver at me.

'*Pour toi.*'

I slope over to the phone and press it to my ear.

'You bloody idiots.'

Sounds like Geoffrey got my text message, then.

'Did I, or did I not tell you, less than twenty-four hours ago, that yer skating on thin ice?'

'I can explain, Geoffrey. There was a lot of vomiting.'

'I don't give a monkey's, mate. You know the rules. If there's one thing I can't abide, it's tardiness.'

But apparently you have no problem with bastardiness.

'You've been one fudge-up after another, you lot. I'm running a business here. You've pushed me too far.'

I lower my voice, and face away from the rest of the band.

'Hang on, what do you mean?'

Geoffrey sighs down the other end of the phone.

'Yeroff the tour. Pack up yer gear, and go 'ome.'

Click-*urrrrr*.

And that's that.

If there is a hell, it surely cannot be far from this. Bleak, fuzzy Euro-balladry drivels through the office radio. Strip-lighting on the ceiling sputters and chokes, its naked glare stinging my eyes. Through the doorway, the ringing of the till can be heard as a Frenchman in a snug-looking ski jacket pays for his fuel, sharing a joke with the sales clerk. As he leaves, he catches my eye and the briefest of pitying looks flashes across his sun-stained face. I'm glad I'm not *that* guy, he is thinking. Only in French, of course.

My phone vibrates in my pocket.

> *Just a quick hello from your Ma, hope you're having an amazing time on TOUR!! We've got some big news, will tell you all when you're home. Lots of love mum (and dad) x.*
>
> *PS. your dad wanted me to ask if there have been any exciting developments!!*

My thumb is poised to write a reply, but I can't think of a single thing to say.

'Hey, Chris…?' says John, sitting next to me and leafing through a dog-eared magazine. As I look round, a glimmer in the gentle blue of his eyes reminds me of home, and I recognise something I used to know, the ghost of some distant idea called hope.

'Yes, Johnny?'

He turns a page in his magazine.

'You smell of puke.'

That's a fair point.

'I know, Johnny. Believe me, I know.'

22

Our suitcases, bags and instruments are piled in silent pyramids around the ground floor of the chalet. Outside the window, half-hearted snowflakes drift through the air and naked trees shiver in the wind. I am slumped on the sofa scribbling lyrics while George scans through text messages in the kitchen. John is reading in a corner.

Padded footsteps sound, and Tony emerges at the bottom of the stairs. His skin is still that unnerving shade of blue-grey from yesterday, his back hunched from exhaustion.

'Morning, lads.'

A tepid chorus of 'mornings' fall from our mouths. In the street, the goat whinnies.

'Can we talk?'

Tony is standing awkwardly in the middle of the room, a slightly pained expression on his face. I flick at the lid of my pen.

'Uh-huh.'

'I'll just come out and say it. There's something I haven't told you.'

Tony is looking sheepish. George puts down his phone, and John sits up in his chair.

'Don't worry,' I reply. 'We know.'

Tony frowns at this.

'We know you're leaving Méribel. We know you've got a gig somewhere else, and you're quitting the band.'

John closes his book and flashes me a serious look. I should have brought him into this.

'You're right,' replies Tony, one hand rising in defence. 'There is a gig somewhere else. A proper festival, not these crappy little pub gigs – five thousand people, maybe more. Tomorrow afternoon. And I'm leaving Méribel to do it.'

George stands motionless in the kitchen. Through the window, the goat stares back at me mournfully. Sooner or later, this moment was coming.

'But I'm taking you buggers with me.'

I sit up, and the goat startles.

'You're what?'

'Taking you lot with me, you lunatic,' laughs Tony, picking up a drumstick from the windowsill and twirling it. 'What did you think I was gonna do, play on my own?'

'I just thought… I don't know, I thought you had some other band on the go.'

Tony pokes out his bottom lip.

'I wouldn't just up and leave you boys in the middle of a tour.'

'But what about the Black Cats? You left them.'

'I didn't quit the Black Cats, they fired me. Besides, they don't care about music – they're just in it for a laugh. You boys are different.'

'So, hang on,' replies George, moving in from the kitchen, 'what exactly are you saying? You've just got us our first festival gig… and it's *tomorrow*?'

'I've got this mate, right,' begins Tony, perching on the window ledge, 'a contact on the European festival circuit from my days playing the gudugudu drums for an industrial bluegrass band. He gets me work now and again, and he called me recently about this top-drawer festival in Chamonix. Money's great, gig's amazing, crowd'll be huge. Levellers are headlining, thousands of people'll be there. He asked if I was in any bands that were good for it, and I told him about you lot.'

He's not a traitor at all. He's a bloody mastermind.

'*Thousands* of people?' I ask, stunned.

'Yep. It'll be at least twice as big as the Astoria. You want a warm-up for the awards ceremony, couldn't ask for much better than this.'

'Hello Wembley!' replies George, grinning. Tony winks at me. The colour is returning to his face.

'If you knew about this before today, though,' I ask, 'why didn't you tell us?'

'Well, first of all, I had no idea you were freaking your noggin about it, otherwise I would've spilled the beans straight away. More importantly, I needed to figure out some way of getting out of the Méribel gigs without turning Geoffrey against us. Course, it turns out we did all that work ourselves.'

He laughs, quietly, then takes a deep breath.

'And look, I've been in music a long time, right, and I've been let down more times than I can count. The industry dangles all these carrots in front of you, but at the end of the day half of it never comes off... and after a while you stop trusting people who promise you the world.' He thinks for a moment. 'I didn't want to be one of those people. Not with you boys.'

Light specks of snow are still falling outside the window, one or two kissing the glass.

'Anyway, to me it just made sense to keep schtum until I was certain. I'm not the sort of bloke to make false promises, never have been. I don't believe it until I'm sitting on the plane, basically. Or, in this case, until I've got a signed contract in my back pocket and a cheque for eight hundred euros in my wallet.'

My mouth drops open.

'*Eight hundred euros?*'

'I had it made out to you, TM. Thought you might like that.'

He passes me the cheque and, sure enough, there's my name, scrawled across the middle.

This is easily enough to pay off our debts and get us home in one piece.

'Thanks,' I mutter quietly, and Tony shrugs in response. 'But... what does TM mean?'

He looks over at me quizzically.

221

'Tour Manager, obviously.'

'So if I've got this right,' begins George, 'tomorrow afternoon we'll be standing onstage in front of thousands of screaming fans, playing through a giant sound system, wearing massive shades and prancing about like rockstars and getting paid eight hundred fat ones to do it?'

'Yep,' nods Tony, tapping the drumstick on his knees.

'You solid gold nugget of genius.'

A huge smile spreading across his face, Tony stands up, spins the stick through his fingers, stops it dead, and slots it into his back pocket.

'Road trip, anyone?'

23

The road to Chamonix is long, winding and beautiful. It cuts hard through the mountains, flanked by steep banks of green and greying pine trees, watched over by lonely wooden huts dotted sparsely through the forest, and all beneath the sweep of a white Alpine sky.

Tony is in the driving seat.

'So what exactly is the plan, Tony?'

'What plan?' he replies, lobbing a fistful of pretzels into his mouth.

'Well… we don't have a house anymore.'

'This is a road trip, TM, we'll sleep in the car. You're not a real band until you've all slept in the same vehicle together. Rite of passage. Car won't ever smell right again, but that's part of the magic.'

He grins widely at this.

'I think we might be a bit lost,' says George from the front passenger seat. 'These directions I found on the web stop at Faverges. We've gone off the map. We're in a vacuum.'

Taking a quick look around, Tony spins the steering wheel and the car pulls a sudden right onto a narrow country lane. George looks back over his shoulder the way we came.

'Is this the right way?'

'Definitely,' confirms Tony, turning on the radio. George is silenced for a moment.

'But… how do you know?'

'General knowledge, mate. See, you've got your fancy coding and your pixels and plug-ins, but when the internet breaks it's the people with the General Knowledge that you'll all come running to.'

George screws up his face at this.

'The internet isn't going to break.'

'Nah, mate, it is. Everything breaks. The internet, washing machines.'

Tony looks back at me, and winks.

'So, anyway, we should be in this little village called Flumet in about half an hour. Passed through there once with Pressgang on the Folk Off and Die tour. We'll stop for nosh and a couple of beers, then push on to Chamonix.'

He lets out a satisfied sigh.

'Man, this takes me back to my early drumming days, y'know.'

In the seat beside me, John is pencilling thoughtful notes into his book. I am counting the spikes of the passing pine trees, silhouettes in the morning sun.

'Why *did* you become a drummer, Tony?' asks George thoughtfully. Tony ponders this for a moment. Hard beams of white sun are slicing through the trees and casting light lines across his face.

'Why did I become a drummer?'

'Yeah.'

'Um… I think… I mean, I was a bit of a rebel when I was a kid, to be fair,' he begins, searching in his pockets for a snack. He pulls out a stick of celery, regards it with mild surprise, then takes a big crunchy bite. 'I wasn't really into pop culture, I thought it was all a bit naff. I liked the old sixties and seventies bands: Cream, The Who, Queen, Led Zeppelin. I didn't know any other kids who were into that stuff, but I didn't care, 'cos I did my own thing in those days. Still do. Probably why I became a veggie.'

The car falls silent. John stops writing.

'You're what?' says George.

'A veggie.'

224

'You're not a vegetarian. You eat like a horse.'

Tony laughs and waves the stick of celery at him.

'*Like* a horse, yeah. Never an actual horse.'

'You can't be vegetarian, though, it doesn't make sense. You eat *all the time.*'

'Mate, when you live off tofu and lima beans, you *need* to eat every ten minutes, take it from me.'

A vegetarian drummer. Well I never.

'Anyway, point is, I always tried to do things my own way when I was at school, so when we finished and all my mates went off to train as accountants and bankers and office types, I didn't want to just fall in line, so I joined a band. Now, all my friends make twice as much money as I do, but most of them hate their jobs. And it's too late for them to do anything about it, 'cos they've all got kids and mortgages and families and whatnot.'

Outside my window the landscape flies past, the soaring hills, the unforgiving mountains. I shift in my seat.

'I think... maybe... some people are just worried that if they chase a dream, they might end up failing.'

Tony shakes his head and changes gear.

'That's not it, though. That's not what I mean. My mates, they bitch at me about work all the time, and so I ask them what they actually *want* to do with their lives, and here's the thing... the problem *isn't* that they're too scared to follow their dreams.'

He slows down at a roundabout.

'It's that they never had a dream in the first place.'

Purposefully, Tony picks his exit and heads straight for it.

'You boys might not have worked this out yet, but most people have no clue what they want from life. They wake up every day, go through the motions, same old treadmill. But here I was, seventeen years old, I knew exactly what I wanted. Play drums, have adventures, see the world.'

He pulls out onto the open road.

'People make excuses, course they do. I don't have the money, my parents want me to be a barrister, all that jazz. But at the end of the day, it comes down to this… If you're lucky enough to *have* a dream, it has to be worth chasing after.'

He reaches into the footwell and produces a squashed packet of crisps.

'Nik Nak, anyone?'

Tony pops open the crisps and shoehorns them into a nearby cup holder. Ahead, a long, clean road stretches out towards the mountains, the distant horizon marrying bright white sky with the peaks of tall trees. A busy stream runs alongside us.

'Also,' he adds, after a pause, 'one day I'll have kids myself, and I'll teach 'em the same lesson. Otherwise, what's the point in even being here?'

I watch Tony drive, one hand on the wheel, the other hanging out of the open window. He is nodding along to his secret drumbeat.

The signpost says Flumet, 13km.

***

'I'm telling you, you're wrong.'

George and Tony are sitting opposite each other, pints of fizzy Alpine lager lined up between them. The room is warm, orange and inviting, a log fire crackling in the corner.

'I'm not,' insists George, with a half-smile. 'Cellar-Door is the most beautiful combination of two words in the English language. It's been scientifically proven.'

'Nah, that's bollocks,' counters Tony, waving him away. 'I'll tell you boys what the most beautiful combination of two words in the English language is, and it's definitely not Cellar-Door.'

John laughs, and shakes his head at me. I chink his glass.

'It's Beer Token.'

We all share skeptical glances.

'Yeah, Beer Token. Or Free Beer works just as well. In fact, Free Beer is probably the greatest band name in history, apart from The Lightyears, obviously. Imagine that sign on the outside of a pub: "Tonight: FREE BEER". You'd sell out every gig.'

226

Le Shamrock is a quirky provincial tavern in the centre of Flumet, cosy and homely and peppered with bearded men playing cards and sharing stories. It's the kind of place you could sit for hours on end, losing time, painting the days.

'Pub Lunch is also up there,' Tony continues, tearing open a packet of Bombay mix, 'and Broccoli Quiche. And then you got your words that should never, ever go together, like Jazz and Funk. Or Smart and Casual.'

'Tony of Pressgang. I was never thinking to see you again!'

A curious-looking stranger is standing by our table, fuzzy-bearded and dressed almost entirely in green and purple tie-dye clothing. He has a thick European accent, possibly German.

'Ludwig Dessler,' replies Tony, his hands spread wide. 'As I live and breathe.'

Tony stands up and embraces the man, who clings onto him for ever so slightly too long, almost vibrating with joy. When he steps away, it becomes clear that underneath his colourful festival garb he is wearing a Pressgang tour T-shirt.

'I am drinking at this bar, and I am thinking there is a man with the face of Tony of Pressgang, and then I am thinking this *is* Tony of Pressgang, no one can believe it!'

Tony laughs and pats him on both shoulders.

'You're looking well, mate! When was the last time...? Christ, what was it, the Noseflute Festival in Ingelmunster, unless I'm mistaken? Crystal healing tent?'

'Yes, of course! Such crazy crazy times.'

The laughter dies down, and Ludwig turns to us.

'And what are these men?'

'Sorry, boys! Ludwig, this is my new band, The Lightyears. George, Chris and John. Boys, this is Ludwig, a Pressgang fan from the old days.'

'We are always following Pressgang *everywhere*, you know!' confirms Ludwig, eyes wide. 'These are the days. Always with the festivals and the crazy times. I remember travelling from Bucharest to Zagreb on the back of a donkey, it took us two weeks!'

Tony shakes his head wistfully, and Ludwig mimics the movement.

'But wait on, are you playing here tonight?'

Tony looks back over his shoulder at the bar.

'What, here? No, no. We've just stopped in for a pint.'

'This is a very great shame. They love live music here, always with the bands.'

Tony searches the room for a stage.

'Really?'

'Oh yes, and they do you good food, maybe some money, hot showers and a place to stay…'

'A place to stay?'

'Yah, yah. They have two rooms upstairs solo for band, four beds, very comfy times.'

Tony turns to the rest of us.

'Whaddya reckon, fellas?'

'I thought sleeping in the car was a rite of passage,' remarks John with a smile.

'Screw rites of passage, I want a hot shower.'

'We are settled, then,' says Ludwig, delighted. 'I am talking with the owner.'

He leaves immediately for the bar and dives into conversation with the manager. We sit in silence for a few moments.

'Well…' says George.

'Nice guy,' adds John.

'Tony,' I whisper, leaning in towards him, 'that bloke is *still wearing a Pressgang T-shirt.*'

'Yeah, Pressgang fans were always very… keen. It's a folk thing. Did I mention we have our own tribute band in Bavaria?'

'Good God,' says George.

'Anyway,' I add, watching Ludwig expertly selling us to the owner of the bar, 'this is perfect. We can run through all the new material before playing it on the big stage tomorrow. It's ideal.'

When Ludwig returns moments later, his smile threatens to engulf his entire face.

'Lightyears, we are all hunking dory.'

He points at the bar owner, who waves back enthusiastically.

'You can play whenever you like, Gustaf thinks maybe eight o'clock, and all the folk are coming, and he will feed you hot stew and you can all sleep upstairs. Oh, and he is telling me to give you these,' he says, carefully arranging a pile of small, rectangular laminates on the table in front of us.

'What are they?' asks George, poking at them. Tony leans back in his chair and lifts his drink to his mouth.

'Beer tokens,' he says, draining his pint.

***

Le Shamrock is absolutely full to bursting. People are sitting on chairs, on tables, under tables, on the bar, in the doorway, even one or two standing in the street. It feels like the entire town has come out to see us.

To the soundtrack of the crackling fireplace, we are pacing through every song we know, filling the small space with careful notes and rich harmonies. Every single audience member is utterly rapt, silent, listening intently to the quietest of notes, the slightest of cadences. We are using a light, simple set-up: George on acoustic guitar, Tony on a pared-down drum kit – a snare-case bass drum and a single washy cymbal. We are sitting on old wine crates and dark oak beer barrels, our faces lit sporadically by flickering candlelight. The sound is stripped back, unfettered and raw. We cycle through new song after new song, the band tightening with every moment, our voices slowly blending, instruments unending in the soft, candlelit dark.

> *I could wait out here all night*
> *'Cos it's not a home, if nobody comes around*
> *I won't wait forever to be found*

George's new song, 'Wait Forever'. A brooding ballad with a harmony-layered chorus.

> *This stampede has begun*
> *'Cos it's not enough, throwing your love around*
> *And I won't wait forever to be found*

Then 'This House Will Burn', a track about fear, betrayal and redemption, a tangle of voices and cascading melodies.

> *And now I talk in my sleep*
> *I tell tales of daring and pain*
> *All of my friends will be gathered in thundering rain*
> *The truth is, my sweetheart, you'll never see my face again*

> *And so you stand and you stare*
> *If you think that I'm wrong, I don't care*
> *I'm pouring out all my heartbreak but nothing is stirring inside*
> *All that I ask for is some sign that I'm still alive*

In the warmth of the fireside the evening drifts by, while outside in the dark the snow slowly falls. I almost don't notice that two hours have passed, until Tony checks his watch and leans in to speak to us.

'What next, boys?' he says off mic. 'I think we're out of songs.'

Everyone looks at me, and I shrug.

'Do you know any covers?' comes a voice from the back of the room. Tony shields his eyes against the light.

'Is that a Flanders accent, mate?'

'*Ja, vriend!*'

'In that case' – he leans over to us and whispers 'I Saw Her Standing There' – '*Laten we nu stap in onze tijdmachine.* This one's a classic by The Beatles!'

Unbelievable. The time machine.

He was absolutely right.

A roar billows up from the crowd, and the song begins.

Half an hour later, after three encores, much dancing and, finally, a hushed version of 'Hallelujah' that leaves the place cloaked in a pin-drop silence, we stand up from our instruments and depart the stage with our bodies tired but our hearts full. The locals get back to the important business of drinking and philosophising, and Tony and John are swallowed into the fold. George and I are standing at the bar being grinned at and shoulder-patted by everyone who passes.

'I think that might have been one of our best ever gigs.'

'Do you know, Christoph, I believe you may be right. Unless you count that jumble sale in Rotherfield Peppard.'

I smile back at him.

'Obviously.'

A Beatles number clicks onto the jukebox, the harmonica riff from 'Love Me Do'. Pockets of people start singing along. 'All we need now is to nail those songs on the big stage tomorrow, and we'll be ready for the Astoria.'

'Ready for the Astoria? Old chum, by the time we're done with that awards ceremony, they'll be scraping people off the ceiling.'

'One thing, though,' I reply, passing a crumpled banknote to the barman. As he pours fresh beers, he shakes his head, smiles at me and pushes the money back across the counter. I nod him thank you. 'That lyric in "Embrace Of Many", I think you got it wrong. It's "*tell me you are terrified*".'

'Oh yeah, sorry about that, old fruit. I should probably go over those words.'

'I've written them all down. Upstairs, middle pocket of my bag.'

'Thanks, Christoph. I'll go grab 'em, you sort me another pint of that disgraceful raspberry beer. See you in a sec.'

He spanks me on the bottom and heads for the stairs. I look around the venue, soaking up the buzz and the laughter, the excitable chatter and the drinks frothing over. Tony and John are surrounded by fans, all talking at once, full of beer and excitement and the fire of live music. My chest swells.

I think we may finally have turned a corner.

Then a sudden twitch in my memory pulls my mind from the room. Something's not right. Something to do with George. I've… oh my god.

Dashing along the bar and pounding up the stairs two at a time, I spin round the banister on the top step and hurtle towards our bedroom. The door is wide open, and I speed through, eyes searching wildly for my bag.

It's too late.

George is standing in the corner with his back to me, completely still, holding the letter.

'George, I can explain.'

He turns round. I haven't seen that look since he found out I was taking Anna Coles to our year eleven prom.

'What's this?'

My letter from the Harley Bourne Group is unfolded in his hands. A darkness clouds his brow.

'It's nothing – I only brought it with me for the lyrics.'

He scans it again.

'It looks like a job offer.'

'It's not. I mean, it *is*, but… it's really nothing.'

He looks at me for what feels like hours. The blue of his eyes has dimmed, somehow.

'Are you going to take it?' he asks.

'No, course not. I didn't even mean to go to the interview, not really. I'd forgotten about it entirely until the other week. I only brought it for the lyrics.'

He reads the letter again and I stand there, helpless, in a silence that twists my stomach.

'Twenty-two grand, that's not bad.'

I walk over and take the letter from him. He lets go easily.

'I don't care about that. I don't care about the money,' I say, folding the paper and shoving it back in my bag.

'No,' he says, unconvinced. For a moment the two of us just stand there, a half-empty room in between us.

'I'm feeling pretty exhausted,' he says, gathering up his stuff. 'I'll see you in the morning.'

'Where are you going?'

'Think I might share with John tonight. You and Tony can have the big room.'

Downstairs, Tony finishes an anecdote in Flemish and a big group of listeners guffaw and applaud. Everyone bursts into song.

'Oh... OK.'

'See you in the morning.'

Walking past me, he steps out the room and closes the door behind him.

24

The roar from the assembled thousands is like nothing I've ever heard before.

The stage seems vast, unending, like the deck of an advancing battleship. A dazzling rig of burning bright lights spirals and reels above our heads, casting a kaleidoscope of colour onto the stage and out into the glistening white slope beyond. A sea of people stretches back along the piste as far as the eye can see, their sun-bronzed faces glowing golden beneath the rainbow-shine reflection of a thousand ski goggles. To our right is a sweeping bank of triangular-peaked super-chalets nestled among a forest of pine trees, and to our left, a heart-stopping vista of mountains and sky.

'This is it, then, lads,' says Tony as we wait backstage for our call. 'The ultimate dress rehearsal. If you wanna be the ones thanking your mums in that award speech next week, we need to win this crowd over. Simple as that.'

George is standing at my side, and I brave a glance in his direction. We haven't talked about the letter.

'This is pretty amazing,' adds John, adjusting his shades.

'Hey, the bass player's impressed,' jokes Tony, prompting a smile from John. George stares out into the crowd. 'Let's just make sure we get this right.'

A mighty roar erupts in the valley as the band before us launch into their final song. I check my watch.

We're on in five minutes. 'Oi, Shakespeare!'

A Glaswegian accent cuts through the air. Turning round, I see a cluster of smirking faces waiting at the base of the stage, and my pulse instantly quickens. It's the Black Cats, all twisted, armed and dangerous, beckoning me down. Behind me, Tony is regaling John and George with an especially animated tour story, so I leave them in the wings and walk down the steps alone.

'What are you doing here?'

'Came to see you lot,' says Heidi, blowing a lock of hair from her face.

'How did you know we were playing?'

'Overheard Judas talking about it at the party,' she replies, pointing up the stairs at Tony. 'And we've got a show in Chamonix tonight, so we thought, screw it, we'll come along for a laugh.'

'OK…'

'Not a bad gig,' she adds, pulling a cigarette slowly from the packet. She touches it between her painted lips and flicks at a lighter.

'I don't think you're supposed to be back here, you know. It's restricted access.'

'Restricted access ma bawbag,' says Duffy. 'We got pals in high pleeces.'

Hamish nods in slow agreement, while Crazy Wee Willy slugs from a bottle of Buckfast.

'Paul knows the bouncer from home,' explains Heidi, blowing smoke. 'He used to work for City Records at the weekends, so he was like, come in, hang out, whatever.'

'Right. But our set starts in five minutes, so…'

Duffy pushes past his bandmates and squares up to me.

'D'yoose no' wanna wee drinkie afore yoose start?'

His eyes nod down to the bottle in his hand. It's whiskey. He's clearly drunk nearly half of it himself.

'I don't think that's a good idea…'

He looks down his nose at me.

'Ah thought yoose boys were supposed tae be rockstars?'

'Well, it's just—'

'Ah mean, we're on tour, rayght?' he slurs, his eyes darkening. 'We're backsteege at a gig, *we're* a rock 'n' roll band… and yooser rock 'n' roll band.'

That smile, the smile of the escaped clown, spreads across his cheeks. When I fail to respond, the smile curls down at the corners into a hard, black line.

'Or is tha' no' whit yoose are?'

'No, no, course we are. Course we're a… rock 'n' roll band.'

Over my shoulder and up the steps, The Lightyears are still waiting by the stage. George has his back turned to me.

'Can't you take a whiskey, Piano Man?' goads Heidi, lingering on the moistened tip of her cigarette. Her eyes are smouldering.

I roll up my sleeves.

'Go on, then.'

The bottle is halfway to my mouth when Hamish interrupts.

'Ah say we make this interesting.'

The rest of the Black Cats nod in agreement.

'What do you mean?'

'A gentleman's drink-off,' suggests Duffy. 'One fer me, one fer yoose.'

'I don't think that's a good plan. I don't like that plan.'

Duffy snakes a sinewy arm around my neck, tightens his grip and pulls my ear in against his lips.

'Ahm gonnae let yoose intae a wee secret,' he says, the heat from his whiskey breath singeing my skin. 'Ah used tae be jis like yoose, ye ken? Boy next door, alwees deein' wit mah ma told me. But this, wee man, this is *the music industry*. And there's nae room in this business fer pussies, yoose follow me?'

The band onstage are reaching crescendo. We don't have long now.

'These days, when ah step intae the room, yoose ken whit everyone thinks, don't ye?'

'What?'

He steps back from me, bottle in one hand, the other on his groin.

'That bastard's a proper rockstar, an' no misteek.'

Heidi is watching me intently behind a mask of cigarette smoke. Duffy passes me the whiskey.

'Don't… think. Just… drink.'

BAM. One. The hot liquid fire stings my throat.

Duffy matches me.

BAM. Two. Duffy matches me again.

The band roars, guitars thrash and drums thunder.

BAM. Three. Heidi is still watching me, her eyes widening as I throw down shot after shot, tensing with every swallow.

BAM. Four, and then five, and then six. And then the world begins to spin.

'Hey you, you're a Lightyear, right?'

A man with a headset is talking to me.

'Huh?'

'You're in The Lightyears?'

'Oooh yeah. Bring it on, cowboy.'

'You need to get onstage, man, you're late. Go!'

With a shove, I'm running up the stairs, stumbling as I go. On the massive stage, my band are waiting for me. Not sure this is a good thing. Effects starting to kick in now. Head feeling kind of like a balloon, arms sausage-flopping.

Black Cats behind me, shouting at my head.

Onstage. Here we go. Thousands and thousands of people watching as I grip my piano. Our biggest ever crowd, waiting under rainbow lights.

'Christoph, where've you been?'

Do a point back over my shoulder.

'Down there for some time.'

'You look weird. You OK?'

'I am totally good, old chum my man.'

No I'm not. My legs have gone wrong. My ears are like jelly and my elbows are fizzing.

'Hello Chamonix!'

Uh-oh. Tony's starting. Why is he starting? What am I doing? Oh yes. Behind my piano. This is a good place to be. The best place.

'We're The Lightyears – you guys having a good time?!'

People are cheering. That's good. That's LOUD. Haven't done anything yet, though. Why is everyone looking at me? What do we play again? Oh, I know. 'Sleepless'. Yeah. That's a flipping great song, that is. Whatever happened to great songwriting? Used to be Paul McCartney and Paul Simon and ALL THE OTHER PAULS and now it's all hip-to-the-hop-to-the-hippity-hop and spelling things with a 'z' instead of an 's'.

Wooooah. Nearly fell over a bit there.

'TM, it's you. Start, for Christ's sake.'

Obviously I'm going to start. Obviously that. Oops. That note doesn't sound right. Is it right? Try hitting it again?

Nope. Definitely not right.

'Sort it out!'

Ooh. Tony glaring at me. Keep playing, keep your head down. That sounds good. That sounds BLOODY FANTASTIC. George is singing now. Everyone's looking.

Everyone's looking at me. They seem angry. What even have I even *done*? Just a little drinkie. What does John want?

'What's going on? What's the matter with you?'

'Johnny! Johnny!'

Keep shouting Johnny.

'Johnny! I'm loving it! I am rocking ouuuut!'

John retreating, shaking his head. Just have to concentrate for twenty minutes, try not to be sick, just get on with my life. What's happening now? Legs feel like soggy otters.

'*Tell me it's a lie, and everything you said was just to make me hurt...*'

Was this is a good idea? Hope it was. All good ideas start with a drink, don't they? The Bayeux Tapestry. Blu-Tack. The American Constitution. Consti*chew*shun. That's a hard word to say, even in my head. So what was I saying? Oh yes. Hope this was a good idea. Otherwise, everything's broken, and it's all my bloody bastard fault. Have to get a job in finance, find a wife, buy a mortgage, buy a dog, kill myself.

'TM. *TM!*

Stage is spinning.

Song is spinning.

Are we nearly done?

We are.

'Christoph. Christoph!'

'Yip?'

'What's with all the bum notes?'

'Bum?'

'OK, um… cheers, thanks everyone!' Tony's voice again. 'That one's called "Sleepless". This next song is—'

'Oi, people, listen up, you…!'

All eyes ALL EYES on me. Sounds like I'm doing some talking.

'So yeah, listen up you twats, you giving us some love or what?'

Is that *booing?* Why are people *booing?* Where's the love?

The band start playing over me. They're drowning me out. Still thousands of booing. This doesn't feel good.

I don't feel good.

'*The stampede has begun…*'

Songs go by, and the gig goes by, and I am extreeemely wobbly. Which is bad. George doesn't look happy. I'm not happy. And all of the time, at the side of the stage, there's a gang of Black Cats, watching my face.

And it ends.

And we are standing in the wings, roadies unloading gear. Everyone is waiting for me. It is all over.

No one is speaking.

'So… what shall we do now?' I say. Tony's face is all hewn rock, dark and hard and unmoving.

'I'm going to the bar,' he says. John looks at me like he's about to say something, but nothing comes out. He goes with Tony.

Now, in the cold and the snow and the noise, George and I are alone.

The mountains are watching us, ready for my next move. Might tug at his arm. OK, done that. He stops. He turns round.

The end.

'What were you doing out there? Are you drunk?'

'I may be drunk, but in the morning *you* shall be sober. No, hang on. Other way round.'

Once, when we were fourteen or thirteen or fifteen, I kissed Anna Coles. I remember, because it was in the middle of East 17's 'House of Love'. Felt bad, though; George liked her. Probably shouldn't have done that. Probably should have thought about that one first.

'Chris.'

Looking at me, hard. Never seen those eyes before. Hard, and sad.

'*Chris.*'

'Georgio.'

'Why are you doing this?'

'Doing what?'

'Ever since we got here, you've become this totally different person. It's like you're trying to prove something, or *be* something, something I don't understand. I'm supposed to be your best friend, but right now it feels like we barely even know each other.'

I try to think of words, but thinking of words is quite hard.

'This isn't you, Chris. You're acting insane.'

'Am I? *Insane?* Gimme an example, m'lud.'

'An example? This whole tour is an example, but... OK, last week you got high on crack and tried to jump off a seventeen-storey building.'

'Well, *obviously* that sounds crazy *out of context...*'

'The next day you get busted for drug-dealing, force us out into a snowstorm when Tony's practically dead from food poisoning and get us chucked off the tour, then I find out you've been applying for secret jobs in London and now you turn up onstage smashed out of your head.'

'I'm just trying to do the right thing.'

'*How?*' he is shouting, his eyes wild now. 'I don't understand *how* you could possibly think that *any* of that was the right thing to do! We're supposed to be a team, aren't we? What happened to that?'

Don't really know where to look now.

His eyes are blue, like an ocean.

'What happened to you, Christoph?'

Four little words, the lightyears between us.

'Just trying to… make this band work…'

'You always say it's you who does everything, and organises everything, and the rest of us just crash about while you pick up the pieces, but lately…'

He stops, just for a bit. Now he's looking straight at me.

'… lately it seems like it's you screwing everything up.'

Words hanging in the air, like snowflakes, and so nobody speaks, for a really long time.

Everything is cold.

I remember now, on the ferry. We were standing on the deck, in the wind and the freezing rain, and George was with me, and he said, 'Just you wait, Christoph.' 'Just you wait,' he said. 'This tour will change everything.'

And it has.

25

Each room needs two teabags, two sachets of regular coffee and two sachets of decaffeinated coffee. Biscuits alternate between shortbread and cookies. Towels go in the laundry if they're left in the bath, otherwise fold and replace. No more than twelve minutes per room. When the hotel is full, aim for nine.

'You all right, my lovely?'

Vera is standing in the door to room 395, holding a mop.

'I'm OK.'

'You don't seem right since you came back from your tour, you know. I don't know what it is. You missed the second pillowcases next door. And in the two rooms before that. Not like you.'

I go back to organising teabags into little straight lines.

'Sorry. Think I must be a bit distracted.'

'Not like you, my duck. Not like you at all.'

You have to work really hard on the mirrors. Sometimes if you catch them in the wrong light, they seem clean. You can think it's fine, I'll leave this, no imperfections on this one. Then you stand at the opposite angle, and the light changes, the sun's cast across it, and you can see it's not right. It's covered in marks and stains you didn't notice the first time.

George called me up the day after we got back from France, and I almost didn't answer. I always answer him on the first ring, but this time I let it go, almost to the end.

'We should talk about the awards ceremony,' he says.

'What is there to talk about?'

'We have to make plans, "cement timings" – that's what you always say.'

I wait.

'But I'm not coming.'

Another pause.

'What?'

'I'm not coming.'

'Not coming where?'

'To the gig. I've arranged a replacement piano player. I asked Tony to find someone for me.'

'Wh—... Hang on, you spoke to Tony?'

'Yeah.'

I can hear him closing his bedroom door.

'And what did he say?'

'He tried to talk me out of it.'

'Of course he did! What are you talking about, replacement piano player?'

I stare out of the window, over the tumbling fields and across the rolling green of Goring's hilltops. A farmer is ploughing the soil.

'A band is a unit, everyone's supposed to work together. Tony said that to us when we first met him, and he was right. And I've pulled the whole thing apart.'

'Christoph, I know things went to crap at the end of the tour, but I didn't mean for *this* to happen. I don't think you've thought it through—'

'I have, and I've made my mind up. You said it yourself: I'm the person screwing everything up. You're better off without me.'

'That's just not true—'

'I don't know who I've been trying to kid this whole time. I'm not a rockstar, and no one's ever going to see me like that, so... that's just the way things are.'

We listen to the sound of each other breathing for a while.

'It's not The Lightyears without you,' he says, finally.

I don't answer.

'Can you at least think about it?'

243

'I'm sorry. I hope it goes well.'

And that was that.

'Tell you what,' says Vera, waddling into the room with her mop and bucket, 'I heard about someone looking for a band while you was away. Wobbly, up at the golf club. Says he needs a fun beat combo for the Ladies' Over-Sixty-Fives Centenary Dinner.'

'We're not really… together at the moment.'

She plants her hands on her sides.

'I thought you and that George were joined at the hip, my lovely?'

I'm polishing the bedroom mirror in concentric circles, pressing hard to lift every stain. There are greasy fingermarks all over my reflection.

'Well, anyway, I tell you this, my duck. Wobbly was very keen, he said you lot are the best band in the whole of the Goring Gap, he said. So I'll tell him you're up for it and he can give you a call. Long as you play plenty of Roy Orbison.'

'Vera, I—'

'Now then! Enough nattering,' she interrupts, flapping a cloth at me. 'Those towels. Four one seven needs toilet rolls, and there's something unpleasant in room two nine five that needs ridding of. Honestly, the things these people get up to…'

It rains heavily on the way home, and I walk into the hallway with my hair dripping wet. From the radio in the kitchen, Terry Wogan's gravelly tones are floating through the house like a ghost.

'You're a bit wet.'

Dad is fiddling with the top button on his shirt.

'Uh-huh.'

'Any exciting developments with the band?'

I don't think the Ladies' Over-Sixty-Fives Centenary Dinner really counts as an exciting development.

'Not right now, no.'

I drift through to the kitchen, where Mum is flicking through *Good Housekeeping* over a pot of tea.

'You're wet, darling. Cup of coffee?'

'Thanks.'

Standing up, she stops and looks deeper into me.

'You OK?'

I just nod.

'You seem a bit off-colour.'

'Tired, that's all.'

Dad walks into the room with a funny look on his face. He looks intently at Mum, who closes her magazine and takes a long, slow breath.

'Remember we said we had some news?' she says, a hand on Dad's arm. 'Well, we wanted to bring you up to speed.'

'Oh… OK.'

They're standing next to one another, Mum looking concerned, Dad looking excited. He claps his hands together.

'We're selling the house, son.'

A tiny sound drops from my mouth.

'Oh.'

'We've thought about it a lot,' continues Mum, 'and we need to move on from the village, now that all you boys have grown up. And your Dad's always had this dream of moving to the coast one day, living by the seaside.'

Dad nods matter-of-factly.

'It's been on the backburner for a long time now, but I said to your father, you've got a dream, you know what you want, it's time to do something about it.' She narrows her eyes at me. 'Does that make sense?'

'Of course, absolutely. It's… great news.'

'And anyway,' she continues, busying herself with the folding of a tea towel, 'things seem to be going so well with the band at the moment, we thought you'd probably be moving out soon anyway.'

'Right… yes, sure. I thought that too.'

'Great. That's great. We wanted to tell you.'

'Yep, absolutely.'

Dad rocks back and forth on his feet, a funny little smile teasing his lips. He exchanges a quick glance with Mum.

'How'd you like to see some of the places we've been looking at?'

'Sure,' I reply, as he disappears into his study.

'I've started a spreadsheet…'

Mum slips an arm around my shoulder.

'You do understand, don't you? You boys are all moving on now, and we need to focus on our own lives. Chase a dream again.'

'Time to get out there and explore the world,' adds Dad, reappearing with his clipboard. A stack of estate-agent brochures are clamped to the front.

'I alphabetised these, so we can flick straight through to, say, Teignmouth, that's in Devon. After Sidmouth, but before Totnes. I might do a digital version too, as a back-up.'

'That's a bit over the top, darling.'

'You can't be too careful. Phil and Margaret had a burst pipe in 1987 and he lost eighteen months' worth of Homebase loyalty-card statements. Bloody nightmare.'

Dad flicks through his collection of property brochures.

'See this place? Underfloor heating. That's the future.'

'Very green of you.'

'Well, exactly. If we switch to underfloor, we're looking at a fifteen to forty per cent reduction in our annual energy expenditure.'

I watch the two of them for a while, Dad extolling the benefits of low-wattage light bulbs, Mum muttering about the proximity of the nearest big Waitrose. A train rumbles past in the distance.

Meanwhile, on the radio, Terry Wogan bids farewell for another day.

Upstairs in my bedroom, the large attic window is playing a never-ending loop of vast, slow-moving clouds, drifting in herds against a bruised sky. Patchy grey rain falls in ten different directions at once. The coffee has gone cold on my desk.

I unlock my phone and scroll through to Favourites, my thumb hovering over George's name. On the end of the bed, the cat glares at me with indifference and yawns.

Sliding the phone back into my pocket, I lie down on the bed and a deep, dark exhaustion wrestles me asleep.

26

Thursday 29 April.

The day of the gig.

In my bedroom, the cat watches as I fold the letter, slide it into the envelope and seal the top. It's done now, cordoned off, immortalised in ink. In sober typeface, the letter states my sincere gratitude and considerable excitement at being offered the role of Junior Account Manager at the Harley Bourne Group, Golden Square, London W1F 9EP, and in turn my acceptance thereof. The starting salary is £22,000 per annum.

The original letter came with an information sheet: a rundown of what to expect from the job and from a career in advertising in general. It's an exciting time. It's an industry with many prospects for upward mobility, an established ladder to climb. A respected vocation, and a challenging one. A lucrative one.

If you set the right goals, the sky is the limit. You'll be rewarded for thinking outside the box, for pushing the envelope, and those rewards will continue to grow handsomely as you steadily climb the ranks. I can see the decades rolling out in front of me, and they make sense.

Things, finally, make sense.

All I need now is a stamp. The currency that will set this letter on its onward journey to London, and deliver it safely to the desk of Dominic Sykes, Creative Director at the Harley Bourne Group. The man with the numberless clocks on his wall.

Reaching into my inside pocket, I pull out a collection of abandoned odds and ends and find a clump of receipts, an old tissue, the desired book of stamps and, lastly, two dog-eared squares of card with string looped through them. Setting the stamps down for a moment, I dangle both squares of card in the early-evening sun, reading the slightly faded text printed on the front.

I remember now. These came from the loft, before we left for France... before everything changed.

I should really put them back.

LB96
ACCESS ALL AREAS
Pro Mori Backstage Pass
GEORGE

LB96
ACCESS ALL AREAS
Pro Mori Backstage Pass
CHRIS

Suddenly I remember, in vivid hypercolour, that forgotten afternoon in the summer of '96. It was the school holidays, and the day of the gig was nearly upon us. We'd spent weeks and weeks rehearsing with Pro Mori for what was to be our first proper concert, and now we were down to the last-minute preparations. We whiled away hours working on the setlist, writing it out in capital letters, drawing stage plans, devising costume changes and making Access All Areas passes. We cut out cardboard squares from old cereal packets, and glued the printed passes onto the front – you can tell because the top corner of Tony the Tiger's head is visible on the back. His eye on George's, his ear on mine. In fact, holding them next to each other, you can see they fit together, like a puzzle.

'Who else needs a backstage pass, then?'

George thinks about this.

'Shelley. Definitely Shelley.'

Shelley was our chief groupie.

'OK,' I reply, pulling another box from the pile. 'One for Shelley. Then Alan and Ben, obviously. Anyone else?'

George stares out the window at the field of cows across the road. The sun is setting sleepily over the valley.

'Nope, just us,' he replies. 'Otherwise it's not special.'

We go back to our respective jobs, George cutting out cardboard squares, me typing on the computer. After several minutes of industrious silence, I turn round slowly on my chair.

'George.'

'Yo.'

'Are we ready for the concert, do you think?'

George pauses with his scissors in a wide V. He looks at me very seriously for a few moments, then smiles his valley-wide smile.

'We ate ready for breakfast,' he replies, and we both burst out laughing.

Nearly a decade later, and it's time those passes went back in the attic for good. Perhaps I'll have a major clearout later, dust away some cobwebs. But, in the meantime, the future beckons.

Setting the passes aside, I open the book of stamps, and find just one left. Peeling it from the page, I place it carefully on the corner of the envelope, taking care to line it up precisely with the right-angled edge, and then it's done. Sitting in the folds of my duvet, the completed package, ready to go. A new beginning. Simply slot this into the postbox at the end of the road, and everything will change, forever.

Very exciting times.

Then, something tugs at my gaze again. The two backstage passes, lying together on the pillow, their frayed strings intertwined. It looks like there's a word scrawled across the back of George's pass.

It says 'West'.

I examine the word more closely. It's George's handwriting, unmistakably. Excitable, semi-legible, scribbled in haste. And he's written something on the back of mine, too: the word 'art', by the look of it. Although... is that 'arted'? *Arted?* And another word follows, 'those' or 'thus', perhaps, or 'these'. Nonsense, then, just random jottings. Nothing important.

But a nagging feeling urges me on, and I pick up the two matching pieces of card and slot them together so that the two strings of handwriting link up. Gradually, the letters shift and click, the years slowly stumble and dance, and a sentence forms in front of my eyes.

A sentence I've heard before.

We started this.

Just like George always says, when he's standing centre stage, looking back at me. Only now it's Tony the Tiger, watching me knowingly from the twinkling corner of his one big, shiny eye. Most people, says Tony, wake up every day of their lives, going through the motions, never knowing what they really want.

But if you're lucky enough to have a dream in the first place, then…

***

I can't make this mistake.

Because it *is* a mistake… right?

My heart is beating loud in my chest as ten years of memories battle noisily for attention. Fragments of time, endless hours of friendship, endless days spent making music in tiny rooms, struggling and failing and winning little victories and struggling all over again. And all the way along, a silent truth reigned: *it was never supposed to be easy.* That was never the point. The point was that the plans we made when we were kids, those big, sprawling, idiotic plans – we had this ridiculous idea that we'd stick two fingers up to the rest of the world and actually go through with them. We dared ourselves to wander unprotected and unprepared into the storm, even though, if you thought about it, we were almost certainly destined to fail. The easy option wasn't the band – the easy option was *giving it up.*

And so I *could* give up on this now, quite easily. In effect I already have. The backstage passes will be going back in the attic. I've written the letter, I've made up my mind. I've missed the gig.

Except I haven't missed the gig. Not yet.

Not… yet.

Everyone talks big when they're a kid. Before the world gets too serious, we all pretend we'll become astronauts, explorers, rockstars. We dream vast and unchained. But when it comes down to it, any idiot can start a dream.

It's keeping it alive that's the problem.

I stand up, sit down, stand up again.

What time is it?

6:10 p.m.

Could I do this…?

Am I doing this?

I could still make it, if I leave now.

Right now.

Am I doing this…?

Pocketing the passes, I grab my phone, dash from the room, crash down the stairs and fly out the front door.

***

I have to phone George.

Tell him I'm coming.

6:16 p.m. I don't have long.

Running down the hill to the train station, I'm grappling with my phone to tap out a text message. I'm up to '*G, I've made a mistake, I'm co*' when the screen blinks at me, then shuts down. Dead battery.

The station has a payphone, but the train leaves in two minutes. I throw in a clatter of ten-pence pieces and smash out his number.

Come on… *come on.*

'*You're through to George's phone, please leave a message.*'

Damn. Try again.

Thirty seconds left.

Still straight to answerphone, no ringing. He must be backstage, no signal.

'George, mate. It's me, I'm… bugger!'

The train pulls into the station and, leaving the receiver dangling, I throw open the phonebox, run across the platform and zip in through the closing doors.

The train trundles along at a maddeningly casual pace, my fingers tapping the tabletop. We're passing through rolling countryside, meandering through meadows, and I watch the familiar valleys and hills through the window, heart beating fast.

From Paddington, a crosstown dash on the Bakerloo and Central lines brings me to the exit at Tottenham Court Road station. London is thrumming with people, and the noise is angry and fast, unrelenting. Black cabs honk horns, bus brake pistons hiss and pop, and music blasts from bars and clubs up and down the Charing Cross Road.

7:39 p.m. The Lightyears are onstage in twenty minutes.

'I need to get in,' I say to the man on the door, noting the sign above his head. It reads LONDON INDEPENDENT MUSIC AWARDS in big red letters.

'Got any ID?'

This face seems strangely familiar. He stands heavy in my path, waiting for ID that I didn't bring, flaring his nostrils like a big angry bull.

'Listen, the thing is—'

'I need ID.'

A sheen of burgundy sweeps through my line of sight.

'That guy! That guy over there!' I shout, pointing at Shawn, who is striding through the foyer in his wipe-clean suit. Like you could dunk him in the bath and he'd come out dry.

'Shawn. Shawn!'

Shawn cocks his head at the sound of his name and, clocking me, stops moving entirely for a second or two. Then he bursts suddenly into life.

'Well I never, it's the Satellightyears!' he exclaims in his triple-distilled Irish accent. His mouth widens into the shape of a laugh, but no sound comes out. 'Just joshing, love the new name. Shouldn't you be backstage?'

'Yeah, I'm just a bit late, I need to get inside…' Shawn digs an elbow into the bouncer's ribs.

'Let the wee fella in. He's a musician, y'know.'

Not looking at me, the bald-headed bouncer shakes his head and unclips the red rope.

Garbling thanks, I dive into the building.

Inside, the Astoria is buzzing with an excitable chaos of journalists, lost-looking musicians, doormen and fans. I'm pushing through the rabble, drenched in noise, burrowing through a hungry scrum of photographers and staff on my way to the auditorium.

Time is running out.

Passing underneath a banner that reads *LIMAs 2004: Highlighting the very best in emerging live music*, I plunge into the deep of the venue, all dark and throbbing, crawling and loud. A thousand bellowed conversations battle with rock music and beer taps, doors swing open and slam, laughter crackles. Elbows prod, feet shuffle, sweat clings. My throat feels dry. Onstage, a rainbow-coloured punk band are thrashing their way through a set of spiky, angry tunes.

And then I see it. A big black door that says BACKSTAGE.

'Ay-maze-ING.'

Smacked over the head with a giant rubber mallet. It's the Noise.

'Oh my ACTUAL God it is SOOOO exciting that you're back how was France I bet France was sooooo wicked did you write any new songs and I totally love the name The Lightyears that is actually SUCH a cool name hey this is so exciting there are photographers here and everything oh my actual God check out my wristband.'

The Noise is, somehow, wearing a VIP wristband.

'How did you get that?'

'Oh my god so there was a competition on the LIMA website and it was like for the Best Super-Fan of the nominated acts to get VIP entry or whatever and I phoned up and it was like so cool because I told them I'd been to every single gig apart from the French ones and I have all the setlists in my scrapbook and I knew your birthdays and star signs and how many brothers and sisters you've got and John and George are brothers anyway so that one's easy and also I know where everybody lives.'

'Oh. Well, that's…'

Striking fear into my very soul.

'…lovely, but I've got to g—'

'I made this for you.'

She is holding up a notebook with leaves of paper sticking out of it.

'What's that?'

'It's a scrapbook of all your newspaper clippings.'

The cover of the notebook reads *The Lightyears Scrapbook April 2004*. It's full to bursting.

'What newspaper clippings?'

'All the press you got while you were away.'

'You mean the *NME* review? I'm not sure I want to see that again.'

'No way it's AWESOME I collected everything but I threw away the *NME* one because it was dumb so I got this one from an e-zine and this one from *Hot Press* and it's all AMAZING and this one tells the story of the band and the one in *Metro* says "The Lightyears are being widely touted as next big things" which is like WAY cool.'

The pounding of music rings in my ears as I stare at the scrapbook.

'That's… all about us?'

She nods giddily and passes it to me. I flick through, stunned. Article after article about us and our award nomination… and *Metro* are tipping us to win.

'Do you want a J2O?'

'Sorry… what?'

Ellen's eyes drop, and she fiddles with the zip on her bag.

'Never mind.'

Onstage there's a changeover, and a seven-piece jazz-funk band in white suits and saxophones start their set. Shawn is hovering in the wings.

'I was thinking… I was thinking maybe after this you might want to go get a milkshake, or something?'

Ellen is talking to me, but looking at the floor. She seems small, all of a sudden.

'I can't, sorry, I've got to dash. Thanks for making the scrapbook…'

I push away through the crowd, Ellen watching me as I go. 7:48 p.m. Faces pass by, my brain pulses with cold fear, bodies brush against mine, boozy voices holler and sing. My heart is beating in my ears as I sink into the sea of people filling the mosh pit, squeezed heat and a rising fever.

'Hohmygosh! Trissy!'

Ugg boots, pink leggings and an England rugby shirt with the collar popped. Araminta air-kisses me, six times.

'I am so excited, Trissy, I almost did a bit of wee there. All the gang are here, Nick Faldo, Jocastles, Tabby Cat, Garden of Eden, Sheebs, and we are *crazy* excited about the gig.'

I glance again at the backstage door. Araminta taps at my arm.

'What's up with you, grumpy-pumps?'

'Sorry, I, um… thanks for coming to see us, it means a lot.'

'Oh, gosh no. We're not here to see you.'

'You're not?'

'Well, yes, I mean, *of course* we'll watch your bit, silly. But our other favourite band's playing too.'

I have less than ten minutes.

'Who's that?'

'Heidi, obvs.'

Heidi? Now hang on just a minute.

'As in… *and the Black Cats*?'

She nods, sipping at her rosé.

'You're a fan of Heidi and the Black Cats?'

'Uh, yuh-*huh*. Why wouldn't I be?'

'Doesn't seem like your kind of thing, that's all.' Her face crumples at me.

'What do you mean?'

'I just imagined you'd be more into… y'know. Chick music.'

'What's chick music?'

'Never mind, I *really* have to ru—'

'Of course, when we found out you were playing too, then like, hello, best night ever. Plus I like *luch'raly* had to break in my new Jimmy Choos. *Regardez!*'

She presents me with an expensive-looking pair of designer heels.

'I won't tell you how much they cost Daddy, but twelve hundred pounds is *quite* the price tag.'

'That's great, Arry. I'll see you afterwards, OK?' I call back as I push away into the mass of bodies, Araminta waving at me as I go. The backstage door is unguarded, so I slip through and leap up two stairs at a time on my way to the dressing room.

Outside the door, a girl with a headset and a clipboard is sitting on a stool. I can hear Tony warming up his voice inside.

'Can I help you?'

'I play piano in The Lightyears, we're about to go onstage.'

She scrunches her nose and consults her clipboard.

'We've already checked in the pianist for The Lightyears.'

'No, that's some other guy… there's been a mistake. I need to get inside.'

'You're too late, mate. They're waiting in the wings. You need to go back out into the main auditorium—'

'Hang on, hang on, hang on.'

Do I have a plan? Any kind of plan at all? She stares blankly at me.

'All right, one sec,' I continue, buying time. 'What about if I said I'd give you my lead singer's phone number? He's pretty hot, right…?'

This is never going to work.

'Give it a rest, mate. I'm not some teenage groupie.' It didn't work.

'Although…' She looks at the floor, and shuffles on her stool. 'If it was the *bass player*, then…'

John, you absolute beauty.

'Here you go,' I reply, scribbling John's number onto her clipboard. 'Pleasure doing business with you.'

She keys in a code, and I walk through.

***

The green room is quiet, and seemingly empty. A mirror framed with light bulbs hangs on the wall, and a mini-fridge full of beer hums frostily in the corner. There's even a basket of fresh fruit.

But no Lightyears.

'People, that was the awesome Nu-Soul Train, give it up!' Shawn is standing centre stage at the mic, whipping the crowd into ear-splitting frenzy. Hundreds of people, probably thousands, jostle in the dark, a rippling sea of heads. Onstage, my keyboard waits for me in low light.

Finally, lined up behind a table on the far side of the venue are the LIMA judges, fingering wine-glass stems and exchanging secret words.

It's 7:59 p.m.

Waving to the crowd, Nu-Soul Train head for the wings and sweep into the dressing room, disturbing the curtain as they pass and revealing four new figures in the black… The Lightyears.

My band. 'George.'

George turns round, just as Tony, John and my replacement walk out onto the stage.

'… Christoph.'

He is standing on the brink, caught between darkness and light.

'You came.'

Shawn begins his introduction, and the rest of The Lightyears take to their instruments. I hear the scuzzzz-*pop* of a lead entering a guitar, and the *clickety-slick* of Tony nervously tickling the hi-hat. I wait, for a moment, in the dark.

'I let you down.'

'That's… OK.'

'No, it's not. I'm so sorry. I let you down.'

'You came, though.'

'Yeah. I mean… I thought about giving up, I was *going to*… and then I found something at home that I… wasn't expecting.' Shawn is listing our achievements to scattered whoops from the crowd. 'We started this, and we started it for a reason.'

George's blue eyes gleam, silently.

'I knew you'd come through, Christoph.'

'Do you think it'd be OK if I… stepped in?' I ask, indicating the stage.

'Of course, old fruit. Big Molly's dead laid-back.'

The silhouette manning my keyboard is surprisingly small, around five foot, and slight.

'*That's* Big Molly?'

'Yeah. Top bloke, got some hilarious stories about prison. Ask him about Shower Tobogganing if you get the chance.'

'He won't mind?'

'Not at all. He's used to it, apparently he was stand-in mandolin player for Dexy's Midnight Runners back in the mid-eighties.'

'Wasn't everyone?'

'Exactly.'

We stand opposite each other, unsure of what to do. George glances at my wrist.

'How'd you get in without a wristband, by the way? The security guards in this place are MEAN.'

Walking over to him, I reach into my pocket, pull out a dog-eared square of card and drop it into his hand. His name is written on the bottom. He reads it, looks up at me, and ten years fall away in an instant.

'I had a backstage pass.'

'London,' Shawn is saying from the auditorium, 'you're a lucky lot, these guys are fresh from their first European tour, and they are hot as hell right now…'

258

'I haven't seen this in a while,' replies George, looping the pass over his neck and slipping it inside his shirt. He nods past the curtains. 'Shall we?'

'Probably should. I think Tony's about to have an embolism.'

He plucks a plectrum from his pocket, and I gesture towards the stage.

'After you.'

Walking out behind George, I move towards my piano and, for just a second, I'm dazzled by bright lights. Then, as my eyes adjust to the glare, I find my band standing around me, Tony looking slightly stunned, John allowing himself a careful smile. Little Big Molly gives me the nod and leaves the stage.

I look out into the Astoria. The crowd must number two thousand people, maybe more. George fires a millisecond of ocean-blue eyes at me, and I stand up straight.

'Ladies and gentlemen… The Lightyears.'

Under the applause I begin a bold, insistent piano riff, the striding chords that open 'Blinded By Light'. My hands feel powerful, electrified against the keys. George steps up to the microphone.

'*Four bedroom walls, we were so small…*'

Magnetic ripples course through the sea of faces as George's voice is submerged in the song. All eyes synchronise, minds begin to fuse, imaginations bubble and rush.

'*Now that I am back here it's the memories that make me feel old…*'

The words, the melodies, the heat from the lights unpick the tightly packed scrapheap inside my head. Fragments of memory float to the surface, tiny screenshots washing past me like driftwood. Finding Tony in the sweat-soaked gloom of the 12 Bar Club. Lashed and defeated by a mountain snowstorm, bloody on cold concrete. Bon Jovi at Wembley, when we were fourteen. Our own stadium concert at the village hall in the summer of '96. Cutting out home-made backstage passes from a torn cardboard box.

'*I've known your heart, right from the start…*'

My voice aligns with George's as we drift towards the chorus. The heart of the song begins to thump, thump, thump, big and bold and unafraid.

'*Now we're growing older, it's the comfort that tears us apart…*'

Then, as the drums drip-feed into piano, the song begins to soar. The band is firing into action, guitar sweeping over spiralling piano chords, rhythms all tumble and roll. Words and chords and harmonies wash over us in waves.

'*Over the fields and beyond, where will I be when you're gone?*'

Beyond George, a sea of people in the dark, moving, breathing, watching.

'*You don't know the weight of your heart on my heart…*'

Plunging into the guitar solo, we're running, travelling, weaving through the song with two thousand miles of momentum behind us. John's bass, rich and warm, sits underneath the sound, the ever-present bedrock. He sends me his quiet smile, then turns back to face the crowd.

The song ends and, over the applause, 'Blinded By Light' becomes 'Sleepless', another insistent piano riff marching in underneath growling guitars. George's voice storms in powerful and towering, and it swoops and dives as Tony slams and hammers the drums, the blacksmith in his forge. The song flies by, pianos rolling, guitars screeching, three voices calling, and soon it washes into 'Emily', our final number.

'We've been The Lightyears. We'll leave you with this one.'

'Emily' kicks off at full tilt, a festival of sunshine-pop, harmonies diving and sweeping, steady beat driving. The sound is warm and bright, crisp and full and ocean-blue. Choruses leap and soar, verses pass in a flash, the guitar solo slips and dips and we soon find ourselves hurtling towards the finish line, a moment many years in the making, waiting in the wings.

In just under sixty seconds, this whole thing will be over.

Between us and the stirring crowd is a line of Shawn's big-necked, black-jacketed bouncers. At the far corner, diametrically opposite me, stands the bald-headed one from the main entrance. Our eyes meet, and I take in the bullish nostrils, the mobile-phone headset, the head like an egg in a call centre… and that's when I realise. *That's* where I know him from. The Rock Garden, on that Thursday afternoon back in early April, before any of this had happened, standing between us and the venue entrance. 'Bands only,' he had told us. '*And you don't look like a band.*'

But now, my friend, *we are* the band. And there's nothing you can do about it.

As our final song nears its conclusion, I look from my piano to the speaker stack at the front of the stage, the music thundering in my ears. Before my brain has time to hold me back, I'm marching towards it. As I pass the front row of the crowd, a raucous cheer fills the room, sending an adrenalin-shot right through me from feet to fingertips. I arrive at the tower and, with a hop, launch myself onto the top so that my chest is perched on the edge, both arms stretched across to grip the opposite side.

Halfway there.

Behind me, the rest of the band continue their inevitable advance towards the end of the song. As more heads turn to watch me climb, a second, louder roar spills upwards from the audience and the bald-headed bouncer turns to look in my direction. He double-takes as he notices me swinging my legs onto the platform and, turning his enormous bulk in my direction, starts moving up the stage steps towards me.

Crouched in a sweaty ball on top of the speaker, I find my footing and stand up, straight as an arrow. The bouncer has been joined by a second, and a third, and like ogres they're closing in on me from all directions. As I stand on the platform, the noise from the floor is deafening and the crowd are swelling, breathing and moving like a boiling black ocean. I'm on the seventeenth storey, climbing a mountain, and I'm right on the edge and all I can see is time and space and endless lightyears stretching out across the sky, and deep inside my stomach I've got this incredible sinking sensation.

Somewhere between fear and hope.

Up above, the lights begin to spin. All around the lamps are flashing, and the band are crashing into the final chord of the song, and Tony clocks me on my podium and thunders into a clamorous drum fill that stretches on, and on, and I'm bending my knees, and the bouncers are closing in, and the crowd are screaming, and the guitar's wailing, and the bass is chugging, and the air is hot with lights and sweat and rock 'n' roll and my brain seems to quake in my skull and four thousand eyes are focused on me and Tony raises his sticks and George hammers the guitar and the tiniest muscles in my feet brace themselves for release and everything goes silent and then…

I'm in the air.

Unstoppable.

Untouchable.

Dropping, falling, flying… and bound to land… somewhere.

And inside a cataclysmic explosion of music and thunder and screaming, I hit the ground, my hands slamming the keys, my whole body crunching with the impact and a blur of hair and sticks and rhythm and bass and voice and hope and fear around me, armageddon ringing in my ears.

And it's all over.

And before I know it we're tumbling off the stage, all four of us, crashing through the curtains in a tangled embrace, body heat, applause, congratulations flying. Hands ruffle hair and slap backs. We emerge backstage, and George slings an arm around me and kisses me hard on the cheek.

'Gentlemen, I think this calls for a round of Massive Desperados.'

I shake my head, choking out laughter. George grins back at me.

'Here,' says Tony, reaching into his trouser pocket and producing a fistful of rectangular laminates. 'Beer tokens. Last one at the bar's a jazz trombonist.'

We stumble towards the exit, Shawn's voice echoing over the speaker system, applause from the crowd still dying out. I am at the back of the group, leaning on George and John's shoulders.

But as I step through the door, a huge hand clamps onto my shirt collar from behind, stopping me dead. Then, a second, similarly huge hand locks onto my shoulder and, as I watch the rest of the band disappear down the stairs, the hands spin me around and bring me face-to-terrifying-face with the bald-headed bouncer.

'Come on, then.'

I wonder what he wants?

'Don't you talk, mate, or what?'

Slightly confusing grammar there.

Might keep that to myself.

'Oi. Mate.'

What happens in a fight? I genuinely have no idea.

'We need to have a private chat, you and me.'

He presses against my ribcage and corkscrews a meaty fist around the front of my shirt. I can see hundreds of tiny, angry pores opening across his nose and cheeks.

Say something. Diffuse the tension.

'Hello there.'

Hello there? *Hello there?* Who says that in a combat situation?

'Bet you think that was a pretty funny stunt, yeah?'

'No, not at all… um… Sir.'

He lifts me two inches off the ground, pushing air through his nostrils like a bull. My feet dangle in space.

'There are two thousand people in here tonight. You got no regard for Elfin Safety?'

I *could* reply that the safety of elves is the least of my concerns right now, but I don't think he'd find it that funny.

'Sorry… I won't do it again.'

'Damn right you won't.'

I could try punching him. Shall I punch him?

I won't punch him.

'I've been watching you,' he says, venting a gust of stale breath into my face. It smells of pork scratchings. On the other side of the curtain heaves the sweaty might of the London Astoria, ripple and pulse, a beast in the dark.

'You weekend rockstars, you're all the same. Think you own the place.'

'No, I…'

'But you don't. You get me?'

One hand still clamped fast around my shirt, he slowly curls the other into a tight red boulder. His gaze darts downwards to admire the fist, then rolls back up to face me.

OK. This is now going to happen.

My lungs empty of air.

Every muscle tightens.

His elbow spring-loads backwards, and I close my—

HANG ON.

Did he just call me a rockstar?

He bloody did. He called me a—

BLACK OUT.

***

'Oi, Piano Man.'

A room fades hazily into focus. A basket of fruit… a mirror framed with light bulbs… an empty beer fridge… and an astonishing cleavage.

'What are you doing on the floor?'

Heidi is standing above me, half-empty bottle of Jack hanging by her hips.

'You alive?'

I consider this for a moment.

'I've never been in a fight before.'

'You just had a *fight*?'

She offers a hand, and I take it. My brain is swimming.

'Ooh… ouch.'

'What happened?'

I stare out across the stage at the line of bouncers surveying the crowd.

'He called me a rockstar.'

'Who did?'

'The security man, the egg man! He said, "You weekend rockstars, you're all the same."'

Heidi takes a swig of whiskey, and her lips glisten as she pulls the bottle away.

'Cheeky bastard. You should've lamped him one.'

'Oh, yeah, I mean, I would've done,' I reply, dusting myself down, 'but my Tae Kwon Do shit is way powerful. I have to use it responsibly.'

There is a deep throbbing pain in my stomach. This is amazing. This is the agony of rock 'n' roll, and I bloody love it.

'You like a fight, then, do ya?'

Heidi is sizing me up, an intense look in her eyes.

Oh God.

She's going to punch me, isn't she?

This is now going to happen.

Second time's a charm.

I close my eyes.

And she kisses me.

Yep, that's right. SHE'S KISSING ME.

She pulls away.

'What are you doing?' I stammer out, my whole body tingling.

'What d'you *think* I'm doing?'

She has a point there.

'You do realise I lost that fight, right?'

'Shut up, Shakespeare,' she says, pushing me up against the wall.

'Ah will be *shaggin'* tonight, boys! Just yoose watch me. A big, fat, filthy shag. And by the time ahm finished wi' her...'

'Oh, shit!' exclaims Heidi, pulling away at the sound of approaching Glaswegians. 'That's my band. You need to hide.'

'Hide?'

'Yeah. Hide.'

I tilt my head at her.

'You do realise this isn't *Scooby Doo*, right?'

She shrugs and, with unexpected force, shoves me backwards into the curtains. I trip on a thick cable, stumble blindly and land uncreremoniously on a plastic chair, the hanging black fabric now obscuring me from view. Seconds later, I watch as Heidi snakes out onto the stage in front of me, followed by her smoking entourage, to boisterous cheers from the crowd.

'People, put your hands together for Heidi and the Black Cats!'

Cautiously, to the thrashing of guitars, I poke my head out far enough to observe the action. As it turns out, I've got a rather good view from my little hiding place, close enough to smell the sweat on the microphones, the musk of dirty jeans.

And, as the gig slowly unfolds, something very unexpected happens.

It's loud.

And intense.

And mesmerising.

Mesmerisingly... *bad*.

The band are all over the place. Out of time, out of tune. Crazy Wee Willy is thwacking his drums with indifference, Hamish is staring listlessly at his twiddling fingers, fag hanging from his mouth, and Duffy leans against the stage wall, detached from the action like he's at a lacklustre rehearsal. At the front of the stage, Heidi is ignoring her bandmates, ignoring the crowd, face down, growling into the microphone. The sound is muddy and listless. And they know it.

I listen, intrigued, as they trudge stiffly through songs, slope around the stage and thud their way through uninspiring guitar solos. At the end of the set, patchy applause rises up from the house and the band stumbles off the stage in a disjointed mess... heading right for me.

Should I still be hiding?

I consider each one of the Black Cats in turn, advancing towards me, big black boots slapping the stage.

They look very angry.

I think I'll stay where I am.

'What the hell was *that*?' spits Heidi as she storms into the dressing room, her band dragging behind. She lobs her whiskey bottle at the wall and it clatters into a forest of guitars.

'You know what you lot are? The Black Twats, that's what.'

Ha! That's actually quite witty.

'Who cares, Heidi? Ahm bored o' this shite. Ah say we go back tae Glasgae an' start that hardcore electro band, eh boys?'

'Aye,' agrees Hamish, blowing smoke into the ceiling. Crazy Wee Willy snaps a drumstick in half, which I think is his way of expressing agreement.

'Fine, you idiots go back to Scotland, see if I care.'

'Yoose ain't got nuthin' withoot us,' scoffs Duffy, cracking open a warm can of beer. 'We *made* this band, sweetheart.'

'Oh yeah? You lot? You've got about six brain cells between you.'

This is getting too weird. I should go.

Tiptoeing out from my hiding place inside the curtains, I sidle past Hamish, ever so slightly brushing up against his back. He turns and looks at me like I've got six heads. I smile awkwardly.

'Sorry, folks, just squeezing by here...'

Duffy's piercing eyes follow me as I pass. His tongue probes the inside of his cheek.

'Were yoose *hidin'* in there, Shakespeare?'

I point back over my shoulder with my thumb and do Surprised Eyes.

'Wha...? In there? Nooooooo. Absolutely not... hiding.'

Hamish turns his letterbox gaze on me.

'Whit *were* you deein', then?'

Good question. What *was* I doing?

'Erm. I was looking for... this,' I reply, picking up a magazine from a nearby table. 'Left it in here earlier.'

I look down. It's a copy of *Lady Golfer* magazine.

So that's good.

'BAR!' barks Crazy Wee Willy, snapping his other drumstick in half. Hamish agrees, stubs out his cigarette on the arm of the sofa and follows Duffy and Wee Willy out the door. Heidi and I are left alone.

'Thanks for screwing this one up for us, mate.'

'Me?' I reply, pointing *Lady Golfer* at my chest. 'What did I do?'

'You Lightyears, you ruined the whole thing.'

'*We*... ruined this... for *you*?'

'Yeah.'

'How?'

She looks at me with raised chin.

'You weren't supposed to be…'

'What?'

'… good.'

Not entirely sure what I'm supposed to say to that. Is she angry with me? Are we going to have a fight? Is *now* the part where she finally punches me?

Nope. She's kissing me again.

This is totally brilliant.

'Ladies and gentlemen,' comes a voice from the stage, 'the judges have reached a decision in the Best New Act category…'

Uh-oh. This could be incredibly awkward. We pause, mid-kiss, both slightly pretending not to care.

'…The winner of Best New Act 2004…'

An expectant chatter ripples through the crowd.

'…going home with a five thousand pound cash prize and a week's recording session at London's RAK Studios…'

Shawn pulls a gilded square of card from a large envelope.

'…is…'

Just spit it out.

'…Speedracer!' Speed-who?

'Let's hear it for Speedracer – well done, lads!'

Heidi pulls back from me, face painted with disgust. The crowd cheer rapturously as 'We Are the Champions' fades up on the speaker system.

'Who the hell's that?'

'I've got no idea.'

We stare at each other for a mini-eternity. Nobody moves. Our chests are touching, our breath quickening, our arms entangled. Body heat warms the air between us.

Beyond the curtain, a rabble of rainbow-haired punks rush the stage, punching the air and hugging.

'What now?' she says, pressing up against me.

Exactly, I think. What the heck now?

27

Slamming the front door shut behind her, Heidi kisses me, hard and hungry, and starts tearing off her clothes.

Our breathing is short, our hearts pumping, our skin still sticky with sweat from pawing at each other in the taxi. I unbutton my shirt and feel the frantic hot press of her arms, cheeks, breasts against my chest.

In seconds flat she is standing before me, naked but for a pair of small, lacy black knickers, hair and make-up plastered across her face. Her lips are slightly parted, and an almost-empty bottle of Jack Daniel's swings down below her hips.

'Talk about sleeping with the enemy,' she says, taking a long, indulgent swig. She slides her tongue along her bottom lip, drags a hand across my chest and, taking the bottle with her, slinks past me into the bedroom.

I got four words for you, people.
Rock… and fuckin'… roll.

***

WHOA.
Whoa there.
OK.
Where am I?
This is not my bedroom.
This is not the Alps.

This is...

Noises from below.

There's a person downstairs. Doing stuff. Clinking around.

Oh my livelong Jesus.

I remember.

It's Heidi.

Heidi from Heidi and the Black Cats.

I stayed here last night.

Slowly, I lift up the covers to inspect the damage. Yep. Butt naked.

'Wanna drink?' she shouts up from the kitchen. I quickly scan the room for signs of my clothes.

'Yeah, yeah, just get me whatever you're having, thanks.' Probably White Lightning, or a Bloody Mary. Or meths.

Heidi's bedroom is all stainless steel, exposed brickwork and album cover prints by the Sex Pistols and Siouxsie Sioux. It's the kind of apartment you see twentysomethings inexplicably living in in romantic comedies. Through the window, a sign on the opposite building reads 'BRICK LANE'. Who did she rob to pay for this place?

Bare feet are padding up the wooden stairs. I run a desperate hand around the mattress for my pants. No joy. Heidi appears in the doorway wearing my shirt, buttoned only once, and nothing else. She is carrying two steaming mugs.

I sniff, like a builder.

'All right, darlin'.'

Darlin'? Tone it down, Del Boy. She pads across the room.

'Made you some tea.'

This is a dangerous impasse, my friend. If you're not careful, she'll work out what you're really like, and then you're done for.

Do something daring, devil-may-care.

'Ah what, tea? Nah, that's not how I roll. I'm a whiskey man first thing in the morning.'

She slips underneath the crisp duvet next to me and her leg brushes against mine.

'Are you a tramp?'

Hmm. That backfired. Still, you're in it now. Just see it through.

Leering at her (that's right, *leering*), I reach down beside the bed and pick up the whiskey bottle from last night.

It's very important that I don't wince when I drink this. 'Don't do that!' she cries, spilling tea on the covers. I drop the bottle from my mouth.

'What?'

'Don't drink that.'

'Ah, come on darlin'…' Still persevering with that one, are we? '… I like a wee swig o' whiskey in the morning.'

Note to self: the Scottish accent does not make you sound like Sean Connery. It makes you sound like Jimmy Krankie.

'*Yeeaah*, gets me going, whiskey does. Gets me fired up for another long hard day of *rark-en-rowulling*.'

She looks at me like I'm slowly turning into a giant lizard. I should just keep saying words.

'What do you think of that then, bitch?'

Oooh, you took that one a bit far.

'It's whiskey o'clock,' I continue, like a stupid, stupid arse. I press the bottle to my lips and glug it enthusiastically. Mid-slug, Heidi snatches it off me and a splash of booze dribbles all the way down my chest, snaking through my wisps of chest hair on its way to my belly button. (While we're on this subject, why give me just a *bit* of chest hair, God? Either loads, or none, is fine. But a humiliating *little bit*? Where's the humanity?)

We both watch the whiskey soak into her fine white sheets. A small quivering puddle has settled in my belly button. I stick out my bottom lip.

Well, this is attractive.

Hang on.

Where's the sting? The searing throat pain? The warm boozy brain-fuzz?

'That tasted weird,' I say, as Heidi slides the bottle back under her bed. 'Is it off?'

A curious look squirms across her face.

'No, it's not off.'

'Oh.' I open my mouth and waggle my tongue around. 'It's just that did *not* taste like whiskey…'

She sighs, deeply, and sets her tea down on the bedside table.

'That's because it's… not really whiskey.'

'Not really…? What?'

'It's not whiskey. Happy?'

Well, this is a queer development.

'What is it, then?'

She fiddles with the corner of a pillow and mumbles a reply.

'Apple squash.'

'Apple *what*?'

'APPLE SQUASH.' She pouts. 'High juice.'

'High juice?'

'Yeah. Got a much higher real-fruit content than regular squash.'

'I know what high juice is, thanks. But why would you put squash in a whiskey bottle?'

'Take a wild guess, Shakespeare.'

Why does everybody keep calling me that?

'I don't know. Smuggling purposes, perhaps? Or maybe… maybe if you were doing an amateur production of *A Streetcar Named Desire* and there's that scene where Blanche finds a whiskey bottle in the closet, and you don't want to get all the actors drunk, but also glass is more readily recyclable than plastic, so maybe it's a green thing, or… um…'

'You're quite a strange person, you know that?'

That's a very fair point.

'Maybe, but I'm not the one drinking pretend whiskey, am I? Except just then, obviously.'

'It's because I can't drink spirits, all right?'

This is most bizarre. It would appear that I have found a smoking gun. And I'm using it to smoke her out of her hole, like a badger. A sexy badger.

'Why not?'

She looks at her tea, instead of me.

'Yeast allergy. Aggravates my asthma.'

Yeast allergy. Ha! One point to me.

'What I don't understand is why you would take a whiskey bottle onsta—'

Oh good Lord. Oh, sweet jubilant Jehoshaphat on high and his heavenly choir of angels. This is more than a smoking gun. This is a warehouse full of Semtex.

'You're faking it, aren't you?'

Heidi adopts a fairly unconvincing look of open-mouthed shock.

'No. No! I am not… faking it.'

My eyes narrow as I search her face for clues.

'Come on, what's going on here?'

'Nothing is going on here.'

She gives me a strange little sideways look. Outside, Brick Lane is beginning to awaken. A girl in a polka-dot headscarf floats past on an old-fashioned bicycle. A misery of goths emerge from a café across the street.

'Seriously, the fake booze, the snazzy flat. What's the deal? And your accent, what's going on with that?'

'What? Shut up. What you banging on about?'

'Normally you sound like a cross between Oliver Twist and Janet Street-Porter. Today you've gone a bit…'

'What?'

'Posh.'

Her shoulders slump and she parks her tea in her lap.

'I sound posh, you idiot, because I… *am*… a bit… posh.'

'You have got to be yanking me.'

Her eyes flicker towards my groin.

'Yanking you?'

'Sorry. You know what I mean.'

I think for a moment, watching the clock on the wall. It is eggshell white, and patrolled by a single silver hand.

'So you're not an actual Cockney, then?'

'Not really, no.'

'And you didn't grow up in East London?'

She pouts again.

'Not exactly.'

'Where did you grow up then?'

'Chalfont St Giles.'

I start laughing. Quietly at first, a gentle titter, and then it grows, becoming raucous, uncontrollable, soon splitting into a guffaw and forcing me to set down my tea so I can smack my hand on the mattress. She watches me in stony silence.

'This isn't funny.'

'No, it really really is,' I reply, wiping a tear from my eye. 'It's hilarious.'

She is fully sulking now. I compose myself and carry on. 'I have to ask you this again, and I want an honest answer... where did you school?'

She eyes me suspiciously.

'St Mary's... then the Brit School.'

'Well I never. St Mary's in Royal Berkshire?'

'Yes, *Royal* Berkshire. So what?'

'I'm willing to bet you knew a girl there by the name of... Araminta Bashforth?'

This is amazing. I have so got her cornered. I'm like the Poirot of keyboard-led rock.

'Maybe. How do you know all this?'

'Just a hunch.'

She sighs, again, and runs a hand through her gorgeous, tousled hair.

'Anyway, yeah, I know Fizzy Fanny. Used to hang with Tabby Cat, Nick Faldo, Cordelia and that lot. They were in Méribel last week, remember? Came to our party. The one where you got high and tried to jump off a building.'

'Yeah, that party,' I reply, clearing my throat. 'On reflection, smoking all that crack may have been a mistake.'

She fails to suppress a smirk.

'But back to you,' I continue, instantly denting her smugness. 'You grew up somewhere named "Giles", you boarded with the Pink Flamingos... next thing you'll be telling me you've got a double-barrelled surname.'

She slides down underneath the duvet.

'Oh my god, you *have* got a double-barrelled surname! This is ruddy excellent.'

She covers her face with both hands. I poke her four times on the shoulder.

'Spill the beans.'

'Fine. But you have to promise – *promise* – not to take the piss.'

'Scout's honour.'

Scout's honour! Ha. How cunning am I? I left the Scouts after the first week because the uniform was itchy.

'My full name' – she closes her eyes like somebody about to admit they're secretly into dogging – 'is Heidi Cecilia Cadence Montgomery-Butler.'

This is just too good. This is totally, massively brilliant.

'That is a WON-derful name.'

'Seriously, how are you doing this?'

'Just a hunch.'

My hunches are watertight today. I'm a Hunching Maniac.

'And since we're doing truths,' I continue, perhaps a little too gleefully, 'how on earth can you afford this incredible apartment?'

'Papa bought it for me, OK?'

She says it like this: Pa-*pah*.

'"Pa-*pah* bought it for me"? Don't you have to be in *Brideshead Revisited* to say that?'

She smacks me on the arm.

'Not funny.'

Was a bit funny, though.

'Wow. This is kind of like that song "Common People".'

'No, it isn't. It's nothing like that.'

I settle down into the duvet to enjoy my cup of tea. Heidi squirms.

'I'm assuming your dad's not really a Nazi then?'

'No, he's not.' She pulls the duvet up under her armpits. 'His name's Clive.'

'And he didn't beat you up as a kid?'

'No, he... he used to take me to Cotswold Safari Park and that.'

275

Cotswold Safari Park. That's basically the *opposite* of the Nazis.

'So what does he do, ol' Clive Montgomery-B? He's an investment banker, isn't he? Or a hedge-fund manager, or he runs a sweatshop in Pakistan forcing slave babies to knit guns for oligarchs.'

She casts me a withering look.

'No, actually, he's in the media. And anyway, you can't talk. Where did *you* school? Probably Uppingham, wasn't it, or Radley, or Eton with all the other floppy-haired Ruperts.'

'I am not a floppy-haired Rupert.'

'Mate, you are. Trust me.'

'Well, anyway, we already had this conversation in the Alps, *if you remember*.' She sticks her tongue out at me. 'It was a tiny comprehensive. You know, one of those funny little places with the free school dinners.'

A reluctant smirk plays on the corner of her lips.

'Peasant.'

'So come on, 'fess up. The *NME* interview. That wasn't… in any way… *dodgy*, was it?'

'Maybe a bit. Papa golfs with the finance director, so…'

'He must have been delighted you told the whole country he's a child-beating fascist, then.'

'Yeah, he… wasn't too happy.'

A truck full of Indian spices reverses, beeping, into Brick Lane. The driver hangs out of the window, cursing at wobbling cyclists as they dodge out of the way. I watch the mini-drama unfold for a few seconds, then return to my investigation.

'This leads me to my final question,' I muse, with a Sherlockian stroke of the chin (damnit, wish I had a pipe). 'What about the record deal? That one legit? Or courtesy of Pa-*pah*?'

She scowls at me.

'You're really enjoying this, aren't you?'

'No, not at all.'

Absolutely loving it.

'OK. Paul used to work for Papa at BSkyB, and Daddy has a table next to some City Records bigwig at the Ivy. So he got Paul the job, and Paul got us the deal. Nothing wrong with that.'

'No, you're right. Nothing wrong with that.'

She thuds her head backwards against the wall.

'Except it doesn't matter now, anyway, because Paul got fired on Monday. Deal's fallen through, the band's gonna split.'

Ah, the brutal cut and thrust of the music industry. One minute you're in, the next you're out.

Mind you, the guy was a tool.

'Don't tell me, he haemorrhaged the company expense account on Bollinger.'

'No, his last signing tanked, according to Papa. Drummer told everyone he had cancer, but turns out he was full of crap. Then the VP said their first single was total bollocks and dropped them.'

I finish my tea.

'Air Biscuit's a rubbish name for a band anyway.'

'How'd you know it was Air Biscuit?'

'Just a hunch.'

'Stop saying that. You're not Columbo.'

I am a *bit* like Columbo. Might not say that, though. Might just think it.

'Well, this is brilliant. You… Heidi, from *Heidi and the Black Cats*, a band so trendy you abuse your own fans at gigs, are Faking It.'

'So what? You're faking it too.'

'No way, baby, I'm a hundred per cent street.'

'No you're not. And it's really obvious, you know.'

'In what way is it really obvious?'

She sticks her hands on her hips and adopts a mock man-voice.

'"*What do you think of that then, bitch?*"'

'Point taken.'

'Plus, I don't know… that clipboard you carry around everywhere?'

Damn you, clipboard.

'I don't carry it around *everywhere*.'

'Yes you do. The boys in my band call you Clipboard Bumboy.'

'Charming.'

The room falls silent. The lonely silver hand on the faceless white clock ticks its pompous tock.

'If I'm just a Clipboard Bumboy, then why are you even hanging out with me?'

'I don't really know. You're not like other boys in bands.'

Oh yeah. She be digging my style.

'You're a geek, for a start.'

Well that's good to know.

'Plus, I dunno. Something tells me you're not as uptight and square as you appear to be.'

HA. In your face. I *am* as uptight and square as I appear to be.

'Sort of glad, though,' she says, fiddling with the corner of her pillow again. 'You're actually all right, you.'

I pretend to brush some dust off the duvet.

'You're all right too.'

The clock ticks three, four, five times.

'You don't mind that I'm just another little rich girl then?'

'No… not really. Because… OK. Here's the thing. I've spent the last six weeks of my life running around being thumped and puked on trying to convince everybody I'm Berkshire's answer to Kurt Cobain so I could beat you in a trumped-up Battle of the Bands, and it turns out you're even posher than I am.'

She blushes slightly.

'I thought it was just me putting on an act, but everybody's doing it. You, me, Ozzy Osbourne.'

Heidi finishes her tea and sets the mug down.

'Ozzy's not faking it. He bit the head off a bat.'

'Sure, allegedly he did, but where's the actual proof? It was probably made of cake or something.'

'Cake? You're not right in the head.'

'All that stuff I was trying to hide, that's just me. That's who I am.'

I hop out of bed and cross over to the bedroom's expansive bay window. Brick Lane is bustling now, and the day has gloriously begun.

'I don't have anything to hide.'

278

'Fine, but do you think you could hide your ball-sack, just for now?'

I glance back at Heidi, who is looking at me with tilted head and raised eyebrows. Down on the street, an elderly lady is holding her shopping and staring up at me through the window. She drops the bag and a cabbage rolls out.

'Right, yes. Sorry. Sorry about that. Not really sure where my pants are, though.'

'Over there.'

She is pointing at a standing lamp in the corner of the room, upon which are perched my underpants.

'Oh, yes. So they are.' I slip them on. 'What were they doing on there?'

Heidi is looking down at her chest, clipping up her bra. Any man would have to admit, she is one smokin' hot chick.

Although it's probably best for everybody if I avoid phrasing it like that out loud.

'You sort of lobbed them through the air last night in the middle of a weird… sexy… dance… thing.'

Must remember – a man who cannot dance clothed should never, ever, ever dance naked.

'Sorry, I do that sometimes. Anyway, how do you remember all this stuff? I was trolleyed last night.'

She gives me a *use your brain* look.

'Oh. Of course. Apple squash.'

The sound of my phone beeping leads me to a pile of scrunched-up clothes hidden underneath a curvy designer chair. I rescue my jeans, and pull them on. The message reads:

> *Christoph, buddy, get your tiny ass to Denmark Street NOW!!*
> *I have news x*

'So you wanna get breakfast or something…?'

I look back at Heidi, one leg inside my trousers, and nearly fall over. Cunningly, though, I manage to segue the fall into a crafty little hop.

'I can't, I've got to go. I'll call you over the weekend, OK?'

She shrugs.

'Where are you going?'

I glance through the window, out across the London skyline, and a shaft of early-morning sun blinks at me from behind the nearest building.

'I'm going home.'

***

All around, in every direction, are musicians. Tall ones, short ones, fat ones, angry ones, old ones, bored ones, beardy ones, greasy ones, the lank-haired, the dark-eyed, the scruffy-jeaned, the pale of face. Music shops are crammed like slum shacks onto both sides of the street, and the pungent tin-foil tang of cheap Chinese takeaway chokes the air.

'What are we doing here?' I ask George.

'When I woke up this morning, Christoph, my brain was full of these hectic little ninjas, bouncing around and ninja-ing the heck out of each other. I was going berserk. You should have seen it.'

I glance down the narrow alleyway creeping down the side of Andy's Guitars. Brown urine stains snake down the brickwork to the gutter below.

'OK. But why are we here?'

'If you recall, my friend, this is where you go when you want to find a band. Fancy a beer?'

'It's eleven thirty in the morning.'

'Exactly. Sun's past the yard arm.'

'No it isn't.'

'It is in Tokyo. We'll just drink something Japanese.'

George smacks me on the bum and walks off in the direction of the 12 Bar Club. I watch him slalom between two pork-armed men in Black Sabbath T-shirts and disappear through the doorway.

'D'I know you?'

Inside the 12 Bar's grubby-windowed entrance booth squats a bloated, leathery woman with bulging bug eyes and a faceful of ironwork.

'Maybe,' I reply.

'You in a band or something?'

I nod back at her.

'Yes. Yes, I am.'

She returns to counting out pound coins from her red tin and, with a shrug, I step into the club.

Sitting at the table in front of me, complete with cold pints, are The Lightyears.

'Wotcha, TM.'

Tony raises his glass. John gives me a nod and a smile.

'Hi guys.'

George slides a beer across the table.

'It's Asahi, Christoph. Japanese. So you're golden. Sit down.'

I take a seat, slowly, looking from one to the other.

'What's going on?'

'Band meeting,' says John.

'Yeah,' agrees Tony, ripping open a bag of peanuts. 'You've been rubbish on the admin front recently, mate. Didn't even bring your clipboard.'

He grins at me.

'Ooo-kay, but… seriously…?'

John leans forward, both elbows on the table.

'My exams finish in a month or so, and I'm looking for a new project.'

George takes a big, hungry gulp of his beer, then wipes his mouth with his sleeve.

'Basically, my little bro will be unemployed with a master's in philosophy, so his options are limited. And an inside source tells me your folks are relocating to Devon, which means it's time you and I moved to London. Whaddya say?'

'Um… OK.'

George drums on the table.

'Which makes this an excellent time to reveal my big news.'

He rummages around in his back pocket, unfolds a crumpled sheet of paper and spreads it out in front of us. 'This is from a booking agent who saw us at the Astoria last night, and wants to sign us up for some top-drawer gigs. Details for a possible *American tour* in August. East coast: Philadelphia, New York. We could go to New Jersey, find Richie Sambora's birthplace.'

'Where did you get that?'

'You may have stopped checking the band emails, Christoph, but the world keeps on spinning. Thought I might have a go at your job, see if it's everything it's cracked up to be. Turns out it's easy.'

He beams at me.

'We'll need our own sound engineer,' says Tony, chucking nuts one by one into his mouth. 'Somebody young I can train up. Who we don't have to pay. I know a bloke, I'll look him up.'

'Right. That all sounds…'

'Diamond?' suggests Tony. I nod.

'Diamond.'

'Moving on,' adds George, 'the real reason for this band meeting is actually to grill you about Heidi.'

Tony slaps the tabletop.

'Yeah, spot on, George. Word on the street, TM, is that you two got off at Glasgow last night. Now, don't take this the wrong way, but… you and Heidi?' He points at my face. '*You*… and *Heidi*?'

'Three words for you, chaps,' I reply, puffing my chest out and leaning back in the chair. 'Ten. Minute. Rule.'

At the jukebox, somebody drops a coin into the slot and Don Henley's 'Boys of Summer' starts up on the speaker system. Tony wipes salt from his mouth and slams his drink down on the table.

'Congratulations, my boy, for today you become a man.' George ruffles my hair.

'But anyway,' continues Tony, 'this tour. We've got three months until we hit the States, so what we doing until then?'

I take a sip of cold beer and sit back, arms folded.

'Seems pretty obvious to me.'

With all eyes in my direction, I look at George, remembering a birthday card from the attic with an aardvark on the front and a dusty, scribbled message written inside. *Just keep on rolling*, it says.

'We should make an album.'

***

As the London sun casts its early-afternoon light across the red-brick buildings of Denmark Street, four Lightyears are strolling up the middle of the road while the city tumbles and thunders around them.

I am scrolling through the calendar on my phone.

'Anyone know any Roy Orbison?'

'Why?' asks Tony, firing peanuts into the air and catching them, every one, in his mouth.

'I've got us a gig.'

He nods and crunches at me, nuts tumbling from his fist.

'Nice one, TM. Whereabouts? 'Cos seeing as we just did the Astoria, by my calculations next stop should be...' He thinks for a moment. 'Wembley.'

John laughs quietly to himself.

'Hello Wembley,' agrees George, matter-of-factly.

Wow. This could be a hard sell.

'It's not *quite* Wembley, no.'

They all wait.

'No, it's more, um... more the Goring and Streatley Golf Club Ladies' Over-Sixty-Fives Centenary Dinner.'

Tony's mouth is frozen full of nuts. Diversion, quick.

'Wait there. I have to go do a thing.'

Hurrying away, I reach the end of Denmark Street and look both ways up the busy main road. Outside the front of a nearby bookstore are two receptacles – same height, same size, different colours. One red, a postbox; one black, a dustbin.

In my bag is a letter, snug in a rich cream envelope, typed address on the front: *The Harley Bourne Group, Golden Square, London.* I examine each receptacle in turn, considering its contents. Then, stepping past the postbox, I stop at the bin and lift the letter to the slot. Feeding it through, I leave it hanging for just a second and, with the bells of old London ringing around me, let it drop into the dark.

Turning around, I walk back along the road towards Denmark Street and waiting for me, on the corner, is my band.

Acknowledgements

The author would like to thank: George, for a lifetime of japery, and for taking me aside and saying, 'I think you should write a book'; The Lightyears, for heroically standing by as I assassinated their characters; my wife, Pip, for listening to me laugh at my own jokes for months on end; my agent Ed Wilson at Johnson & Alcock; Abbie Headon and the whole team at Farrago; Karen and Caroline at Red Button Publishing; Sophie Scott at the Sophie Scott Literary Consultancy; the late, great John Howlett; and of course my multitudinous and ever supportive family. Finally, because great teachers don't get enough thanks, Jerry Owens, Jane Watret, Maureen Lenehan and Professor David Punter.

***

The Lightyears are a real-life rock band based in London. Together they have toured the world, played Wembley Stadium and been named Best Pop/Rock Act at the UK Indy Awards.

Find out more at www.thelightyears.com.

About the Author

Christopher Russell is a writer and musician based in London. Since forming The Lightyears in his teens he has toured the world, playing everywhere from Wembley Stadium to Glastonbury Festival. He has worked as a music reviewer and features writer, and is currently writer-in-residence for Byte the Book. As well as *Mockstars*, Chris is the author of a successful series of novels for young adults: *Songs About a Girl*, *Songs About Us* and *Songs About a Boy*.

Note from the Publisher

If you loved this book, don't miss out on *Pit Stop*, a bonus short story in the Mockstars series – in which things don't all go to plan for The Lightyears...

To get your free copy of *Pit Stop*, and to receive updates on further releases in the Mockstars series and comparable series to make you smile, sign up at
www.farragobooks.com/mockstars-signup